HACKER'S RAID

Creative Texts Publishers products are available at special discounts for bulk purchase for sale promotions, premiums, fund-raising, and educational needs. For details, write Creative Texts Publishers, PO Box 50, Barto, PA 19504, or visit www.creativetexts.com

HACKER'S RAID
by Jared McVay
Published by Creative Texts Publishers
PO Box 50
Barto, PA 19504
www.creativetexts.com

978-0-578-46520-3

HACKER'S RAID

By
JARED MCVAY

CREATIVE TEXTS PUBLISHERS
Barto, Pennsylvania

The characters in this book are the product of the twisted mind of the author.

Jared McVay, born and somewhat raised in the southeastern part of Kansas, grew up with tales of the old west and as a young man helped break and train horses, [rode in rodeos] mostly bulls and bareback broncos. In addition, at the tender age of eleven, he rode as a jockey in quarter horse races because he was light and didn't fall off. He even won a few races.

Because he has always loved reading western books, it has been his longtime dream to write some. This may be only the first of many, depending on how well the readers like this story.

THANK YOU FOR CHOOSING THIS BOOK

If you want your western to contain good versus evil, this is the book for you.

If you want a family torn apart by one man's stupid pride thrown into the mix, this is the book for you.

If you like your western to contain twists and turns, this is the book for you.

If you like your western tale to have people you can identify with, this book is for you.

And let's not forget the long-lost love that comes back into our hero's life with an unexpected twist....

If the above tempts you into reading my ramblings, all I can say is, I hope you enjoy HACKER'S RAID.

Thank you
Jared McVay

Acknowledgements

To all of the people who have researched and written down the history of the Old West with all the pictures and facts for me to use as background, I say thank you.

To all of the dime novelists from the past, I also say thank you because you have given me a different slant on the characters of the Old West.

And to all of the people who made the western movies I've enjoyed over the years, I also say, thank you.

I would like to express my gratitude to all of the western writers who have given me many hours of pleasure while reading your books. I can only hope this book will, in some small way, bring the same enjoyment to its readers that your many books have brought to me.

A special thanks to my publisher Dan Edwards at Creative Texts Publishers, for having faith in my writing and me.

To my good friend and fellow writer, Howard Bellew, for his most valuable help and advice, thank you, brother.

To Jerri Burr, my best friend, my love and companion, you're the best.

And last, but by no means least, I want to thank my daughters, Tresa, Debra, Irene and Ronda for their encouragement those many years ago for me to become a writer and storyteller.

And to all the readers of this book, I hope you enjoy reading it as much as I did in the writing.

Thank you and happy reading...

Jared McVay

TABLE OF CONTENTS

CHAPTER ONE

"Aiee, you look berrie good, berrie good now, much better than when you came in."

The little Chinaman fussed over the man standing in front of the full-length mirror as he picked a small piece of lint from the lapel of the man's suit jacket before stepping back to admire his handiwork.

Wong felt proud of himself. Indeed, the stranger did look much better than he had when he walked in from the street. The man's eastern styled suit had been rumpled and dirty, and the man himself was unshaven and smelling like many days of sweat.

Wong chuckled to himself as he remembered thinking the man had looked like a walking bag of dirty laundry.

Justin Hacker was twenty-eight years of age with sandy-red hair, deep blue eyes and a ruddy complexion that was enhanced by a roguish grin, which caused many a young lady between Nogales, Arizona and New York City to give him her most alluring smile. And being a young man who adored the ladies, he had returned each and every smile with eager enthusiasm. Over the years he had often thought to himself, ' Ahhh, the wonders of women, they are both a delight and a mystery.'

What he saw in the mirror made him give a nod of approval. For the first time in over a week, Justin Hacker looked and felt clean. It had been seven days since his last bath and shave, which in his mind was much too long. He preferred to bathe daily when, and if, means were available.

But this trip, which was going much too slow, had pushed all thoughts of bathing or anything else from his mind - until this layover in El Paso, Texas.

Turning to the little Chinaman, Justin had a wide grin on his face and said with a strong Irish brogue, "Well now, Wong, me buck'o, tis ah fine job ya do I don't mind tellin' ya. And especially pleased, I was, with the two mugs of cold beer ya brought without me askin', as I leisured in me tub of hot water with ah fine cigar. T'was ah grand way ta pass the time, and it's thankin' ya kindly I am."

Reverting to the Irish brogue of his ancestors was a game Justin liked to play from time to time. It made him feel like one of those actors he'd seen on the stage. And people being what they were, would believe anything if you sounded sincere enough.

Digging into his pocket, Justin pulled out a wad of bills and peeled off several and laid them on the counter.

Wong eyed the small stack of bills the young man with the strange accent laid on the counter and counting it quickly in his mind, concluded it was twice what he'd asked for.

Bowing and smiling widely to show his appreciation, Wong reached over and picked another small piece of lint from the sleeve of the man's jacket.

"Aiee, you come back see Wong again maybe next time you come to El Paso."

Justin Hacker turned and looked at the beautiful young lady who was standing in the doorway to the laundry room. It was obvious she was the one who had cleaned his suit and washed and ironed his shirt, along with his unmentionables.

Justin took the three steps that put him directly in front of her and even though she stood her ground, the look in her eyes said she would bolt if he said, boo. Instead, Justin reached out and gently took her hand and placed two dollars in it, then winked and gave her one of his most heart melting smiles.

The young woman didn't look at the money. Instead, she stared adoringly back at Justin with passion in her eyes as he turned and headed for the front door, cocking his derby hat at an angle down over his right eye - whistling as he went.

Wong watched the stranger leave and then looked toward his daughter who was staring after the young man in the eastern styled suit and funny hat. Though she was only seventeen, for the first time, Wong realized she was a young woman now. And she was beautiful.

There was a gleam in her eyes, a wistful smile on her lips and a glow about her that left little doubt to what she was thinking - that is, to anyone except her father.

"He berrie nice man," Wong said. "He much happy with our work. See, he leave berrie big tip."

Wong held up the money for his daughter to see, waving it in the air as he went on. "He not say so, but I believe he have many worries. And can you tell me daughter, why he not let us clean his hat, but do it himself? I find that berrie strange. But I think he berrie nice man anyway."

The girl hadn't heard a word her father had said. In fact, she didn't seem to notice him at all. She was thinking of the stranger with the deepest blue eyes she'd ever seen - eyes that could see straight into the very depths of her soul, causing her to feel naked and vulnerable. The stranger's eyes had spoken to her - had drawn her deeply into his arms where she had gone willingly. He'd kissed and caressed her in places she'd never been touched before.

Suddenly, she felt faint and her knees got weak. She turned and hurried back into the laundry room, straight to the nearest bench and sat down, leaning her back against the wall. Dreams of this handsome young man would fill her head for many nights to come. She could only hope the man she would someday marry would be as handsome.

Wong shook his head back and forth as his daughter left without saying a word. He was puzzled over this younger generation that held so little respect for their parents. The only solution he could come up with was, this is America and everything is totally different here. But he missed the old ways where children honored their parents. Wong was glad his father was not here to witness such disrespect, especially from a female.

Wong looked at the clock on the wall and noted the time. He then hurried over to where a basket filled with clean and folded sheets and towels sat on a bench. As Wong picked up the basket and headed for the back door, he called out, "Wife, come to front please and take care of customers. I have clean laundry to deliver."

"Hurry back, husband. I have much ironing to do," she called after him.

As Wong hurried down the alley, he hoped the young man in the fancy suit would be all right. "He have serious problems," Wong said to himself, "but he no discuss with me, no, he keepa his problems all inside. And what so special about his hat that he not let me clean it for him?"

"Hurry up with that laundry, Wong," a female voice called out from the backdoor of the saloon.

Wong looked up from his thoughts and saw the large Madam standing with her hands on her hips. She would not be giving him a tip for his hard work, he thought to himself as he hurried on in her direction. "She never in nice mood; always in a hurry, and always grumble about price."

CHAPTER TWO

As Justin stepped out of 'Wong's Bath and Laundry,' the heat overpowered him like a blast from a Pennsylvania steel mill. A large thermometer hanging next to Wong's front door read one hundred-four degrees. Under the steps leading down to the street, an old, tan colored, slick haired dog lay panting in what little shade there was to be found. The poor old fella's eyes were closed and his tongue hung limp over the side of his jaw.

Justin started off down the wooden sidewalk just as a trickle of sweat began running down the middle of his back and the inside of his nose felt the burning of the hot, dry air, reminding him of his final destination - a place that gave the appearance of being a waterless wasteland, but in truth was a land full of life for anyone who had the knowledge and courage to challenge it. The Indians had known how to survive there for untold centuries, while the white man was still a struggling newcomer.

He knew well this place that was fraught with danger, not only from blazing heat, hidden water holes, scorpions and rattlesnakes, but also from the fierce Apache who had ruled that part of the world long before the white man came trespassing on their land, trying to bend both the Indians and the land to his liking.

It was the white man who brought the army to drive the Apaches from their land. But, other than greed, Justin couldn't conceive of any reason why the white man would want this wild, uninhabited territory that was so fierce that if you didn't learn to survive, you died. It was only the Apache and a very few others who were truly at home here.

Of course, there were the Mexican Banditos who came across the border to steal and the Comancheros who found profits throughout the mountains and deserts where they raided the white man of his horses, cattle and arms, which they traded with anyone who offered them gold or silver.

Justin sauntered down the sidewalk, his mind drifting to what he could expect in the next few days. He knew his returning might cost him his life because his own father had vowed to shoot him on sight if he ever came back.

It had been some time now since Justin had given his father much thought. Had he forgiven his father for forcing him to leave his home? He wasn't sure. A lot would depend on what his father did when, and if, he ever got back to Nogales. Justin didn't think he'd ever hated his father, it was more like he felt sorry for him for being the way he was. Another burden his already troubled mind had to worry about.

Next, there would be the Mexican warden to deal with, the one who was holding his younger brother, Jeremiah, in that hellhole prison just south of the border.

The telegram had said the warden was planning to hang Jeremiah for rape and murder. And, of course, Jeremiah was innocent, at least that's what the telegram had said, and knowing his cousin Ben like he did, he had no reason to disbelieve him.

Either way, he couldn't let his younger brother hang. His father would probably blame him for that, too.

Justin's timepiece read ten minutes until four and the conductor had said the train would leave at four sharp. Justin slipped the timepiece back into his vest pocket, and then flexing taunt hard muscles that had been too long without the feel of vigorous use, switched the satchel to his other hand as he walked toward the depot.

Dressed in an eastern styled suit with a derby hat perched at a cocky angle on his head, Justin Hacker did resemble a greenhorn from back east - possibly a bank teller, or maybe a storekeeper - even a drummer, anyone but the man he really was.

To the casual observer, Justin Hacker with his boyish smile and easy manner about him was very misleading. He rarely went looking for trouble, and had been known to give a man the opportunity to settle their differences by both of them walking away. Even though he tried time after time, he found it rarely worked.

The train sat like a huge dragon waiting to swallow up anyone who came too near. The train engine pulsated a slow rumble, waiting to be called into action - bellowing heat and black smoke into the already scorching air.

A small group of people, those about to board the train, and the ones seeing them off, stood on the platform suffering from the unbearable, searing Texas heat.

A cowboy, the size of an oak tree and the personality of a bear with a thorn in his paw, exited the depot. He made a sound in his throat and hacked up something putrid and then spit it in the direction of the people.

Both the ladies and the men turned their backs on him, trying to ignore his bad manners, hoping he would continue on his way and not cause any trouble.

But as luck would have it, the giant cowboy noticed the greenhorn in the eastern suit and derby hat coming toward the steps leading up to the platform near where he was standing. A grin spread across his face as he headed in the young man's direction.

Just as Justin started up the steps leading to the platform, the hair on the nape of his neck stood on end - a forewarning of danger he'd had all of his life and it had never failed him. Within two heartbeats, the giant cowboy stepped in front of him, blocking his path.

Justin stopped and looked up at the oversized cowboy and what he saw was a high crowned, sweat stained, wide brimmed Texas cowboy hat sitting atop an unshaven face that was lined and weather beaten and held a pair of watery, bloodshot eyes. The man had a wide slit for a mouth, with very thin lips, uneven teeth that were yellow-brown and covered with tobacco stains. His breath reeked strong enough of whiskey to put a horse to his knees - plus the man had enough body stench to gag a maggot. Justin wondered how a man could let himself get in that condition?

The bandanna around the man's neck was old and filthy, and the ragged shirt he wore had once been blue but now it was sun bleached and thin. Weather beaten leather chaps hung below a pot gut, covering a pair of worn Levis. His boots were scuffed and bent over at the heels. A brace of Navy Colts in an old Mexican style holster rig was strapped around his waist with both holsters tied to his legs for faster drawing.

If the man didn't stand at least six feet four inches tall and weigh close to three hundred pounds, Justin would lose money in a bet. And without a doubt, the man was a drunk and a bully. Every town he'd ever been in had one and he'd seen too many just like this one not to recognize him, especially when he stood directly in front of him.

This whole process had taken no more than five seconds while the man stood directly in front of Justin, grinning like a cat that had cornered a mouse.

Well, there it was. This was the danger his senses had warned him about and he wanted no part of it. This was stupid. And it wasn't because the man stood at least seven inches taller than him and outweighed him by more than a hundred pounds, no sir, not by a long shot.

Barefoot, Justin Hacker stood five feet nine inches tall and tipped the scales at one hundred-eighty pounds and there wasn't an ounce of fear in him. In fact, there were places where he was considered, by many, as pure hell in a knockdown drag out fight. But Justin always tried to stay true to a statement his grandfather had told him, "Ah smart man never looks for trouble cause there's too much of it ta be found without tryin."

How well he knew the truth of that statement. Standing in front of him was a prime example of what his grandfather had talked about, but he wanted no part of it. He was sure there would be plenty of that later. Besides, it was too damn hot.

The small group of people on the platform had gone quiet, waiting to see what was going to happen. Without actually staring, they hung their heads and watched out of the corners of their eyes.

The ladies twisted hankies and adjusted their sunbonnets, while several of them pretended to smooth the wrinkles out of their dresses, trying to seem unconcerned.

The men looked skyward and stared into the empty space or searched through their pockets for some unknown object, anything that would keep them from getting involved while watching from their peripheral vision.

The sun continued its vengeance against man and earth alike as tension began to build and the small crowd of people waited for what they believed to be the inevitable outcome for this young man from somewhere back east.

The giant cowboy glanced over his shoulder, eyeing the small group of people, making sure he had an audience. When he was satisfied, he looked down at the man in the fancy suit and spoke with a deep voice that sounded like it was coming from the depths of a dark cave.

"Now ain't you real purty like," he said with a slur, and loud enough so the crowd could hear. "All dressed up fancy like in yer citified suit and cute little derby hat."

The big cowboy gestured toward the small crowd, "I ain't never figured out what them little derby hats are good fer, but I always had me ah hankerin' ta have one."

With that said, the big cowboy reached for Justin's hat - but what he got was a steel grip on his wrist and his arm pushed aside. Astonished, the cowboy looked at the greenhorn and saw something in the man's eyes that told him leave it be and just walk away, but that would be out of the question. He'd made his play and it would be all over town if he backed down from ah man half his size. Especially ah drummer from back east, or wherever he was from.

"Jest give me the hat and I'll let ya be on yer way," the big cowboy said in a voice low enough so the small crowd of people couldn't hear.

The color of Justin's eyes had a habit of turning slate gray when he got angry and he was beginning to feel the anger well up inside him. It wasn't the principal of the thing, nor was it feeling ashamed in front of the small crowd of people that kept Justin from giving the big cowboy his hat. Giving this man, or anyone else, his hat was a thing he would not do and there would be no discussion on the matter. Besides, trying to discuss anything with this tub of guts would be like asking an aggravated rattlesnake not to strike. It simply would do no good.

Besides, the derby hat held much more importance than anyone could imagine. He would keep his hat and that was all there was to it.

Thoughts of how he was going to get out of this situation flitted through Justin's mind like a wild bird trying to escape from a cage, but nothing jumped out at him. Then, an outrageous thought popped into his head. What would happen if he just continued on and boarded the train like the big man wasn't even there? Sure, why not? Maybe there wouldn't be any trouble. Maybe the man would just let him board the train without trying to stop him. And maybe it would snow in El Paso, Texas in the next five minutes.

As much as he hoped it would be as easy as just walking on passed, he knew he was just fooling himself.

Justin realized that just boarding the train was his only option short of teaching this loudmouth a lesson. After just a moment, Justin opted for option number one, but as he turned to step around the town bully, the big man reached out and grabbed Justin by his arm.

"Whoa there little fella, I ain't finished with you, yet."

Justin sighed and said in a frustrated voice, "Yes, you are."

The big cowboy didn't believe what Justin had just said and leaned down and   asked, "What'd you say, city boy? You gettin' smart mouth with me?"

Jerking his arm free, Justin turned back and stared the big cowboy straight in the eyes, trying once more to warn him to back off, but the man chose to ignore the look. Instead, the cowboy spoke again, in a very low voice that Justin had to strain to hear.

"Don't be stupid, boy. Jest give me the hat and I won't haf'ta mess ya up right here in front of all these nice folks."

Justin glanced over at the small group of people standing a short distance away, looking embarrassed about their fear of this man. Justin thought they probably were nice people, but for the life of him he couldn't understand why folks put up with bullies like this poor excuse that called himself a human being.

Like it or not, he was going to have to get this thing over with before he died of the heat. So, with the decision made, Justin looked up and spoke loud enough for everyone to hear, "Mister, I'm not lookin' for any trouble, but I'm not givin' you my hat and that's my final word. I just want 'a get on that train and be on my way, so why don't you be a good boy and go find somebody else ta pick on - maybe somebody who'll put up with your big mouth, bad manners and foul body odor."

There was an audible gasp from the people standing on the platform. They had never heard anyone stand up to the town bully before and they weren't sure what to do. They were sure this man; half the bully's size had lost his senses. It had to be the heat.

And to say the expression on the big cowboy's face was that of stunned disbelief, would be putting it mildly.

The mere fact that someone had talked back to him was bad enough, but the things he said about him having a big mouth and bad manners and, well he might stink ah little bit, but he didn't have ta go tellin' all those people about it.

Just as Justin thought he would, the big cowboy became instantly outraged and roared like some wild animal as he drew back his ham sized fist like a sledgehammer, ready to crush Justin's head.

"You little pimple of ah man, I'll break you like ah stick and when I'm finished I'll feed what's left of ya ta the buzzards!"

Justin dropped his satchel to the platform as he slipped easily under the slow roundhouse punch the big cowboy was throwing - and in the same movement stomped down hard on the man's instep with the heel of his shoe and heard bones crunch.

The big man let out a scream of pain and doubled over, only to meet Justin's hard right fist smashing against his nose.

Once again, a bone broke, but this time it was followed by blood gushing from the man's nose and covering the front of his shirt. Both of the man's eyes instantly swelled almost shut making it difficult for him to see. And in his state of pain and confusion the man hopped around on one foot while holding his nose, looking like one of those bears that dance at the circus.

Justin reached over and lifted the big mans two colts from their holsters, then raised his right foot and kicked the man squarely in his pot gut, which caused him to stagger back.

The big cowboy was close to the edge of the platform and when he stepped backward, he stepped into nothing but air, and for just a moment he was airborne, arms and legs flailing as though he was trying to fly.

In no more than the blink of an eye, the cowboy hit the ground like a giant tree being felled. The earth shook and a cloud of dust rose into the air, and then settled over the man like ash from a volcano, mixing with the blood on his face and shirt.

The big cowboy lay there, unable to move as he tried to regain the breath that had been knocked out of him; gagging, he tried to spit out the blood that had gone down his throat but it barely cleared his lips and dripped from the stubble of whiskers on his chin. Down at the cowboy's foot, a small piece of bone protruded through the leather of his boot. Blood was seeping from the hole.

The small crowd of people stood in awe, unmoving, unbelieving - not sure of what had just taken place. Everything had happened so fast, and with so little effort on the part of the greenhorn that they had been caught totally unaware. It was completely the opposite of what they imagined would happen.

Justin smiled as he saw the shocked looks on their faces. Over the years, he'd become used to that kind of reaction. They would do a lot of talking later about how a young greenhorn dressed in an eastern suit, wearing a derby hat had bested the town bully.

Justin would bet that if he came back to El Paso a year from now he would be able to hear at least ten different versions of the story.

Justin grinned as he tossed the big man's pistols onto the roof of the depot, and then without a word to anyone, picked up his satchel and headed for the train just as the conductor called out, "All aboard!"

As he went up the steps, the conductor, a smallish man in his sixties, who walked with a limp, patted him on the shoulder and said, "Thanks."

CHAPTER THREE

A little after nine o'clock that night the train pulled into Lordsburg, located in the southwest part of the Territory of New Mexico.

It was the conductor who informed Justin of yet another delay. He'd said it could be two or three days at the least, maybe longer, this time.

Among the Apaches, there were a few young bucks still not willing to bow to the white man and his ways and were not afraid of the iron horse and had torn out the rails in several places between Lordsburg and Benson, Arizona.

Justin considered buying a horse and heading out alone, but leaving Lordsburg by horseback by himself was not only dangerous, but also insane. Between Lordsburg and Benson was more than a hundred miles of mountain and desert terrain that was home to the fearsome Apache tribes where small bands of hostile Chiricahua Apache warriors still terrorized the area. It was an area soon to become known as the Sonoran desert. It was filled with desert, rocky hills, cactus, mesquite, scrub brush, and precious little water. Other than snakes, lizards and scorpions, along with a hawk or two, there wasn't much wild life. In the mountain areas, a man might find a bit of wildlife, such as wolves, mountain lions and other small critters, but all in all, it could a difficult place to survive, especially for a white man who was unaccustomed to such living.

There would also be the possibility of running into bands of Mexican banditos, or Mescalero, who robbed and murdered anyone they found within their territory and then disappeared into no man's land like a puff of smoke on the wind.

Even using all his skills and knowledge of the country, his chances of survival would be small. But sitting around Lordsburg for several days, wasting even more time, was not the answer either. He was a man with a mission.

The train would have taken him to Tucson, which was north of where he wanted to go. But since the train would make a stop at Benson, which he guessed to be somewhere around sixty miles as a crow flies from Nogales, he could save at least two days, maybe more by getting off at Benson, buying a horse and riding on down to Nogales. But now, those plans were spoiled by yet another delay. What the hell was he supposed to do now? His mind was in turmoil as he gathered up his bag and headed for the exit door.

As he stepped onto the platform, the conductor helped Justin make his decision when he informed him the Southern Pacific Railroad was offering free passage by the Butterfield Stage Line to Tucson for anyone who didn't feel they could wait.

Justin definitely didn't want to wait. There had been enough delays already, and the stage would pass through Benson, where he wanted to go in the first place. Plus, riding on the stagecoach would be better than trying to travel by horseback alone or pacing the sidewalks of Lordsburg, doing nothing.

The Southern Pacific Railroad began offering service in this part of the country during the year eighteen hundred and seventy eight and was slowly driving the stage lines out of business because trains were more comfortable to ride and had less chance of being robbed - if you didn't mind the delays.

The stage line would provide a man to ride shotgun and along with himself, some of the other passengers might also be armed. In this country, an extra gun or two could make the difference between living or dying.

Justin checked into the hotel, then went down to the crowded dining room where he ate his supper, alone. After his meal, Justin had a nightcap at the bar before heading to his room, leaving several ladies of the evening pouting and looking sad.

Around six o'clock the following morning, Justin and two drummers boarded the stage that was scheduled to take them to Benson where he could buy or rent a horse for the last leg of his trip. Justin had gotten up early and had gone down to the dining room and eaten a good breakfast and was now ready to be on his way. He handed up a package to the driver. The hotel clerk had asked him to give it to the driver. The driver stored it on top of the stagecoach with a grin. Must be some private secret, Justin thought.

Instead of storing his satchel on top or in the luggage area at the rear of the stage, Justin kept his own satchel with him as he climbed inside and settled into the far corner, putting his satchel on the seat next to him. If an attractive woman boarded, naturally, he would move his satchel to make room for her. If not, then he would leave it where it was. He would need space in case there was trouble and in this part of the country you needed to be ready for anything.

As his two fellow passengers approached the stagecoach, Justin looked them over very carefully and decided they didn't appear to be much. Neither of them looked like he would be much help in a fight. Justin figured them to be the type who was afraid of their own shadow. But he also conceded that looks could be deceiving, which in the case of these two, he sure hoped so. Otherwise, if trouble came, it would be just him and the man up top, riding shotgun.

Justin's hopes that the two drummers might be of some help, if there was trouble, were dashed even further when they climbed inside. Both smelled of whiskey and it was just past six am. This was not a good sign. A drunk could be the worst kind of help in a gunfight.

On the other hand, maybe it would be just another boring ride.

CHAPTER FOUR

The Butterfield stage bumped and rattled its way over the trail through the mountain and desert areas that lay between them and Benson, Arizona. It was not yet noon and already the air was stifling. The starched collar of Justin's shirt was chafing his neck and his body was clammy with sweat, which didn't put him in the best of moods.

The two drummers sitting across from him were nursing a bottle of rotgut, hoping to calm their nerves, each wishing he'd waited for the train.

Thaddeus P. Jones was a small, wart of a man who had married late in life for money. His bride had been the daughter of a Cincinnati man who manufactured ladies corsets. And, after only a few months of being married to an obese, sex maniac, who drove him crazy, Thaddeus suggested to his father-in-law that he go west to introduce their line of corsets to the women of the frontier to broaden the business. And, of course, he must leave his wife behind. The Wild West was no place for a delicate flower like her.

The other drummer, Elmer Beeler, looked like a walking cadaver, stood six feet six inches in his stocking feet and weighed one hundred forty pounds with all his clothes on. Elmer's outstanding feature was a hooked nose that curved around so far that he could touch it with his tongue. Elmer was traveling west to introduce a new line of satin lined caskets for the genteel that wanted to rest in splendor for all of eternity.

Between the heat and the whiskey, the two drummers were getting happily drunk as meaningless conversation floated back and forth between them.

Justin was in no mood to engage in idle conversation or advertise his problems, and drinking whiskey in this heat was definitely out of the question. For the moment, he was content with staring out of the window of the stage. As far as he could see, giant Saguaro cactus stood proudly like huge sentinels of the desert. Some were close to fifty feet tall with arms ten feet long pointing skyward. Here and there, scrub brush fought for existence. A large rattlesnake slithered his way across the barren floor of the desert as a roadrunner raced along parallel with the stagecoach for a short distance, chased by a dust devil that was kicking dirt high into the air. At the sight, a small chuckle erupted from Justin's throat.

Justin stuck his head out of the window and looked forward through the dust the horses and wheels were kicking up, trying to see the outline of the Peloncillo Mountains in the far distance ahead. He knew they were there but the dust impaired his vision.

Dust came through the open windows and filled everything inside the coach. The canvas covers could have been lowered to help keep the dust out but the heat would have made it even more unbearable.

Justin pulled his head back inside and leaned back against the seat. He would try to get a little rest before they got to their stop over, which were still several hours away. He was just about to pull his hat over his eyes when Thaddeus nudged his foot, "You want a drink, young man?"

Without opening his eyes, Justin said, "No."

In his drunken state of mind, Thaddeus P. Jones was not about to be put off by this young upstart. "What's the matter? Are you one of those uppity preacher men who don't believe in enjoying the qualities of good Kentucky corn liquor?"

Elmer Beeler was encouraged by his new friend's banter and decided to jump into the conversation. "Maybe he's one of them sissy fellers that's got ah little woman waiting on him and don't want her to smell liquor on his breath because she might take ah frying pan to him."

Both men thought this was very funny and busted up laughing as Justin pulled his hat down over his eyes.

Seeing Justin retreat under his hat made the two drummers believe their opinion had been correct, which urged them on, causing their mouths to disconnect with their brains.

Thaddeus nudged Elmer and said, "He certainly isn't well bred in the manners of social conversation, is he?"

"On top of that, he isn't very friendly," Elmer, said. "Maybe the little woman doesn't allow him to talk to strangers," Elmer continued, which caused both of them to burst into laughter, again.

By this time, Justin had heard enough and lifted his hat from over his face and stared hard at the two drummers through slate gray eyes. The look caused both men to shut their mouths and become deadly quiet. Elmer Beeler's adams-apple bobbled up and down as he swallowed several times, trying not to soil himself.

Justin decided it was time to put a stop to all this nonsense as he reached across and clamped down on Thaddeus's knee, digging his fingers in deep. "The way I see it, my private life is of no concern to either of you. Nor am I in the mood to be made sport of." Justin increased the pressure and saw a wet spot appear on Thaddeus's pants. "Have I made myself clear?" Justin asked in a stern tone of voice.

Shook to the core, each one of them nodded his head, yes.

Elmer, who was holding the bottle of whiskey, turned and threw it out of the window.

Justin released Thaddeus's knee and gave it a pat, then leaned back against the seat and changed his thoughts to the young oriental girl back at Wong's Laundry and Bath House.

Elmer scooted back against the seat and as far into the corner as he could get, glad he hadn't been the recipient of the young man's wrath. A quick sideward glance at Thaddeus revealed tears in his friend's eyes and a pained expression on his face.

Thaddeus was badly shaken. The young man's grip on his knee had been like a vice and the look in his eyes made him feel like he was close to death itself. The liquor had given him false courage and bad judgment. He was glad Elmer had thrown it out of the window. Out here in this God forsaken country a man wasn't always what he looked like - a piece of information to be well remembered.

The two drummers sat in silence as the stagecoach entered the Peloncillo Mountains, heading for Apache Pass Way Station where they would get a bite to eat, along with fresh teams of horses. There was a vital spring there, the only one for many miles in either direction. It had been ole Cochise himself in his efforts to live in peace with the white man, who had allowed the Butterfield Stage Line to travel this route and build a way station here.

Things had gone alone fairly well until February of eighteen sixty-one, when a hotheaded lieutenant fresh out of West Point by the name of George Bascom accused Cochise of stealing cattle and abducting a twelve year old boy from a ranch eighty miles away, which no one but Bascom believed.

Cochise was trying hard to keep the peace with the white man, and of course denied the whole thing. Bascom chose to ignore what he believed to be an ignorant heathen Indian. His superiors had told him to bring the boy and livestock back by any means he saw fit and that is what he intended on doing.

Bascom called for a meeting with Cochise at Apache Pass and when he tried to arrest him, Cochise pulled his knife and slit a hole in the back of the tent and escaped in a barrage of pistol fire.

Instead of dropping the matter for lack of evidence, Bascom took six of Cochise's companions' prisoner. There were two squaws, a boy, his brother and two nephews.

Bascom thought he now had the upper hand over an ignorant heathen who would return with his hat in hand, so to speak, and return the boy and the livestock. How dare this Indian lie to him like a child to his father when the father knew Cochise was guilty.

When Cochise heard the news, he captured several white people to trade in an even exchange. When negotiations failed, he killed his prisoners and left them where they could be found. Shortly thereafter, the six prisoners were hung close to where the white people had been killed and the peace treaty was over. The prisoners were left hanging there until July of eighteen sixty-one.

As far as Justin Hacker was concerned, it was men like Bascom and the other people like him, who took no time to learn about the Apache people or their ways that started the trouble. Like Bascom, they believed all Indians were ignorant heathens and the only good Indian was a dead Indian.

Justin knew these people to be a hardy race who loved their wives and children, and in many ways, had far more compassion for their fellow man than the whites.

It was General Sheridan, of the union army, who made two statements about the Apache people.

First, he stated, "We took away their land, their means of support, broke up their mode of living, their habits, then introduced disease and decay among them - and it was for this they went to war. Who among us can blame them?"

Second, after fighting with them, he said, "The only good Indians I ever saw were dead."

The first quote was from understanding the situation and the second quote came from frustration at trying to defeat them.

The stage pulled into the way station and without a word, the two drummers went straight to the bar and began drinking again.

Justin washed his face and hands at the water basin close to the well, and then dried himself on the roller towel mounted on a nearby post. Finally, he went inside to the dining table where he found the driver and the man riding shotgun already seated and eating heartily. They nodded as Justin sat down and began filling his plate. He was hungry and the food smelled good.

Both the driver and the man riding shotgun, glanced toward the bar and shook their heads, but decided it was none of their business.

The German couple that ran the place was a credit not only to the company, but to themselves as well. Unlike many people living so far from civilization, both the man and the woman were clean and neatly dressed and friendly. In fact, the entire place was clean and orderly. The food was simple, but superb - a stew with potatoes and fresh vegetables from the woman's garden, along with venison meat, covered with a rich brown gravy. The bread was dark, and freshly baked. The butter was sweet and smooth. For dessert there were large slices of rhubarb pie and strong, black coffee.

How the lady had found the seasonings to create such a delicious meal out here in the middle of nowhere was a mystery. Justin was impressed and told her so. He also left her a nice tip.

She was beaming with pride as Justin returned to the stage, which had been given a good cleaning and had fresh horses harnessed and ready to go.

There hadn't been much conversation during the meal, but as they walked out to the stage Justin looked around and said, "A few short years ago a white man would never have dared ta come close to this place. Now he comes here on a regular basis."

The driver, a tall, lanky man in his late sixties, with skin like worn saddlebags, spit a stream of tobacco juice into the dirt and said, "I was jest ah yonker, ridin' shotgun on the first stage ole Cochise let come through here."

He took a moment, lifting his face to the sky, letting the memory filter through his mind. After a pause, he continued. "I'll admit it now. I was ah mite skeered at first, even with all them blue-bellies ridin' with us. But ole Cochise his-self was standin' right here ta meet us. And you know what? He was ah right friendly fella. Shook all our hands, he did. It was ah real shame what happened ta him and his people, yes sir, ah real shame."

The driver shook his head and spit another stream of tobacco juice at a beetle of some kind that was crawling across the compound. "Them Paches' are ah right proud people and ta be pinned up like cattle, havin' ta beg fer food. . ." He let the sentence trail away as he climbed aboard the stage and gathered the reins in his hands.

Justin nodded as he watched the two drummers stagger out of the building, and with a great deal of difficulty, board the stage.

The shotgun rider, who had been checking the harness, signaled his approval and then climbed up to the driver's seat and took up his weapon as Justin climbed inside the stage and closed the door. The two drummers were already asleep and snoring loudly. The stationmaster and his wife stood in the middle of the compound, waving as they watched the stage go through the front gate. A very large mountain boomer lizard ran for the safety of a large boulder as the stage rumbled past.

CHAPTER FIVE

Even though the interior of the stage had been swept clean, within five minutes the dust was back and Justin was restless. The hair on the back of his neck began to stand up as he reached into his satchel and pulled out his gun rig. The holster had been handmade especially for him eight years ago by a Mexican craftsman by the name of Gomez, a man he had shown friendship.

Justin ran his hand over the smoothness of the leather as he let his mind drift back to the day he'd come across Gomez, lying face down and unconscious in the desert with a broken leg. Ten feet away a burro lay dead from a rattlesnake bite.

He later found out that Gomez had been on his way to Nogales when a large rattlesnake struck the poor creature on the leg. The burro bucked and pawed at the snake, and when its heart finally gave out, the old fella fell on the snake and killed it. During all the bucking and jumping around, Gomez jumped off and landed awkwardly, breaking his leg. He'd crawled away a short distance, then passed out. Justin had come along shortly thereafter and found him. Justin had made a splint and tied his leg up as best he could, and then had taken him to see the doctor in Nogales.

As it turned out, the man's leg had healed as good as new and the custom-made gun rig was his way of saying, thank you.

On the other hand, his pistol was a brand new Walker-Colt six shot he'd bought in New York City the day before he headed west. It was currently considered the finest handgun made and had been named the Peace Maker. Every Texas Ranger he'd heard of swore by it. The action was smooth and easy. He loaded all six chambers and then spun the cylinder. Normally, he would have left one cylinder empty, but not the way he was feeling. He wiped it clean with the cloth it had been wrapped in and then slipped the Colt six-shot into the holster. He buckled the rig around his waist, hoping there would be no cause to use it. Yet, the hair on the back of his neck was still trying to give him a warning, and in this country, a man who didn't listen to that something inside you that warned you of danger could find himself all alone, buried under several feet of desert. Or, he might just be left for the meat eaters to fight over.

With nothing else to do, Justin leaned back against the seat and pulled his hat down over his eyes, hoping to get a little sleep before they reached Benson.

The trail angled southwest, crossing a stretch of desert before facing yet another mountain range called the Dragoon Mountains. And just beyond the Dragoons, was their next stop, Benson, where Justin would depart the stage line.

The trip through this part of the country was boring for the driver and the man riding shotgun. They had traveled this route many times before, and with the heat and the rocking motion of the stage, both the driver and the man riding shotgun nodded off, allowing the horses to follow a trail they too had traveled many times before.

Near the summit of Dragoon Mountain, was a small area where they could pull over and let the horses catch their wind. But a short distance before the rest stop, the stage had to travel through a narrow pass not much wider than the trail itself. And when the horses saw the tree lying across the trail, they slowed down and stopped.

Both men, thinking they were at the rest spot, came awake. But when they saw the tree lying across the trail, the man riding shotgun pulled back both hammers of his double barreled Greener shot gun and looked around for trouble.

Two shots rang out slamming the driver and the man with the shotgun back against the seat. Both men were dead, shot through the head. Both men's bodies toppled sideways to the ground, one on each side of the coach. A Mexican bandito stood up from behind the fallen tree and grabbed the reins of the horses, speaking to them in a quiet voice to keep them from bolting.

Inside the coach, all three men came instantly awake. But it was Justin who flung himself to the floor with the Peace Maker in his hand, motioning for the two drummers to do the same. But instead of heeding Justin's warning, they just sat there with their eyes wide and their mouths hanging open, still in a somewhat drunken stupor.

Black clouds swept over the mountaintop. Thunder rumbled and the rain began to fall. Somewhere out on the desert, lightning struck with a loud crack.

From a nearby boulder, a man speaking English with a Mexican accent called out to them. "Senors, the driver and the other man are dead and cannot help you. Throw your guns out of the window and get out of the stage with your hands in the air and no one will get hurt. You have my word on this."

Justin watched as Thaddeus reached into his satchel and pulled out a thirty-two caliber pistol, while Elmer retrieved a small derringer from the inside pocket of his coat.

"They're not much, but they're better than nothing I reckon," Justin said. "Do you know how to use those things?" he whispered.

Both men looked at each other with confused expressions on their faces, then looked at Justin and shook their heads, 'no,' but it was Elmer who spoke.

"Young man, we are not men of violence. We carry these pistols only for show. Mine isn't even loaded, and whoever is out there has the drop on us with loaded guns. Not very good odds are they? Plus, the man said he would not harm us if we comply with his wishes. I, for one, would rather be robbed than killed in a gunfight, especially one where I have no bullets in my gun."

Before Justin could reply, both men threw their weapons out of the window and Elmer opened the door and began to get out of the coach with his hands in the air.

Justin reached for him, but he was too late.

The rain was falling hard and Elmer slipped as he stepped onto the wet ground. His arm went up to catch himself just as a shot rang out and a bullet pierced the middle of his chest. The bullet drove Elmer back into the coach where he lay face up with eyes that could no longer see.

Justin threw two quick shots in the direction of the shooter, then shoved Elmer outside. As he closed the door, bullets began slamming into the coach. Thaddeus was shaking from head to foot as another wet spot appeared on the crotch of his pants.   Justin hauled him down to the floor just as several bullets passed through the windows of the coach.

A Mexican bandito known as Snake-eye was crouched behind a large boulder some twenty feet or so above the stagecoach, while a second bandito was hidden behind a tree not far below it. And the third bandito, was lying behind the tree that blocked the trail, holding the reins of the horses and speaking quietly to them.

Over the past few years, Snake-eye had gained a reputation as one of the most feared of all the Mexican banditos to cross the border in search of American riches. To say the man was ruthless would be laughable. The name Snake-eye was given to him after a young Apache girl cut a jagged line down across his face from his forehead to just below his left eye with a piece of flint rock. He had been raping her at the time and when he finished he gutted her like he would a fish, leaving her for the coyotes to feast on. When the wound healed the scar resembled a snake, and so the name Snake-eye became more famous than his real name, Ramon Jesus Gonzales ever was.

The storm continued to build as Snake-eye pondered the situation. He was sure there were only two men left inside the stagecoach and reasoned that only one of them had a gun. He began firing through the windows of the coach to keep them pinned down while motioning for the man behind the tree to get around to the far side of the coach so they would have them in crossfire.

Justin saw something moving among the trees and fired a shot in that direction, but just as he fired, the bandito slipped and fell down, which saved his life as the bullet whizzed over his head by a narrow margin.

Justin swung his pistol and fired two more shots toward the boulder, sending slivers of rock into Snake-eye's forehead. Snake-eye yelped and moved to the opposite end of the boulder for better protection, cursing because the gringo's bullet had almost ended his life. He would be more careful until this white man was dead.

Justin was hunkered on the floor of the stagecoach reloading his pistol when Thaddeus made his decision to try and escape. He had come to believe he would be saved from death if he were not inside the coach when the shooting was over. His life would be spared if he were not with the young man with the gun. Surely, when they found out he had no weapon and had not shot at them, they would allow him to live.

Very slowly, Thaddeus inched his way toward the far side door and then opened it and started out, but by then the third bandito had reached a vantage spot on the far side of the stagecoach and saw Thaddeus opening the backside door.

Thaddeus was only head and shoulders out of the coach when the bullet struck him in the head.

At the sound, Justin jerked around and began to raise his pistol for a shot at the bandito who had just killed Thaddeus, but at the same time, Snake-eye began firing from behind the boulder and Justin had to duck to keep from being shot, as bullets were coming through the windows of the coach from both sides. One of Snake-eye's bullets struck Thaddeus in the back and drove him face first out the door of the stagecoach. Fortunately, for Thaddeus, he never felt the pain of this second bullet ripping into his lifeless body.

Justin fired two shots out the backside of the coach, and then swung around to fire at the bandito behind the boulder. He was lifting his pistol when a bullet struck him in the head at a strange angle, not hard enough to puncture bone, but enough to knock him out and cause an ugly wound. There had been one sharp pain, then blackness.

A short time later, Snake-eye approached the stagecoach with great caution, his pistol drawn. When he saw the two men lying on the floor of the coach he called to his men. "Strip them completely. Leave nothing. And when you are finished, lay them here on the ground so the animals can feed on them. And bring me this one's pistola and clothes," he said, pointing at Justin. "I will have them for my own."

As the rain fell, the bodies were dragged onto the ground and stripped. The horses were unhitched and led away. Within minutes, the banditos had disappeared over the crest of the mountain, leaving the bodies for the meat eaters who would come soon.

The heavy rains were unusual for this time of year in this part of the country, but in truth heavy storms could appear out of nowhere, fill the arroyos and then disappear as quickly as they came. Flash floods would run through the arroyos like a herd of panicked buffalo, overpowering anything in its way, leaving a toll of uprooted plants and trees as well as the corpses of any animal caught in the raging water, leaving it as evidence of the force of its power and destruction.

A fast moving stream of water flowed past the five exposed bodies stretched out on the ground next to the stagecoach. Blood from the dead men turned the rainwater to a pale reddish color. Wild animals such as wolves and mountain lions, would come to feast on the dead men, leaving little to identify their remains but washed over bones scattered about the area.

CHAPTER SIX

The sound of growling from deep in the wolf's chest slowly penetrated the inner workings of Justin's brain, warning him of danger. The voice screamed at him "Wake up! Wake up!"

Justin tried to open his eyes, but only the left one would work, and then only just enough to peek through the slit. The sound of growling came again, and through the slit he could make out a big wolf standing no more than six or seven feet to the left of where he lay. The wolf's lips were drawn back, showing vicious looking teeth and slobbers were dripping from his lips.

Justin reached slowly for his pistol only to realize he had no weapon. In fact, he had no clothes, either. They had stripped him naked and left him for the wild animals to eat. Only a low life would do something like that, but he didn't have time to dwell on that right now. He needed to find something to defend himself with, and quick. As that thought crossed his mind, his hand touched a good-sized stone. He let his fingers curl around it. Yes, this might do, he thought.

The growl came again, only closer this time. He knew he had to act now or it would be too late. He took a deep breath, then sat up and yelled, "Yaaaa," while at the same time, he hurled the rock at the wolf. He was surprised when the rock slammed into the side of the wolf's head hard enough to knock him off his feet.

The big wolf yelped and scrambled back onto his feet and ran toward the safety of the trees on wobbly legs. Justin grabbed another rock and this time hitting him on the hindquarters, drew another yelp, causing the wolf to retreat even faster.

He fell back down, exhausted. He was safe for the moment from wild animals. It was the weather he had to deal with, now. He was shivering from the cold rain. His teeth were chattering so bad he was afraid he would break a tooth. He had to get inside the stagecoach and get warm.

With great effort, he rolled over onto his hands and knees and crawled through the mud to the open door of the stagecoach, then dragged himself to his feet and climbed inside.

By the time he had crawled onto the seat, Justin felt like he was going to pass out, again. It took several moments to shake the feeling. He touched the wound on his forehead. It was very tender and still bleeding. He looked around, and then tore one of the curtains from the window to make a bandage, which he wrapped around his head.

Finding nothing to cover himself with, Justin curled up on the seat to try and get some much-needed rest as the sound of rain beat against the roof of the coach.

It was a restless night. First, his body felt like it was on fire, which caused him to sweat. Next it was the chills, which caused his body to shake uncontrollably. In his delirium, Justin dreamed about his brother sleeping under a warm blanket in his cell.

Daylight came and Justin sat up and looked around, trying to get his bearings. When he looked out of the window it all came back to him. There had been a hold-up by some Mexican banditos and everyone had been killed except him. The bloody wound to his head and the fact that they hadn't checked him closely had probably saved his life. Little consolation since he would probably die of exposure, anyway.   He stared out of the window at the four bodies. They would have to be taken care of before the wild animals came to gorge themselves on man meat.

He figured it would be several days before anyone could get here to find them and by that time there would be nothing but bones scattered around the area.

His head hurt and it was hard to think. He knew he had to do something. But as he reached for the door handle, everything went black. The next time he opened his eyes the rain had stopped. The sun was shining brightly, and from its height in the clear blue sky, Justin judged it to be around nine in the morning. His head ached, but his mind was clear and his body no longer shivered from the cold. He opened the door of the coach and climbed out. He had a job to do.

It was close to noon by the time he placed the last rock on the pile that covered all four bodies. Exhausted, his head reeling with pain, Justin sat down on the step of the stagecoach to catch his breath. Dark clouds began to roll in again as thunder rumbled overhead. After a few minutes, Justin stood up and looked at the pile of rocks. "That's about all I can do to protect you until the people from the stage line show up," he told the dead men beneath the rocks. After a moment, he turned and started walking up the mountain road - just as the first drops of rain began to fall.

All day Justin trudged through the rain and mud and by nightfall he'd reached the top of the mountain, exhausted and looking for a place to find some relief. The only good thing about the rain was that it had helped cool down the raging heat that was going on inside his body. That and the water he could drink from the many small pools that had accumulated along the trail.

That night, Justin sat under a ledge just beyond the crest of the mountain, his knees drawn up and his arms wrapped around his legs to try and stay warm. He spent a miserable night with only short bits of rest. High fever switched to cold chills, then back to high temperatures again, causing his muscles to jerk with spasms. Around four in the morning, the rain stopped and Justin climbed wearily to his feet and trudged through the mud down the far side of the mountain, guided only by moonlight.

It was close to daybreak when he found himself standing at the bottom of the mountain. The only clothing he had to protect him from the elements was the piece of canvas wrapped around his head.

Justin watched a bright sun that promised to be a scorcher, climb above the horizon, already beginning to heat up the desert that he was about to try and cross. He'd had no water since a drink earlier from a small pool of rainwater, and he hadn't eaten since the way station one or two days ago. He couldn't remember for sure. And, even if he was lucky enough to find some prickly pear cactus, he had no way to skin it or burn off the spines, and for sure, he couldn't eat it with the spines left on.

The big problem with water was, there would be none, unless it rained again and he could find a pool cashed somewhere - not impossible, but almost. Just thinking made his head throb and his legs feel weak, so he couldn't even consider his brother. It would be hard enough fending for himself. He was beginning this day already exhausted, with still a long way to go. But the stubbornness in him wouldn't let him give up. It just wasn't in his makeup. The word quit had never been a part of his vocabulary.

The next mountain looked to be a million miles away and it wasn't going to get any closer as long as he stood there doing nothing. Justin judged the trek would be at least a day and a half, maybe two days, depending on his strength. Surely, he would be able to survive that, as long as kept his wits about him. To Justin, it would be just another challenge and during his twenty-eight years, he'd had his fair share. He picked up a small stone and put it in his mouth to help keep his tongue moist and started walking.

By late afternoon, Justin was half walking, half crawling. He'd long ago lost the stone and his tongue was swollen, his body was on fire from the blistering sun, and his head felt like his brain was being roasted over a blazing fire. He only knew he was climbing another sand knoll because he had to lean forward. Then near the top his will gave out and he fell forward, face down on the burning sand. He could go no farther. The world spun around until finally he slipped into blackness where there is no thirst or hunger or pain. From high up among the trees on the mountain behind him, a wolf's mournful cry floated eerily across the desert, but Justin was in a place where he heard nothing.

Somewhere in his delirium, Justin's mind ventured back to the day his younger brother, Jacob, who was only sixteen at the time, had gone to the Mexican side of Nogales and got himself killed by another young hothead, in a shootout over a young lady of the night - an occurrence that seemed to happen more often than people liked to talk about.

Jacob's death had been a senseless thing. From what the sheriff could gather, a young vaquero was just passing through on his way to where, no one seemed to know. But the exotic and strikingly beautiful young prostitute, who went by the name Juanita, had made the vaquero's blood run hot.

The problem was, Jacob had been seeing Juanita twice a week for more than a month and fancied himself to be head over heels in love. When he found her in bed with the young vaquero, he called the vaquero out.

The young vaquero had been faster on the draw, and when the smoke cleared, he mounted his horse and rode away, leaving Jacob dead and bleeding in the street.

Juanita had stood on the front porch of the saloon and watched the whole thing. She had been excited that two boys were fighting over her. But when it was over, she shook her head and said, "Stupid boys."

Juanita turned and sashayed back inside the saloon, holding the arm and smiling up at a portly man in a suit. "It is so good to see you again, Senor Bookman," she said in good English.

Two Mexican men hoisted Jacob's dead body onto the back of his horse and then walked the horse slowly toward the sheriff's office on the other side of the border as the sound of music once again filled the saloon. The young gringo, Jacob Hacker was, except in future stories told by the bartender, forgotten.

The town blacksmith, Elijah Hacker and his wife, Elizabeth, had three sons, Justin, Jeremiah and Jacob. It was well known that Jacob was his father's favorite and therefore a son to be doted on, which in effect was part of the reason Jacob was so wild. Of his three sons, Justin, being the oldest, was given the responsibility of watching over his younger brothers. Jeremiah had never been a problem, but Jacob had a wild streak and every chance he got he put Justin at peril with their father by drinking and fighting down below the border and expecting Justin to bail him out. The only thing was, when Jacob got himself in trouble this time, his big brother happened to be fifteen miles away. When the sheriff finally tracked him down and told him what had happened, it was Justin who had to take Jacob's body home and explain to their father what happened. The sheriff wanted no part of it.

Justin's father was working on a horseshoe at the fire pit and had his back to Justin when he rode up.

His mother, who was working in her garden, looked up from her work and saw the body draped over the horse. Her instinct told her who it was, but she had to make sure. She went straight to Jacobs' body hanging over the horse, and at the sight of her youngest son, dead at just sixteen, her heart began to beat heavily in her chest and she felt the tears streaming down her cheeks.

Jeremiah, the middle brother, was forking fresh hay to the horses when he heard someone ride up. He pitched the fork full of hay to a horse, and then looked up just as his mother came running over. Justin was still sitting on his horse and had a stern look on his face. When Jeremiah saw his mother begin to cry, he recognized Jacob's horse and had a good idea what had happened. He stuck the pitchfork into a stack of hay, and then hurried to his mother's side and put his arm around her shoulders. By now, she was sobbing heavily.

Elijah turned to see what the commotion was all about. When Elijah saw his son draped over the back of his horse, his eyes began to glaze over.

When Justin tried to explain to his father what had happened, the only thing Elijah Hacker understood was that Justin had let his younger brother get killed over some tramp down below the border.

If it hadn't been for Jeremiah and Elizabeth, Elijah would have shot his oldest son out of his saddle, right then and there.

Elizabeth tried to reason with her husband while Jeremiah pushed Justin out of the barn, telling him to stay out of sight until their father cooled down.

The next day, Elijah was still grieving and went looking for his eldest son and found Justin eating breakfast at the restaurant down town. In front of at least ten people, Elijah pointed his shotgun at Justin and told him in no uncertain terms to pack his belongings and get out of town before noon, and never come back. Elijah also informed his eldest son, if he ever laid eyes on him again, he would shoot him on sight. An hour later, Justin rode out of town.

The sun was just rising above the horizon when Justin stirred and looked around from where he had fallen. He was disorientated at first, and then realized he had been dreaming.

That day, in his dream, had been seven years ago, and now here he was, belly down on the desert, wondering if he would ever get back to help his younger brother who was facing trouble of his own, a crazy warden in a Mexican prison south of the border.

Justin sucked in a deep breath and willed himself the strength to go on, hoping his father had had time to realize Jacob's death had not been his fault.

He got slowly to his feet and made his way to the top of the sand hill and looked out across the desert. In the far distance, Justin saw something that he couldn't quite make out, but his instinct told him it was something that didn't belong there. With legs that felt like they had heavy weights attached to them, he started walking towards the distant, dark mound on the desert.

The sun had not yet reached its peak when Justin staggered up to the prospector and his mule. Both had arrows sticking out of them. He fell to his knees as once more fatigue took him to that place of darkness.

The sun was low in the western sky when Justin finally stirred himself awake and rose to his knees. He looked around; taking a moment to get his brain focused, then crawled over next to the mule where he found a full water skin still attached to the pack.

He took two tiny sips, feeling his swollen tongue and throat respond to the tepid liquid. Next, he poured a small amount over his head, careful not to waste much. After a minute or so, he took a longer pull of the precious liquid and was happy when it went down easier this time.

After a few minutes, he felt some revived and began looking through the pack, where he found some deer jerky. He bit off a piece as best he could and let it settle in his jaw, the juice mixing with saliva that he swallowed eagerly. It took close to an hour of sipping water and eating small bites of jerky before he felt well enough to get to his feet.

Fortunately, the miner was a mite heavier than him, so the clothes he found in the pack fit fairly comfortably over his sunburned body, and the boots were the right size.

Along with the clothes, Justin found some coffee, a pot, a knife, a pistol and some ammunition. The pistol was old, but in reasonably good working condition. There was also some tobacco and papers, along with a tin of matches.

Justin broke the wooden pack apart and in short order, had a fire going. He would soon have coffee and some food in his belly. Hope rose within him. He just might survive.

Justin put a pot of coffee on to boil, then cut a large piece of meat off the mule's hindquarter, not yet gone bad. Soon, he heard the sizzling of cooking meat which made his stomach grumble. The Apache preferred mule meat to horsemeat and Justin figured if it was good enough for them, it was good enough for him.

Between the coffee, a full stomach, the warmth of the fire, warm clothes and a smoke, his wounds somehow hurt a little less. Wrapped in a blanket he'd found among the miner's things, Justin was able to get a decent nights rest.

That night, he dreamed of his dearly beloved Julie, the girl he planned to marry before his father ran him out of town. In his dream, they had a nice little horse ranch and a strong, sturdy son.

The next morning, after another meal of mule meat and coffee, Justin rolled a smoke and puffed slowly, wondering if Julie had really gotten married in his absence. He'd gotten a letter from his cousin, Ben, a short time after he'd left that said she had, but in his heart, he'd always hoped it wasn't true. After finishing off what was left of the coffee, Justin let his mind come back to the job at hand.

Climbing to his feet, he said to no one in particular, "Well, me bucko, 'tis time ta head for that mountain yonder. As ya can see, it's loaded with trees and shelter from this blasted sun and ye'll be wantin' ta get there as quick as possible."

Dressed in the miner's clothes, the water skin slung over his shoulder, the knife in its sheath tucked into his belt at his back, the pistol stuck in his waistband and a sack filled with other essentials, he headed for the mountain, feeling better than he had in some time. His head wound was scabbed over and the thunder in his brain had slowed to a dull roar. Even though his skin was still red and tender with blisters, the miner's clothes helped protect him from the burning sun, and he knew that everything would eventually heal.

It was close to noon when Justin stopped for a drink of water. As he stood there, he studied the distance and judged the safety of the trees to be not much further than a few hundred yards. He grinned. It wouldn't be long now and he could sit in the shade, feeling the cool breeze as it wandered through the branches and across his ravaged body.

Just as he was replacing the stopper in the water skin, Justin heard a scream and looked up.

Three Apache braves on horseback came charging out of the trees and were headed straight for him. One began shooting at him with a rifle, the bullet splattering sand just in front of where he stood. The other two were firing arrows, which landed well short of their mark.

Justin shook his head in disbelief - the train delays, the Mexican bandits, the burning desert, and now this. When would it all end? Right here and now his brain told him, if he didn't do something real quick, as he grabbed for the pistol.

Pulling it from his waistband, he dropped to one knee while aiming at the Indian shooting at him with the rifle. As he squeezed the trigger, Justin felt the gun buck in his hand and heard the loud report of the big forty-four. The slug dug its way into the chest of the young brave, and knocked him backward off his horse.

Just as he swung the pistol in the direction of the next closest brave, Justin felt the sting of an arrow as it lodged itself in the upper part of his leg.

"Damn!" he said, squeezing the trigger and once again, watched as the forty-four slug knocked its victim to the sand.

He didn't have time to worry about the arrow in his leg, the third Apache brave was off his horse and charging him with a knife held high in the air. Justin swung the barrel of his pistol in the brave's direction and squeezed the trigger.

Other than the click of the hammer slamming down, nothing happened. By then, the brave was on him, trying his best to sink his knife blade into Justin's chest as they rolled over and over. Justin grabbed the wrist of the hand with the knife and with his gun hand he stuck the barrel of his pistol against the brave's ribcage. He cocked the pistol and squeezed the trigger a second time. This time when the pistol bucked in his hand there was a loud roar. The young brave was propelled off of him and onto to the sand. As quickly as it had begun, it was over.

Justin sat up, gasping, scanning the area for more attackers. He found the desert empty except for the three horses standing nearby looking around for something to eat or drink.

He was glad to discover there were no more braves waiting to take his scalp, because he wasn't sure he had enough strength left to fight many more battles. Pain from the arrow in his leg was beginning to rear its ugly head and Justin looked down at the feathered shaft protruding from the leg of his pants.

He felt relieved when he realized the arrow had missed the bone and only gone through flesh. He could see the tip of the arrow sticking out through the backside of his pant leg as he bent to the task of removing it - a chore he dreaded, but had to be done.

Justin took a long pull from the water skin, again wishing it was whiskey, as he gritted his teeth and pushed the shaft until the head of the arrow was fully clear of his leg. Pain exploded through his brain and almost caused him to pass out, again. After a moment, his head cleared and he was able to finish the job. He broke the arrowhead off and dropped it to the sand, then took another deep breath, grabbed the shaft and jerked it from his leg, letting out a loud scream as he did.

If only he had some whiskey to help defuse the pain, along with flushing out the wound. Since he had none water would have to do. When the wound had been washed, he took the miner's bandana and used it as a bandage, tying it tightly around his leg. With the doctoring job completed, he rolled a smoke and sat there waiting for the pain to subside.

He knew he couldn't sit there long or his leg would get stiff on him. It took some doing, but Justin got to his feet, then poured water into the miner's hat and held it out in front of him as he approached the horses, speaking in a soft tone. He watched as they smelled the water and turned in his direction. A few minutes later, Justin rode one of the horses and led the other two as he headed for the shelter of the trees.

His eyes scanned the mountain in search of more Apaches, but the forest was quiet, save for a cool breeze that rustled the leaves.

What he did not see, high on the mountain, sitting on their horses and just out of sight were the Mexican Banditos who robbed the stage and killed everyone but him. Snake-eye was dressed in Justin Hacker's clothes, with the derby hat perched atop his head. He chewed on the stub of a cigar as he watched Justin and the three Indian ponies disappear into the shelter of the trees. After a moment, Snake-eye reined his horse back into the forest and rode away without a word. His two henchmen followed a short distance behind him.

CHAPTER SEVEN

High on the mountain, in the shelter of the pine trees, Justin sat next to a small fire - watching what little fat there was drip from the rabbit stuck on a stick, just above the hot coals. Each drop caused a small hiss when it landed.

The night was quiet except for the noise the three men who had been tracking him made. He'd first heard them shortly after he'd ridden into this place where he now camped. He figured they could use some lessons on sneaking up on a person. But, right now, their tracking skills weren't what were important. Finding out who they were and what they wanted was. He sat quietly, watching the rabbit, while he waited for them to show themselves.

When the noise of their walking stopped, Justin waited a moment, figuring they were sizing up him and the situation. He called over his shoulder, "Come on in, and welcome. I ain't got much but I'm willin' ta share."

As Snake-eye and his two companions walked into the light of the fire, Justin noticed that the one with the scar down across his face was wearing his clothes and they were a mite too large for him. He also noticed his derby hat perched on top of the man's shaggy head of hair and it would also be too large for him if it weren't for his hair. The others seemed to be nothing more than two, tired and hungry, Mexican banditos. They wouldn't be much to deal with when, and if, he saw an opportunity.

Snake-eye motioned for one of his men to pick up the rifle lying within arm's reach of the young man who seemed to have more lives than a cat.

Justin smiled and said, "You wouldn't happen ta have any taters, would ya? I'm plumb out and I sure could use some."

The three banditos walked across to the opposite side of the fire and squatted down on their heels. After a long staring contest, the one with the scar reached out and took the stick with the rabbit on it from the fire. He looked at it for a moment, took a bite, and then handed it to his men who devoured what was left.

This didn't set well with Justin. He was hungry and they had just eaten his supper, but this was not the time to voice his opinion on that subject.

Snake-eye swallowed his morsel of rabbit, then reached into the inside pocket of Justin's jacket and pulled out a cigar. With a small piece of burning wood, he lit the cigar while staring at the young gringo. What made this one so different from all the others he wondered?

Justin remained seated and stared right back at the man he knew to be the one who had robbed the stage, killed the driver, the man riding shotgun, the two drummers, and had also presumed him to be dead. This was no social call. The bandito had been following him for one reason and one reason only. He wanted to make sure he was dead this time. Justin also knew that if he wanted get back to help his brother, he'd better make a move, and damn quick.

Snake-eye grinned as he blew out a long trail of cigar smoke and said, "Amigo, what are you doing up here all alone? Do you not know there are Indians and banditos all around this place? It is not safe. Especially for gringos."

Justin took his time before answering. "I ain't lookin' fer no trouble. I'm just passin' through," he said with a wide grin, sizing up the three men sitting opposite him.

Snake-eye turned serious. "Senor, the pistola and the knife, I will have them. You were brave at the stagecoach and you survived the desert, somehow, and today you fought off the attack by the Indians. You are a brave man for a gringo, but do not be foolish now. I will kill you if you force me. I do not enjoy killing people, but. . ." he let his words trail off.

Like he hadn't wanted to kill those men back at the stage, Justin thought to himself. Raising his hand, Justin said, "Easy now. I'm not plannin' on doin' anything stupid. I know when I'm out gunned. Like I said, I ain't lookin' for trouble."

Very slowly, Justin reached behind him and retrieved the knife. He'd made his decision and now was the time to do something. Holding the knife handle by his thumb and first finger, he tossed it, not at the banditos but into the fire.

When the sparks flew up, Justin drew his pistol and fired three quick shots, shooting each man in the chest while rolling out of their line of fire.

Snake-eye's bullet was the only one to come close as it passed through the air right where Justin had been sitting. The other two bullets went harmlessly into the trees.

Justin came up on one knee, ready to fire again if he needed to, but all three banditos lay staring at the moon with unseeing eyes.

Justin moved back to the fire and stood looking down at the three dead men. What a waste of human life. In the past few days, he'd seen eleven men who had died at the hands of violence. Just like that, they had departed this world; and for what, a few measly dollars or a small piece of hair to show their bravery.

Justin bent over and picked up his derby hat, dusted it off and checked inside. His life's savings was still there, all twelve thousand dollars sewn into the lining. He didn't care about the suit but his hat was a different thing altogether. It held what he hoped would be a new beginning, maybe a horse ranch that might possibly include Julie. That is, if he could rescue his brother from that prison and possibly make amends with his father. These were big odds, and not in his favor, but they were all he had.

Dressed in his clothes again, Justin mounted Snake-eye's horse and led the other horses by tying each horse's reins to the tail of the horse in front of it. It was slow going by the light of the moon. He hoped he could finish the trip without any more trouble, because the throbbing in his head was beginning to affect his eyesight, and his leg wound felt like there was a fire burning inside.

As he rode along, his stomach began to growl. The banditos had eaten his rabbit and during all the excitement, he'd forgotten to eat anything. He reached into one of the saddlebags and pulled out a small sack that held some hardtack and a few stripes of venison jerky he'd packed from the old miner's things. There would be no stopping to make coffee. Water would have to do.

The creaking of the saddle and the plodding of horse's hooves were about the only sounds in an otherwise quiet night. Justin allowed his horse to make its way down the mountain while he bit off a piece of hard tack and gnawed on the jerky. He needed to stop and get some sleep, but that was not a luxury he could afford right now.

When the horses left the mountain and began to find their way slowly across yet another stretch of desert, the sound of snoring could be heard by any

Apache who might be listening. The sound floated through the night air like someone sawing on a large piece of wood, as Justin, without realizing it, had fallen asleep in the saddle. The past few days were taking their toll on the young man in the eastern styled suit and derby hat.

The sun was still low in the morning sky as Justin rode into the yard of Lopez, the sheepherder. Justin had been awake for some time now. He'd seen the ranch from the crest of the hill a mile or so back and headed directly for it.

Lopez was standing next to the water trough and watched in silence as the man dressed in an eastern suit and funny little hat got off his horse and asked, "Se habla ingles?"

Lopez doffed his hat and said, "Si, Senor, I learn at the mission."

"Any chance I can fill my canteen and water the horses?" Justin asked.

"Si, Senor, have all you want, it is a good well."

Justin used the gourd hanging on the bucket to get a drink, and then filled his canteen. By then, the horses, smelling the water had nosed up to the watering trough.

Lopez noticed the bodies tied across the backs of three of the horses, but asked no questions. After all, this was a gringo and he did not question the affairs of gringos.

Maybe this one was a lawman, even if he did not look like one. He had heard of some new lawmen that dressed in suits. He thought they were called Pinkertons.

After Justin had satisfied his thirst, he reached into his pocket and took out a coin and flipped it in Lopez's direction.

Lopez caught it easily and his eyes brightened as he looked down at the twenty dollar gold piece in his hand.

"Name's Justin Hacker. Had ta shoot these three hombres in self-defense. They robbed the stage and killed the driver, the man ridin' shotgun and two drummers, then left 'em for the wolves. I covered the bodies with rocks so's the wolves and other critters couldn't get to 'em before people from the stage line can get up there. I'd appreciate ah favor. That twenty-dollar gold piece is yours if you'll see to it these three men get buried, and you can keep the horses as a bonus for your trouble."

Lopez lifted his sombrero. "Si, Senor; mochas gracias," he said.

The stranger gave him a nod, then stepped onto his horse and rode away in the direction of Nogales.

Lopez waited until the man called Senor Hacker got out of sight, then looked the three dead men over carefully. After he was sure, he mounted one of the Indian ponies, and leading the three horses with the dead men on them, rode away towards the south just as storm clouds, thunder, lightning and rain once again came rolling in from the north.

CHAPTER EIGHT

An hour or so outside of Nogales, the storm caught up with Justin and drenched him and the desert, causing nearby arroyos to flood. And when he rode down the main street of Nogales, his horse walked along in mud up to its hocks.

A dispute of some kind seemed to be taking place. Four men covered with mud were swinging away at each other in the middle of the street right in front of the saloon. Justin guided his horse over to the hitch rail and swung down. He tied the big roan to the rail, then stepped onto the wooden sidewalk next to where an old man sat in a chair, watching the fight and swinging at imaginary enemies.

"Say there old timer, would you happen ta know ah fella by the name of Benjamin Hacker?" Justin asked.

Without taking his eyes off the fight the old man said, "Maybe, maybe not."

Justin chuckled, "Well now, if you did happen ta know him, where do you reckon he might be this time of day?"

The old man spit a stream of tobacco juice into the street and then looked up at Justin and said, "And jest why should I tell you, mister drummer man?"

"Because, you old reprobate, I'm Justin Hacker, son to Elijah and Elizabeth and cousin to Ben. What's the matter? Don't you recognize me? " Justin said with a big grin.

"You don't say!" the old man said, standing up to take a closer look. Before he could say anything more, one of the men from the fight was knocked onto the sidewalk close to where Justin and the old man were standing. The old man spit another stream of tobacco juice into the street, then looked down at the man at his feet. "Ben," he said, nodding toward Justin, "this feller here is lookin' fer ya; says he's yer cousin."

The mud-covered cowboy looked up and said, "Justin?"

Justin shook his head and said, "Ben? Is that you under all that mud?"

Ben began to laugh and started to get up as the three men he'd been fighting with came toward them. "You sure are dressed funny. And you don't look none too good, yourself," he said.

Justin reached out and took Ben's hand and was helping him to his feet as one of the men from the fight stepped onto the sidewalk and took a roundhouse swing at Justin. Justin released Ben's hand and gave the cowboy a left hook to the jaw that sent him sprawling back into the other two cowboys. All three cowboys landed on their backs in the muddy street.

Again, Justin reached out and grabbed Ben's hand, and hauled him to his feet.

"Friends of yours?" Justin asked.

"Not really," Ben said. "Just ah little difference of opinion, that's all."

"Well, let's get it settled so we can go someplace and talk," Justin said, as he stepped off the sidewalk and limped into the muddy street, swinging a hard right fist to the jaw of the first man to get back on his feet.

The old man on the porch was excited as he watched the five men slip and slide around, with most of the punches doing little harm because of the slick mud. Finally, the three men held up their hands in surrender. They'd had enough. They all shook hands and then turned and headed for the saloon. Drinks were on the losers. As they walked toward the saloon, Ben noticed Justin was favoring what looked to be a leg wound.

Justin and Ben took a place down at the end of the bar, away from the others, so they could speak privately. Justin was telling Ben about his ordeal when the bartender brought them each a mug of beer. As the bartender turned and went back to take care of his other customers, Ben said, "No wonder you were attacked, you look like ah dude in them eastern clothes." He grinned and added, "Finish your beer and we'll go see if doc is back in his office yet. He's been out to the Baileys. Ma Bailey is havin' number eleven."

Justin shook his head as he swigged down the last of his beer and turned for the door. His leg wound was making it more and more difficult to walk, but he tried not to show it.

As they stepped through the bat-winged doors, onto the sidewalk and headed for the doctor's office, Justin said, "Tell me about Jeremiah."

Ben shrugged his shoulders and said, "He's got troubles, Justin, real troubles."

Justin looked up at the sky and realized it had stopped raining. "I gathered that from your telegram," he said, turning to look at Ben. "That's why I came back. What kind of trouble has he gotten himself into?"

Ben thought for a moment, and then he said, "It seems he's been seein' this woman down across the border by the name of Maria Gonzales. She wasn't one of them loose women." Ben blew out a breath and continued. "I guess he'd been seein' her for almost ah year. O'course yer pa didn't know anything about it, so that wasn't ah problem. But, there was ah couple of other problems. The first one bein' she was ah married woman. The other was the feller she was married to."

"And he's in love with this woman?"

Ben nodded his head. "Claimed he was, and she him."

Justin looked at his cousin and said, "What'a ya mean, was? Has something happened I don't know about?"

Without answering, Ben pointed to a sign that read, 'DOCTORS OFFICE,' then opened the door and held it open for Justin as he limped in. The doctor was sitting at his desk doing paperwork. He looked up when he heard Ben close the door.

"Hello, Ben. What can I do for you boys?" he asked, centering his attention on Justin.

"Doc," Ben answered, "you remember my cousin, Justin? He just got back inta town and along the way it seems he ran inta ah bit of trouble. He picked up ah couple of wounds that needs lookin' at. So I brung'im down here to you. Mrs. Bailey alright?"

"Yea, she's fine. Twins." the doctor said as he stood up and approached Justin with a curious look on his face. "Justin Hacker, is that really you under all that mud and dressed in them fancy duds?"

"Yea, Doc, it's me alright," Justin answered.

The doctor grabbed Justin's hand and began pumping it up and down. "I sure never expected to see you in this town again. How you been? Where have you been? Does your pa know you're back in town? How long have you been back? Are you in trouble? Are you running from the law?"

"Whoa! Hold on, Doc," Justin said. "One question at a time. I've got ah couple of small wounds that need tendin', but other than that, I'm fine. And no, pa don't know I'm back in town and I'd just as soon nobody told him, yet. And no, I'm not runnin' from the law and I'm not in any kind of trouble."

Ben scratched his chin and said, "I wouldn't be too sure about that last part," as he turned and looked Justin face on. "Didn't you say that one of them Mexicans you shot had ah big scar down across his eye?"

"Yea, down across his left eye. Why?" Justin asked.

Ben rubbed his finger under his nose. "That scar didn't happen to look like ah snake, did it?"

Both, the doctor and Ben had concerned looks on their faces as they waited for Justin's answer.

After a moment, Justin said, "Come ta think about it, it did resemble ah snake. Why? Is that somethin' important?"

The doctor walked over to his desk and took a bottle of whiskey from the bottom drawer. He took a swig, and then walked back to where the two men were standing and held the bottle out to Justin, who took a swig, and then handed it to Ben, who took a long pull.

When Ben finished taking a drink, Justin asked, "Is somebody gonna tell me what the Sam hell is goin' on?"

"Don't know as it'll do much good fixing you up," the doctor said, looking Justin square in the eyes.

Justin looked back and forth between the doctor and his cousin. "What kind of answer is that?" he asked.

Ben took a long, pregnant pause before he answered. "What the doc is saying is, you killed ah Mexican bandito known in these parts as, Snake-eye."

"So?" Justin said. "I killed ah Mexican bandit with an ugly scar on his face, and a stupid name, so what?"

Ben shook his head. "Let me put it another way, cousin. You may be in a lot more trouble than you realize. You remember me tellin' you about that woman down across the border that Jeremiah has been seein'?"

Justin nodded his head. "Yea, so?"

Ben took another sip from the bottle before he answered. "Well, ya see, it was like this, Snake-eye was her brother in law. And both him and his brother, Manuel, the woman's husband, testified to the law down there that Jeremiah raped and murdered Maria. And now that you've gone and killed Snake-eye, why naturally they'll think you done it for revenge. And when Maria's husband finds out you killed his brother, he and his friends will come gunnin' fer ya. Comprende'?"

"I see," Justin said. "And with Jeremiah locked up in jail down there, you think they might do something to him, too."

"It's called ah prison, son," the doctor interjected. "One of the worst hell holes you can ever imagine. And they say the warden loves to torture gringos until they beg to die, before he sends them on to meet their maker. You get my meaning?"

Justin looked down at the floor and nodded his head. "Yea, Doc, I reckon I do." He looked the doctor square in the eyes and said, "You jest patch me up and let me worry about the rest."

Turning to Ben, Justin said, "Soon as Doc finishes with me, we'll see about gettin' Jeremiah outta that hell hole you all call ah prison."

Ben nodded and handed Justin the bottle of whiskey. "Here, maybe this'll help ease the pain."

CHAPTER NINE

The old man was panting when he ran into Elijah Hacker's blacksmith shop and had to take a moment to catch his breath before he could tell him what he'd seen and heard.

Elijah gave the old man a stern look as he reached out and grabbed him by his shirt. "Are you sure it was Justin?"

The old man pulled himself loose from Elijah's grasp and walked to the front door of the barn where he spit a stream of tobacco juice into the muddy street. "Said his name was Justin Hacker and young Ben said it was him, too. Seems purty clear ta me. We all went inta the saloon fer ah beer, and then they went down ta the doc's place. Saw'em go in there, my own self. Then I come right down here ta let ya know."

Elijah spit a stream of tobacco juice into his fire pit and listened as it made a in his eyes, he reached into his pocket and pulled out some money and handed it to the old man. Next, he took his shotgun down from the rack on the wall, checked to make sure it was loaded, then headed out the door with the old man trailing behind him.

Justin's mother, Elizabeth, was pulling weeds in her garden when she saw the old man run into the barn and she immediately felt a chill. She had just pulled off her bonnet and apron when she saw her husband leave the barn. He was headed for town with his shotgun in his hand. The old man was following a few steps behind.

Elizabeth whispered to herself, "Justin's back," as she ran toward the front gate. After she went through, she hiked up her skirts so she could run faster. She had to catch up with Elijah and stop him somehow, before he did something crazy. There was a wild desperation in her normally bright blue eyes because she knew Elijah was not the kind of man to go back on his word. He was proud and stubborn, but so was she, and she would do everything in her power to stop him from shooting her eldest son.

The pin that held her hair in a bun fell out and her once bright red hair, now laced with gray fell down over her shoulders as she hurried down the muddy street, hoping she could stop her husband from committing murder.

Elijah walked at a brisk pace, and when Elizabeth finally caught up with him, she fell in step with him as best she could. "And might I be askin', just where do ya think you'll be goin' with that scatter-gun?" she said.

Elijah didn't bother to look at her or even slow his pace. "Justin's back in town," was all he said as he continued on down the road.

Elizabeth stopped dead in her tracks and put her hands to her face. It was true then, her worst fear had come to pass. The chill she'd felt earlier was real. What could have made him come back, she wondered - especially with him knowing what his father would do? It had to be about Jeremiah being down in that Mexican prison. He'd come back to help his one remaining brother. As she realized this, one part of her swelled with pride that her son would risk his life for his younger brother, while another part of her feared she might lose her last two sons, one because of a crazy warden on an absurd, trumped up accusation and the other by his own father's hand.

She was frozen in shock for no more than the blink of an eye before she hiked up her skirt and chased after her husband again, pushing the old man aside as she ran past him. After she had run a few steps past Elijah, she whirled and stood directly in front of him, her legs spread and her hands on her hips, blocking his way. "And just what is it ya think ye'll be ah doin' with that shotgun?" she asked again, even though she knew the answer. It was the only thing she could think to do to stall for time.

It worked, because he stopped and stared down at her with fire in his eyes. For a long moment, they just glared at one another while the old man stood to one side looking down at his muddy shoes.

After what seemed to Elizabeth to be an eternity, Elijah stepped to his left to go around her, but quick as a cat she moved in front of him again. "Well," she said in as stern a voice as she could muster, "tis an answer I'm waitin' for."

Elijah gave a sigh and tried stepping around her once again. He didn't want to discuss the matter with her, especially not here in the middle of the street with people staring at them. Besides, he'd made his call and had no intentions of backing down. The whole town knew what he'd said he'd do and he hadn't changed his mind even one iota, but here she was, standin' right in front of him, trying to interfere.

Elizabeth reached out and tried to grab the shotgun out of Elijah's hands.

She was a strong woman, but not strong enough to jerk the shotgun from her husband's grip. They wrestled with the gun for a minute or so before Elijah finally gave a yank and pulled it free. "Go back to the house where ya belong, Elizabeth."

She glared right back at him and said, "I'll not be goin' anywhere til we get this foolishness settled. Now give me that scatter-gun and come home."

Elijah looked at his wife for a moment, then brushed her aside and continued on down the street. "Stay outta this woman," he said as he walked past her.

"Stay outta this? Are ya daft, man? What kinda nonsense is that?" she said to his back.

Elijah gave his wife no reply. He was only concerned with his mission.

Elizabeth gave the old man a pleading look, but he just hung his head. "Ughhh, men!" she said as she lifted her skirts and chased after her husband one more time.

When she'd caught up with him, again, she grabbed him by the arm. "Now you listen ta me, Elijah Hacker, you'll be comin' home with me right now and you'll be puttin' that scatter-gun away. You'll not be harmin' that boy as long as I'm still alive!"

By now, Elijah was fairly dragging his wife down the muddy street and the look on his face said he was getting fed up with her interference. Finally, he gave a mighty swing of his arm that caused Elizabeth to be thrown backward. He was already moving on by the time she landed on her rump in the middle of the rain soaked street.

A good-sized crowd was standing along the side of the road, watching another episode in the Hacker saga. Some were even turning their heads to laugh. Elizabeth paid them no mind. She had more important things to worry about than what people thought, or that the back of her skirt was now a muddy mess.

The old man reached out his hand and helped her to her feet. She mumbled, "Thank you," as she wiped herself off as best she could, then slapped the old man across his face with so much force that it almost knocked him down. "And why can't ya be mindin' yer own business ya old sot? This is all yer doin. And how will ya be feelin' when me son is lying' dead in the street?" she yelled.

Whispers and murmurs filtered through the crowd as Elizabeth hurried down the road. Elijah's hatred for his son, along with a well-known twenty year feud with his older brother, Ephram, was known by almost everyone in town. No one, including Ephram, seemed to know what the feud was about, only that Elijah wouldn't talk to his brother or allow him on the property.

In every other way, Elijah Hacker was a good man. He worked hard and ran an honest blacksmithing business. His prices were fair and his work was excellent. It was just his attitude towards Ephram and Justin that caused people to whisper behind his back.

After watching the scene on the street between Elijah and Elizabeth and hearing the buzzing from the crowd, one of the men turned and hurried off in the direction of the sheriff's office.

The boys were in a good mood as they walked down the sidewalk talking. Justin was still in the same clothes he'd arrived in and sported a bandage on his head. Along with a new hat, he was carrying several packages.

Indicating the packages, Ben said, "First we'll see about getting you ah bath and then inta them decent clothes we gott'cha. While we have dinner, we can try ta come up with ah plan fer rescuin' Jeremiah."

Justin nodded, and then asked, "How's ma?"

"I'm sure she misses ya ah lot, but she never says anything. You know how she is," Ben answered, shaking his head.

By now, they had nearly reached the corner and Justin stopped in front of the dry goods store.

Ben reacted by stopping and turning back to look at Justin, who finally asked the question that had been on his mind for some time. "How's pa?"

Elijah, the old-timer and Elizabeth were now approaching the same corner from the opposite direction and saw Ben and Justin standing on the sidewalk. The boys were engrossed in conversation and had no idea of the danger they were in.

Elijah, in his illogical state of mind, put the stock of the shotgun to his shoulder and sighted down the barrel. Just as Elijah squeezed the trigger, Elizabeth ran over and pushed Elijah's arm upward. The roar of the twelve gauge shotgun could be heard all the way down main street as it sent pellets into the Mercantile sign above the boy's heads. Both Ben and Justin looked up at the gaping hole in the sign, then turned and ran for their lives. As they headed back in the direction they came from, Ben yelled, "I think he's still mad at ya!"

Later that same evening, Justin stepped out of the small pond just a few miles outside of town and toweled himself dry. The temperature had already dropped several degrees, causing goose bumps to pop up all over his bare skin. It wasn't the bath he'd hoped to have, like the one he'd had back at Wong's, but it was better than no bath at all. He was just stepping into his pants when he heard the hoof beats.

Justin grabbed his pistol and squatted down behind a nearby bush and waited. From just outside the firelight, a voice called out, "Justin, don't shoot. It's me, Ben, and I've got some food." Justin eased the hammer down on his pistol and stood up, grinning. "Hope you brought some coffee, too," he said. "I sure could use some, and maybe ah nip of somethin' ah bit stronger."

Ben reached into his saddlebag and brought out a bottle of whiskey, which he tossed to Justin. Justin uncorked it and took a long pull, then smacked his lips and said, "This should help lower the throbbin' in my head, and make the goose bumps on my skin go away." After taking a second, shorter drink, Justin passed the bottle back to Ben.

Ben took a hefty swallow from the bottle, then said, "I'll get supper started while you get dressed."

After a supper of beans and beef, Justin and Ben sat around the fire letting their meal settle. They were both enjoying strong, hot, black coffee while Ben smoked a cigar and Justin cleaned his pistol.

"Reckon yer pa is still mad at ya, cause he said fer you ta stay outta town or he'll shoot ya on sight," Ben said with a pained look on his face.

Without a word, Justin finished cleaning his pistol and then slipped it into the smooth leather of the custom made holster. After a moment of reflection on what Ben had said, Justin stood up and went to the fire, where he poured himself more coffee. For a long while he stood staring at the starlit night, saying nothing, wondering how his pa could hold grudges for so long. After what seemed to be an eternity, Justin turned to Ben and said, "Finish telling me about Jeremiah."

Ben snubbed out what little was left of his cigar and took a swallow of coffee while he adjusted his thoughts. "They've got him in ah hellhole of ah prison about twenty-five miles below the border. The word is, the wardens gonna hang him cause they say he raped and murdered Maria Gonzales."

"Killin' ah woman don't sound like Jeremiah. And unless he's changed ah whole lot, I don't believe he did it," Justin stated.

Ben shook his head and said, "I don't believe it, either, but I can't bust him out by myself. That's why I sent you that telegram. But, hell, I'm not sure we can even bust him out together. That place is like ah fortress, with outrider guards all around the place."

Justin finished his coffee and rolled himself a smoke as he stared into the glow of the fire, thoughts of his younger brother filling his mind. "None of this makes any sense," he said to no one in particular. "How could he let somethin' like this happen?"

Ben lit another cigar as he thought about the facts, as he knew them. "When I got word Jeremiah was in jail down in Vasquez; that's the little village where Maria lived, I went down there to see if there was anything I could do, but by the time I got down there he'd already been tried, convicted and sentenced. He was just waitin' ta be transferred ta the prison a few miles west of Vasquez. That's where the hangin's ta take place. They say the warden loves hangin' gringos." Ben took a couple of puffs from his cigar before he continued.

Justin said nothing, but waited patiently to hear the rest of the story.

"Anyway," Ben said, "they let me in ta see'im." Ben swallowed before going on. "Justin, he was beat up might bad, but he could still talk some, and he told me he was there that night, but he hadn't raped or killed Maria. He said he couldn't have done it cause he loved her. And I believe him."

"I can't believe he done it, either, but why was he down there that night, anyway? And who did kill her? Did he know?" Justin asked.

Ben stood up and stretched a kink out of his leg after which he walked around a bit before continuing. "He tole me she'd sent word fer him ta come down there and see her that particular evenin'. The note said to meet her in the barn.

Jeremiah said he sat on his horse at the top of ah small hill where he could see the barn, checkin' ta see that it was clear. Said he spent close ta ah half an hour up there. And when everthing looked all right, he rode down and tied his horse around ta the back of the barn, then eased his way inside. He said the place was empty, cept fer ah couple of horses and some donkeys. So he sat down ta wait."

Now that the cramp in his leg had settled down, Ben sat down again. "Said he didn't have ta wait long afore Maria come in, lookin' kinda nervous like. He said when she saw him, she rushed over and dropped down next to him and gave him ah kiss. He said she tole him she had ta wait til her husband was asleep afore she could sneak out."

Justin looked at Ben, "But she was alright, not angry with him or afraid of him?"

Ben grinned. "Afraid of him? I don't think so. And I'm pretty sure she wasn't mad at him. Accordin' ta Jeremiah, they did some huggin' and kissin' and he told her about how she was the most beautiful woman he'd ever seen and how much he loved her and stuff like that. But then he noticed that she was tremblin' and he asked her what was wrong. She tole him she was scared. She said she thought her husband suspected something, and if he found out, he would kill'em both."

Ben's cigar had burned down to nothing and he lit another before he continued. And after a couple of puffs, he said, "Jeremiah said he'd been thinkin' on this idea he'd had fer some time and guessed now was as good ah time as any ta tell her. He said he asked her to run away with him that very night. Go up to Montana, or maybe Canada. He figured they would be safe up there. And he tole her he would take care of Manuel or his brother if they come lookin for'em."

Justin took a sip of coffee and waited.

Ben sipped his coffee too, took a long puff on his cigar, then blew smoke into the night, watching it drift away. Finally he said, "Jeremiah tole me she was excited and thought that would be ah wonderful idea." Ben paused a moment before he said, " But what they didn't know was, Manuel, that was her husband's name, had followed her and was watchin' through the window of the barn and had heard everthing. The next thing they know, Manuel comes inta the barn, holdin' ah shotgun and sayin somethin' about love bein' so wonderful. Jeremiah said she looked at her husband and said words to the effect of him not lovin' her and only married her so he could take over her father's business.

"Well, apparently Manuel was in the mood ta play the game cause he looked at her and said somethin' about Maria stabbin' him in his heart with her hateful words, even if they were true. Manual agreed that her father was a very influential man and he was grateful to him for dying in that accident at such a young age, and leaving both his daughter and his business to him. Then I reckon he got serious, and asked how it would look if she was to run away with this gringo. He reckoned it would be very bad for both him and the business.

"Jeremiah said that about then, the barn door opened and this mean lookin' feller with ah scar down across his eye come ah walkin' in with ah pistol in his hand. And when Manuel saw him, Manuel looked down at Jeremiah and grinned, then repeated what Jeremiah had said about takin' care of Snake-eye if he tried ta interfere. Well-sir, then ole Manuel makes ah big sweep of his arm and introduces Snake-eye ta Jeremiah as the roughest, toughest badass bandito north or south of the border.

"Well, you know Jeremiah, he's ah lot like you and wasn't about ta back down and he said, 'So, you're the famous bandito called Snake-eye. You don't look like much ta me.

"I reckon both Manuel and Snake-eye thought this was funny cause they both begun ta laugh. And while they were off guard, Jeremiah said he decided ta launch his attack and rammed his head inta Snake-eye's stomach and sent him sprawlin' onta his back. When he turned to face Manuel, Manuel slammed the barrel of the shotgun down on Jeremiah's head and he went out like water on ah fire. Said the last thing he could remember was Maria screamin.'"

"Well, they obviously didn't shoot him," Justin said.

"And, that's ah fact," Ben said. "No, he said when he come to he was tied up and propped up in ah horse stall. He said Snake-eye was standin' over Maria and she had a cut lip and puffed up eye. He said Manuel walked over and spit on Maria and told his brother ta do whatever he wanted to with her, then kill her, but ta not do anything ta Jeremiah cause he had some special plans fer him."

"And all Jeremiah could do is sit there and watch," Justin said.

"Jeremiah said he struggled somethin' awful when he saw Snake-eye beginnin' ta undo the belt on his pants, but couldn't get loose and when Snake-eye finished rapin' Maria, he slit her throat."

"And set Jeremiah up as the patsy," Justin commented.

"Jeremiah said Snake-eye knocked his brother around ah little bit ta make it look good, then the two of them took turns beatin' on him til he blacked out again."

"All nice and proper. He'd heard Maria screamin' and him and Snake-eye got there just in time ta see Jeremiah down between Maria's legs and cuttin' her throat ta shut her up. Jeremiah didn't stand ah chance in hell of winnin' that one," Justin said as he crushed out the butt of yet another cigarette.

Ben shook his head in agreement. "And they're gonna hang him soon if we don't find ah way ta get him out and back across the border."

"Have you checked the place out, yet?" Justin asked.

"Only from ah distance," Ben said. "The place sits out in the middle of the desert and they have guards on the walls and guards on all the approaches."

Justin got up and shook out his bedroll. "I'm bushed. Let's get some sleep. We'll have ourselves ah look-see tomorrow."

The kerosene lamp glowed brightly in the dining room of the Hacker house as Elizabeth stood over her husband, who was sitting at the table, trying to drink a cup of coffee. There was fire in her eyes.

"You've got ta get over this stupid vendetta you got against yer son. Ya know in yer heart that you're wrong. He didn't get Jacob killed. He loved his brother. Besides, Justin is yer son, too, yer own flesh an blood."

Elijah placed the palms of both hands down on the table in frustration. "Will you jest stay outta this, woman. It don't concern you! And I'm not wrong!"

Elizabeth paced back and forth across the room as she spoke. "Stay out of it? Stay out of it, ya say. Are ya daft, man? He's my son, too, ya know. Or have ya lost yer senses and forgot that little fact?"

Elijah stood up and yelled at his wife, "He may be your son, but he'll never again be called ah son of mine, not ever again! I should'a drowned him the day he was born!"

Elijah gave her a look of self-righteousness indignation, started to say something, but then changed his mind, and after a strained silence he stormed into the kitchen.

Elizabeth stared at the doorway for what seemed an eternity, waiting for him to return. When she heard the back door slam, she slumped down onto a chair and began to cry.

CHAPTER TEN

The following morning, just as the sun was climbing over the horizon, Ben and Justin rode southwest into Mexico to take a look at this famous prison everyone kept talking about.

Other than the sound of the horses and the creaking of saddles, it was just two men riding along together in silence. Everything had been said last night and there would be no further need of conversation until they reached their destination. Part of the prison's fame was that no one had ever escaped from it except through death, and no one in his right mind would want to break into it.

But they hadn't considered Justin Hacker – loyal to his family, especially when they were innocent.

A blistering sun that kept their horses to a walk was reaching its zenith when Ben held up his hand and brought the mare to a halt near the bottom of a tall sand hill. "This is about as close as we can get without getting' spotted," he said. "We can see the prison and outriders from the top of the hill, yonder."

Justin stepped out of the saddle and dropped the reins over his horse's head so he could eat what little he could find, but not wander too far. He took a pair of binoculars out of his saddlebag and hung them around his neck, then nodded to Ben. The two of them climbed the tall sand hill so Justin could get his first look at his younger brother's residency.

When they neared the top, Ben motioned for them to drop down on their bellies and crawl the rest of the way. "We don't want ta be seen by their outrider guards," he whispered.

Before looking over the area beyond the crest of the hill, both men pulled off their hats and laid them on the sand. The sand was hot against their stomachs and the sun burned its way into their backs and hatless heads. It was the price they had to pay if they didn't want to be seen.

Justin scanned the area and spotted several men on horseback keeping guard on the prisoners working just beyond the entrance to the prison. There was a garden of sorts to one side and a graveyard directly in front. Prisoners were working in both. Two guards with rifles patrolled the road leading to the prison, not far from the sand hill they were hiding behind. The prison sat in the middle of the desert with no other buildings anywhere near. Justin lifted the glasses to his eyes for a closer look at the prison, itself. The gate was open and reminded Justin of some gigantic beast with its mouth open, waiting to swallow up anyone who came near. Guards with rifles patroled the top of the walls.

"Like I told ya, there's no way ta break in," Ben said in a low voice. "Guards along the road, and more guards on top of the walls. And all of'em armed to the teeth."

Justin lowered the binoculars from his eyes and nodded. It did look like there was no way to break in and he could see how it had gotten its reputation. The walls were at least twenty-five feet high and several feet thick – wide enough for guards to walk from one corner to the other, and gun holes in the wall to shoot from in case anyone was stupid enough to try an attack. The guards could hide behind the wall and shoot through the holes at their targets, who would have no place to hide. For the guards, it would be like target practice.

From what Justin could see, there was only one way in and one way out. The front gates looked like they were made of heavy logs tied together with metal bands, and appeared to be around fifteen feet wide and the same height as the walls.

Justin had, without thinking about it, laid the binoculars down on the sand with the lens facing the prison. When one of the guards turned and stared in their direction, Justin grabbed the binoculars and began to scoot down the hill toward the horses. "Damn, I think one of the outriders saw a glare off the lens of the binoculars." he said.

When they reached the horses, they threw the reins over the animal's heads and stepped into the saddles urging their mounts into a fast retreat back in the direction they came from.

After a half a mile of hard riding Justin slowed his horse down to a walk, allowing the poor creature to catch his wind. It was already beginning to lather up, and saliva was dripping from its mouth, plus it had stumbled twice.

"No use wasting our horses in this heat. There's nobody followin' us," Justin said.

Ben hauled up beside him as he looked over his shoulder to make sure for himself, and then nodded in agreement. Ben took a cigar from his shirt pocket and lit up, then said, "I reckon you see what I was talkin' about when I said the place was ah mite tough ta break into."

They rode on down the road in silence for at least another ten minutes before Justin said, "But what if they just open the gates and let us come in?"

Ben stopped his horse in the middle of the road and stared at Justin's back. He threw what was left of his cigar into the desert and then chased after Justin who had nudged his horse into an easy lope.

"Hey, wait a minute! Why would they do that?" Ben yelled.

All the way back, Ben tried repeatedly to get Justin to explain his earlier statement about the guards opening the gates and letting them just waltz in, pretty as you please, and take Jeremiah out without so much as a by your leave.

Each time, Justin would just hold up his hand and say, "I'm thinkin'," and then ride on.

Once they got back to the campsite, Justin unsaddled his horse and gave it a rubdown with a piece of burlap he'd soaked in the pond, then put a hobble on it's front legs and turned it out to graze. After this was finished, he stoked up the fire and put a pot of coffee on to boil. When Ben finished turning his horse out to graze, he came over and squatted next to the fire and said, "Well, you finished with yer thinkin' yet?"

Justin rolled and lit a cigarette as he explained the plan he'd come up with.

Ben stared into the fire for long while, then stood up and began pacing back and forth.

Justin was pouring himself a cup of coffee when Ben finally broke the silence. "You're insane. You do know that, don't you?"

"Nobody said it would be easy," Justin said as he walked over and sat down next to his bedroll, placing the cup of hot coffee on the ground next to him.

Ben poured himself some coffee and sat down close to the fire. Silence hung in the air like a humming bird hovering in front of a flower, as Ben rolled a cigarette, lit it and took several puffs. He was out of cigars. Finally, he looked at Justin and said, "I got me ah weird feelin' that this plan of yours ain't gonna work. I mean, there's too many holes in it – too many what ifs."

The calls of a night bird in a tree next to the pond were answered by a very large sounding bullfrog. Justin grinned, then looked at Ben and said, "If you've got a better idea, I'm all ears."

For a long time, Ben stared at the flames as they dwindled down to just glowing coals.

"And what happens if this fool scheme of yours doesn't work?"

"Maybe they'll hang all three of us on the same day," Justin said as he stood up and tossed his coffee grounds onto the coals.

"That ain't funny," Ben said, as he stood up and did the same.

"If you're finished with your coffee, let's get some shut-eye. I don't know about you but I need my beauty rest," Justin said as he rolled up in his blankets.

During the time the boys had been checking out the Mexican prison, things were happening at a different location south of the border that would influence the outcome of Justin's plan.

Manuel had just walked out of the front door of his store when he looked up and saw Lopez come riding in his direction, trailing three horses with three bodies tied face down across their backs.

Manuel stepped into the street and waited as Lopez rode up and stopped in front of him. Lopez pulled off his hat as he indicated the three bodies. "Your brother and his friends, Senor."

Manuel walked over and checked for himself. "Who did this?" he asked.

Lopez had not been invited to get down, so he remained on his horse as he spoke. "They were killed by an Americano called, Senor Justin Hacker. He told me he shot them for robbing a stagecoach and killing the passengers."

How do you know this Senor Justin Hacker?" Manuel asked.

"I swear by the saints, I do not know him. He rode into my yard with their bodies over these same horses and told me to bring them here. That is when he told me what he had done. I think he is the brother of the man who raped and killed your sainted wife, Maria. God rest her soul," Lopez said as he made the sign of the cross across the front of his chest area.

By now, a small crowd had gathered and the looks on their faces told the story. They were not unhappy to find out Snake-eye was dead, although none of them voiced their opinion - at least not in front of Manuel.

Manuel pondered the information Lopez had given him before he finally said, "And where is this Senor Hacker now?"

Lopez hung his head and said, "I do not know. When last I saw him he was riding southwest from my small ranchero, Senor. That is the direction to Nogales, but I do not know for sure that is where he was going."

"Well I do know where his is going," Manuel said as a smile spread across his face. He took the reins of the lead horse holding his brother's body from Lopez, then reached into his pocket and pulled out a small amount of money and handed it to Lopez. "Go to the barn and get yourself a fresh horse, then ride as fast as you can to the prison. Tell the warden what has happened and also tell him I said to expect Senor Hacker to try and help his brother escape. Tell him I do not know when or how, but it will be soon."

Lopez bought a small bucket of beans, peppers and tortillas from a woman he knew and five minutes after that, he was headed for the prison. By then, Manuel had handed the bodies of his brother and his two compadres' over to one of the men who worked for him, telling the man to get some help to bury them.

Manuel had been on his way to the saloon for a drink when Lopez interrupted him. Now that this unpleasant business was finished, he could enjoy his drink. Maybe he would even buy a round for the house, a toast to his late brother, Ramon.

It was too bad about his brother, but in his line of business one took certain risks. It was his bad luck to run into this Senor Justin Hacker, who was apparently a difficult man to kill. But his luck was soon to run out and Ramon's portion of the hidden loot was now his.

The worst part was that his brother would be bringing no more money for him to hide. So be it, he thought. There was already enough hidden away for him to retire and live in Mexico City like a king. All he had to do now was to go to the prison and retrieve his share.

He would wait until the warden had dealt with the Hackers and was feeling good about killing two more gringos.

Manuel nodded to Juanita, who came over and stood close to him. She was very beautiful, and young. He handed her some money as he whispered something in her ear. She giggled as she ran behind the bar and grabbed a bottle of tequila, after tossing a coin on the bar.

She followed Manuel out the front door, and then arm in arm they walked back to Manuel's store, where he hung a closed sign in the front window.

Thinking of all that money had caused him to feel aroused, and Juanita was just the girl to help him take his mind off things.

CHAPTER ELEVEN

It was early morning and the sheriff was sitting at his desk, enjoying his first cup of coffee when Elijah stormed in and planted himself directly in front of him.

"You seen Justin?" Elijah asked.

The sheriff sighed and shook his head no.

"And yer sure he ain't picked up thet reward money?" Elijah persisted.

The sheriff downed the last of his coffee and slammed the empty cup down so hard it caused the last drop to pop out of the cup and land on a piece of paper lying near the front edge of the desk. "Elijah Hacker, how many times do I have ta tell ya. For the tenth time, no! He ain't picked up no reward money."

Elijah looked around the office. "If''n he's got ah reward comin', why ain't he come by here ta collect it?" he said, swinging his head back to look the sheriff square in the eyes.

The sheriff walked over to the stove and poured himself another cup of coffee, and then went back and sat down in his chair. After taking a sip of the hot brew, he said, "It might have somethin' ta do with you blastin' away att'em with that scatter-gun and orderin' him outta town, again. And on top of that, we only have doc's word that Justin was the one who was supposed ta have killed Snake-eye and his gang. Now, if Snake-eye is actually dead, why ain't nobody seen the corpse? I got ta have ah dead body before I can turn over any reward money. It's called, proof. That's the law. And ain't nobody brought me no body, nor has anybody tried ta claim any reward money."

That was the most words he'd put together at one time for as long as he could remember.

Elijah paced back and forth for a few minutes, looking out the front window of the sheriff's office like he was expecting someone to show up. Finally, he stopped in front of the sheriff's desk, again. "Did Doc say where Justin and Ben was off ta?"

"All Doc would say was that Justin and Ben left town, and if he knew where they was ah goin', he didn't say," the sheriff said in a quieter tone.

"Probably off doin' the devil's work," Elijah said as he walked over and poured himself a cup of coffee without asking. "He's gonna lead Ben right down the path of sin, jest like he did his two brothers. Then Ephram is gonna blame me fer bringin' sech ah hell raiser inta the world."

Elijah took a sip of coffee, then set the cup on the sheriff's desk and pulled up a chair.

The sheriff had a flustered look on his face and his cheeks were turning red. "Dammit to hell, man! You know as well as I do, Justin ain't never done nuthin' outside the law! Not around here nor anyplace else I know of."

Elijah's jaw tightened and his cheeks puffed up. "You're talkin' bout man's law. I'm talkin' bout God's law. He took Jacob ta thet house ah sin down across the border when he weren't no more than sixteen. And that's where he introduced him ta rotgut whiskey and sinful women. Then poor Jacob got hisself killed tryin' ta be like his older brother. Justin ain't never done nuthin' but bring shame ta me and his ma. He don't deserve ta live and it'll be my Christian duty ta shoot him on sight the next time I lay eyes on'em."

The sheriff shook his head in disbelief. "Elijah Hacker you're nuthin' but ah dumb, hardheaded ole fool with some crazy, mixed up notions roamin' around in that thick skull of your'n. And you ain't gonna shoot that boy, cause if you do, I'll see to it personal that the law hangs you for murder."

The sheriff walked over to the front window of his office and looked out at the street. His hands were shaking while he tried to light a small cigarillo to calm his nerves. After finally getting it lit, he stood at the window for a minute or so before he turned to Elijah and said, "You know as well as I do that Justin had nuthin' ta do with that gunfight Jacob got hisself into. Jacob was ah young hot head on the prowl, and that's the pure fact of the matter."

Elijah bit off a piece of chewing tobacco and settled it into his jaw. "I know thet Jacob is dead. And I know thet Justin was supposed ta be lookin' after him, but he weren't. Thet's what I know. And I also know it was Justin thet led the boy astray in the first place."

Elijah stood up and walked over and opened the front door of the wood burning stove and spit a stream of tobacco juice into the fire, which made a loud sizzling noise.

"Jacob always wanted ta be like his big brother Justin, and look what it got him. Dead. Thet's what it got him."

The sheriff stood by the window, staring at Elijah, wondering how a man could get himself so mixed up that he would shoot his own son, for no sane reason.

Elijah's pent up frustrations flew out of his mouth like swallows out of a barn. "And what about Jeremiah? He always wanted ta be like Justin, too. And where is he now? I'll tell ya where. He's sittin' in ah cell down in thet Mexican prison, waitin' ta hang fer rapin' and murderin' thet Mex gal."

"You can't blame Justin for that!" the sheriff said in an astonished tone. "He's been gone for seven years now. And you know that Jeremiah didn't rape or murder that woman. He's not that kind of man. How can you even think that?"

Elijah walked over and stood right in front of the sheriff. "I can't say thet I know what Jeremiah did or didn't do, but as fer as Justin is concerned, I can blame him, and I do."

With that said, Elijah turned and left the sheriff's office, slamming the door as he went out.

The sheriff sighed and shook his head from side to side. "Why, of all the towns I had ta choose from, did I pick one with a crazy man in it?"

What the sheriff wasn't realizing was, there had never been such a town and never would be. Every town that has ever been, has always had at least one person everybody looked sideways at because somehow a screw inside his or her head had come loose and they just didn't see things like normal folks do.

CHAPTER TWELVE

Just south of Nogales, a small stand of Arizona Cypress grew tall and sturdy in the water thirsty desert. Hidden among the tallest branches of one of the trees, a young female gray hawk built her nest, safely away from predators. She now left the nest and climbed high into the sky, catching a wind current that would allow her to glide well above the desert floor in search of a fat lizard, a small rodent, or maybe even a snake - anything to give nourishment to the eggs inside her.

A few miles to the southwest, she saw a large structure with men and animals. Instinctively she veered off to her left. She didn't know why, only that something inside her told her that danger awaited where men were concerned. Unaware of what was going on below, she soared away, farther into the desert where she might find the prey she sought.

The warden stood barely five feet tall, but inside him was the ruthlessness of a man twice his size. His office on the upper area of the prison was a large room with an oversized desk that sat on a raised platform, facing the door. Like his desk, the warden's chair was an extra-large, overstuffed affair.

On this particular afternoon the warden sat glaring down at Lopez, who stood with his head bowed, wringing his hat in his hands. The fact that he was afraid of the warden was evident. Fear oozed out of him like sweat.

"My dear friend, Lopez, I want to thank you for warning me. Senor Hacker will be in for a big surprise when he arrives. It will please me greatly to watch his face when I hang his brother. And he will beg me to put him to death before I am finished with him."

Lopez said nothing as he allowed his head to move up and down. The warden was a ruthless man and Lopez had no reason not to believe him.

The warden reached into his desk and took out a wooden box. He counted out some coins and put them into a small bag, which he tossed to Lopez.

Lopez caught the bag and took a step backward without taking time to count it. "Muchas gracias, Patron. I hope you catch this Senor Hacker. I do not want him to come for me."

As Lopez backed for the door, still wringing his hat in his hands, the warden spoke. "Do not worry, Lopez, Senor Hacker does not know it was you who informed me and I will not tell him. You give this gringo far too much credit for intelligence. Besides, I will personally see to it that the gringos will never leave here alive."

Lopez nodded his head again, then turned and reached for the door latch. He was anxious to get away.

A loud roar exploded in his ears, followed by a sharp pain when the bullet struck him in the back.

"And neither will you. I do not part with my gold so easily."

The warden was pulling the small bag of coins out of Lopez's dead hand when one of the guards came rushing in.

"He tried to attack me and I had to shoot him," the warden said as he walked back to his chair and sat down. "Have the prisoners dig a hole and throw him in it. Let them see what happens to anyone who tries to attack me."

The guard saw that Lopez had no weapon, but kept his mouth shut. He called for a second guard, who came on the run. The two of them carried Lopez's body out onto the walkway, and then closed the door before ordering two prisoners to take the body outside to the ever-growing graveyard and bury him.

The warden felt good. After putting the coins back in the wooden box, he called in the captain of the guards and informed him to be on the lookout for this Senor Hacker, who was Senor Jeremiah's brother and not to kill him. He wanted this gringo alive. He also told him he would be spending the night. He wanted to be here in case there was an attempt to break Senor Jeremiah out.

As the captain turned to leave, the warden said, "Send someone to tell my wife that I may be spending a few days here. I do not want to miss the capture of this foolish gringo who thinks he can break into my prison and steal someone away, just like that. Such stupidity and bravado. It will be interesting to see what he is made of."

Next, he ordered some supper. For some reason, shooting someone always made him feel full of energy and hungry. Plus, there was the added excitement of capturing this Senor Justin Hacker. What arrogance this gringo must have to think he could match wits with him. He would see that this gringo died a slow, painful death. Yes, he would give this much thought. He retrieved a bottle of tequila from the bottom desk drawer to drink with his supper.

Outside the prison walls, the prisoners quickly took Lopez into the shadow of the sidewall, where they stood him on his feet. One of the prisoners pulled a thick piece of wood from inside the back of Lopez's shirt. There was a bullet lodged in the middle of the wood. Lopez, himself, removed another piece of thick wood from inside the front of his shirt. "I was afraid something like this could happen," Lopez said. He was trembling form head to foot.

Lopez looked at the piece of wood with the bullet lodged in it and shook his head. "The bullet hit me so hard that I wasn't sure the bullet had not killed me. May the saints be blessed, it only knocked me out.

He turned to the prisoner who had removed the board with the bullet. "Muchas gracias, mi amigo. If you had not noticed me breathing, I would be in a hole, buried alive."

Lopez tried to pay the man, but he would not take any money. "Just get word to our people. Let them know we are still alive," he said, waving his arm toward the other prisoners. Maybe they will come and kill the warden. That will be payment enough for us."

Later that day, during the time most of the guards were taking their daily siesta, an empty supply wagon rumbled through the gate, headed for Nogales. A large pile of canvas was lying in a heap in the back. Lopez lay hidden under the pile of canvas. He lay very still and held his breath, hoping the guards would not find him, praying he would get back to his small ranchero alive. He silently promised god he would never go near these people again. In fact, he made a promise to himself to never go south of the border without an army of men to protect him. And since he was not rich, there was no chance he could ever hire an army to protect him. So, he would be content to stay north of the border, where hopefully, he would be safe.

CHAPTER THIRTEEN

Aided by a billion stars shining brightly, a quarter moon ruled the night as Justin and Ben belly crawled to their positions at the top of the sand hill not far from where a guard sat, smoking a small cigar.

After checking to see that the guard was alone, Justin crawled off to one side and edged his way up to about ten feet off to the side of where the guard was sitting. When Ben saw that Justin was in position, he stood up and began dancing around in the bright moonlight like some mad man who'd lost his senses. Slowly, Ben waltzed his way down the hillside in the direction of the guard, the moon glow creating eerie shadows.

At the local dances, Ben was considered quite the stepper, and the women lined up for a chance to sway around the room in his arms. Ben liked to dance because he would get to hold a woman close and smell the different perfumes. The waltz was his favorite. The women would smile as he swirled them around the floor.

The guard stood up, mesmerized as he watched Ben dance down the road leading to the prison. By the time the guard came to his senses and started to raise his rifle, Justin moved up from behind and clubbed the guard on the back of the head with the butt of his pistol, not hard enough to kill him, just enough to render him unconscious. The man would have a good-sized headache when he came to.

Justin stripped the guard of his uniform and put it on, then he and Ben headed for the second guard a little further down the road, closer to the prison.

As they approached the second guard, Ben held his hands in the air while Justin prodded him forward with the end of the first guard's rifle barrel.

The guard looked at them and said, "Que pasa?"

Before the second guard could react Justin poked him in the gut with the barrel of his rifle, and then followed with a hard uppercut to the chin with the butt of his rifle. The guard landed on his back, unconscious.

Ben had just finished changing clothes with the second guard when they saw the wagon with the relief guards come through the front gates of the prison.

The guards were riding in a small wagon pulled by a single horse. Justin moved to a prone position in the ditch next to the road while Ben moved a short distance up the road, and then stood relaxed, like a guard waiting to be relieved.

The guards were laughing and talking as they passed Justin lying in the ditch. They had no clue what was about to happen.

Once they'd gone past, Justin got to his feet and ran up quietly and climbed into the back of the wagon. At the same time, Ben reached out and took hold of the horse's halter, bringing him to a halt.

"Keep real quiet and you just might live to see another day," Justin said in a quiet, serious tone.

Ben pointed his rifle at the guards. "Drop the reins easy like and climb down."

The two men did as they were told and stood quietly while Justin emptied their rifles of ammunition, put the bullets in his pocket, and then handed the rifles back.

"Just stand where you're supposed to and pretend you're guardin' the road. There's ah friend of ours with ah rifle layin' at the top of that hill, yonder, and if you try anything stupid, he'll shoot you. He's not too fond of Mexicans. He had an uncle who disappeared inside that prison bout ah year back and ain't nobody seen him since."

Ben and Justin had left a rolled up piece of canvas and a rifle lying on the desert, at the top of the knoll with the rifle pointing toward the general direction of the road, hoping it would fool the guards.

Both guards turned and looked at the top of the hill where they saw a dark object. It was hard to tell. With only a quarter moon and at that distance, it could be a man with a rifle. They were not what you might call brave men to begin with, so they would take no chances. Besides, the captain of the guards had told them to let any gringo pass unmolested if he showed up.

'Even two gringos would not be enough to rescue Senor Jeremiah,' one of the guards thought to himself as he shook his head from side to side.

"That's real good." Justin said as he climbed onto the wagon and sat down next to Ben who was already seated with the reins in his hands.

The inside of the prison yard was illuminated by torches, which made anything in the prison yard an easy target for the guards on the wall walkway. And when Ben drove through the gates, neither he nor Justin had a problem seeing Jeremiah standing on a gallows platform with a hangman's noose around his neck. Close to the handle that released the trap door stood a prison inmate, with one hand on the handle.

Ben brought the horse to an abrupt halt and when they looked at the top of the wall, they saw at least twenty rifles pointed at them. Ben shook his head. "Looks like we were expected."

"Looks, like," Justin answered as he rolled and lit a cigarette. One of the guards ran over and took control of the horse. Two other guards ran over and took Justin and Ben's weapons, then stepped away from the wagon like it was carrying the plague.

Once it was safe, the warden strolled up to the wagon and looked at them with a bemused smile on his face. He made a big dramatic display, waving his arms in a wide sweep. "What have we here? New guards?"

When the laughter died down, the warden turned and looked at Ben and Justin with contempt. "Stupid gringos. You have made a very serious mistake."

Ben whispered out of the corner of his mouth, "Yea, that's what I been sayin' all along."

Justin just smiled that boyish grin of his and shrugged his shoulders.

After a moment, the warden turned and began to walk away. "Bring them to my office. And the one on the gallows, also."

Jeremiah's relief at having the noose removed from around his neck was evident as he grinned at his cousin and big brother. "Hope you got some kind of plan," Jeremiah said as he walked down the steps of the gallows.

"Nope. Just come by fer ah visit ta make sure you ain't sufferin' much," Justin said with a grin from ear to ear.

When the guards ushered Justin, Ben and Jeremiah into the warden's office, the warden was already sitting in his overstuffed chair behind his huge desk, puffing easily on a cigar. He stared at the three men standing in front of him. Blowing smoke in their direction, he said, "Sometimes I think gringos are all very stupid. And you must think I am stupid, also. Yes? Did you think you could just walk into my prison and take your brother out without anyone noticing?"

They returned the wardens stare and made no attempt to argue with him. Sometimes it was better to keep your mouth shut and see what happened. This was the warden's show. They would bide their time.

The warden blew out another long stream of smoke. "Which one of you is Senor Justin Hacker?"

Justin stared at the warden a long moment, and then took a step forward. "I am."

The warden got out of his chair and strutted around the desk to where Justin was standing and stopped directly in front of him. He blew out another stream of cigar smoke, this time directly into Justin's face. Justin paid no attention to the smoke and stared right back at him.

What was so special about this gringo? He was not a giant with huge muscles that could tear down the walls and rip the bars apart. He must have a cunning mind, the warden thought as he walked around, sizing him up. But if he was so smart, why had he and the other one come driving into his prison like no one would notice? Did he think they could over power all of his guards just by telling them to put down their guns? No, he could not be that stupid. This Senor Justin had a plan, of that he was sure, and he would discover what it was. After all, he had all the time he wanted to take, and after the torture he had in mind, this gringo would beg to tell him what that plan was.

"So, you are the famous American bandito who is wanted for killing three of our Mexican citizens. The people of Mexico will be able to sleep easier once I have made your death public."

When the warden resumed his position in front of him again, Justin said, "The way I hear it, they were wanted criminals with a price on their heads."

The warden grinned. "A mere technicality."

"Besides, I shot them in self-defense, on American soil, so none of your citizens have any cause ta lose sleep over whether I'm dead or alive."

The warden turned and walked behind his desk and sat down in his chair. "No matter. There are other charges to consider. Breaking into a Mexican prison with the intent to help a prisoner escape, also carries a death sentence."

The warden's attention moved to the two guards standing by the door. "Take the prisoners to one of the large cells down along the back wall," he said with a wave of his hand. "I will deal with them later."

The guards immediately moved over and began pushing Justin, Jeremiah and Ben toward the door. Just as one of the guards reached for the door handle, the warden spoke again.

"Senors, I have just decided - I will hang all three of you with great fanfare two weeks from tomorrow, to celebrate my wife's birthday. Is that not a wonderful gesture?"

The guards ushered Ben and Jeremiah out of the warden's office, but before leaving, Justin turned and took a couple of steps back into the room. "One little thing, warden. If we do hang, you won't be alive ta see it."

Without allowing the warden time to reply, Justin spun around and marched out the door, leaving the warden to his thoughts.

As they marched along the catwalk, Jeremiah poked his older brother in the ribs, "Big brother, you always did have more gall than any three men I ever knowed."

Ben nudged Jeremiah in the arm. "Yea, that's what I tole him."

"Quit yer complainin', we're still alive ain't we?" Justin said through a grin.

"Yea, but I weren't sure how long that might be when I saw the two of ya come drivin' through the gate," Jeremiah came back with.

"Me neither," Ben said. "When we saw ya standn' on them gallows with thet rope around yer neck I figured all three of us was goin' ta meet our maker right then and there for sure."

"Naw, puttin' Jeremiah on that gallows with ah rope around his neck, that was just ta get us ta surrender," Justin said as they came to a large cell with four bunks.

One of the guards opened the cell door with a key from a ring that he wore on his belt. When they were inside, he closed and locked the door, then walked away, talking to the other guard.

CHAPTER FOURTEEN

A few miles northeast of Nogales, the small community of Patagonia, Arizona was no more than a wide spot in the trail, with a total population of twenty-four. But it was an important wide spot because of the rich silver mine that had opened a few years back.

Ephram Hacker, older brother of Elijah Hacker and father to Benjamin Hacker, was the prime reason Patagonia was such an important wide spot in the trail. He was an important man. He owned the general store a few miles north that supplied the miners with whatever they wanted or needed.

Ephram was checking some crates of mining equipment when he noticed the shadow cross the floor. He looked over and saw a Mexican peasant standing in the doorway with his sombrero in his hands.

"Buenos dias. Que quieres?" Ephram said in fluent Spanish.

"I speak English, Senor. My name is Lopez and I bring you information about your son, Benjamin."

Ephram put down the pad and pencil he was holding and escorted Lopez into the back room where they could talk and have a cold beer. After Lopez related the story of Benjamin and Justin getting themselves thrown into the prison, without the part about him being there and why, Ephram stood up and paced around the room for a minute before speaking.

"And you're sure it's my boy, Ben, down there in thet prison?"

Lopez stood up and looked down at the floor as he spoke. "Si, Senor. My cousin is a guard at the prison. He told me himself. And I came here right away to tell you, with much danger for myself if the warden should find out. He is a very evil man, but I think it is my duty to come here and tell you."

Ephram stepped closer to Lopez. "And the warden said he was gonna hang all three of'em on the same day?"

Lopez began to ring his hat in his hands, again. "Si, Senor, in two weeks, to celebrate his wife's birthday."

Ephram went to the cash register and took out some money and handed it in Lopez's direction, who just stood there as though he wasn't sure what to do.

"Go ahead, take the money. You earned it. And don't you worry none, I won't tell anybody who I got the information from."

Lopez reached out and took the money, then backed towards the door. "Thank you, Senor," he said as he turned and hurried out the door, grinning to himself about how easy it was to make money selling information. Except for the incident with the warden, it was much less work than raising sheep.

Less than thirty minutes later, Ephram was standing on the front porch of the general store talking to Warren, the young man who worked for him. "Now remember, if'n anybody asks, I've gone fishin'."

Warren nodded his head. "Whatever you say, Mister Hacker, but you sure don't look like you're goin' fishin'. You ain't even got a pole. And I ain't never seen nobody go fishin' with ah rifle and ah hand gun."

"Don't you worry none bout thet, boy. You jest keep yer mouth shet and do like yer tole, elsewise you'll be lookin' fer ah job someplace else. You got thet?"

"Yes sir. Whatever you say, Mister Hacker. You've gone fishin' and I don't know when you'll be back."

Ephram nodded, then stomped down the steps, untied the reins from the hitch rail, stepped into the saddle and rode off in a southerly direction.

Night comes quickly in the desert. One minute it's light, then the sun just disappears and in its place, the moon shines brightly.

Ephram Hacker was glad for the darkness of night and the coolness that came with it. It helped settle his nerves a little. His horse seemed to know where they were headed and kept a brisk pace. It had been awhile since the animal had stretched his legs and Ephram allowed him his freedom.

During the trip, Ephram allowed his mind to dwell on several things. The feud between Elijah and himself had been a mystery to him for the past twenty years and Elijah would only say for him to think about it and he would understand. Well, over the years he'd given it plenty of thought and still didn't understand. Then there was the vendetta Elijah had with Justin. He blamed the boy for everything that displeased him. Something had gone wrong with Elijah and he had no clue as to how to fix it.

Foremost in his mind, though, was Benjamin being in that Mexican prison a few miles south of the border. He guessed Justin must have come home and Ben and him went down there to try and rescue Jeremiah. That was the only logical explanation, but for the life of him, he didn't understand how they had let themselves get caught.

Well, no matter. It was up to him now to see to getting the boys out of there and back home, again.

Ephram nodded off a bit as his horse slowed to a walk. This was the longest ride he'd taken in some time and it was taking its toll.

CHAPTER FIFTEEN

The guards placed them in a cell that had four bunks, two along each wall, with a walk space in between. After the guard locked the door and walked away, Justin sat down on the floor in the far corner of the cell and took off one of his boots.

"You are allowed to sit on the bunk," Jeremiah said with a bit of sarcasm.

Justin smiled as he took something long and slender out of a slot inside his boot, and then put his boot back on. "Ben, keep ah lookout, " he said as he stood up and went to the cell door.

After a nod from Ben, Justin reached his hands through the bars and began to try to pick the lock with the object he'd taken from his boot.

Jeremiah walked up to Justin and asked, "Are you doin' what I think yer doin'?"

Justin grinned at his younger brother and said with a ring of sarcasm, "Hello, big brother, it's good ta see ya again. Thank you for comin' down here from wherever you been these past seven years, just ta get me out of this hell hole."

Justin's smile disappeared. "Little brother, we came down here ta get you out and that's what we're gonna do. I learned this little trick from ah fella back in New York City."

Jeremiah was a bit embarrassed that he hadn't greeted his older brother formally yet, but things had happened pretty fast. "It is good to see you Justin, and thank you for what you're tryin' ta do, but I think you've lost your mind. Even if you do pick that lock, how do you plan ta get past the guards, out the gate, and back across the border?" Jeremiah queried in all seriousness.

Before Justin could answer, Ben whispered, "Somebody's comin'."

They moved back and sat down. Justin and Jeremiah took one of the bunks, while Ben took a seat across from them. Justin had just slipped the pick back into his boot as the warden and three guards with rifles walked up and stopped in front of the cell. Two of the guards pointed rifles at them while the third guard unlocked the door and swung it open.

The warden entered the cell, followed by one of the rifle toting guards, who was carrying a small bundle of prison clothes.

The warden indicated the clothes with his head. "You will remove your clothes and put these on."

Ben and Justin stripped down to their long johns and put on the prison clothes, which are not much more than rags.

One of the guards immediately began to search their clothes and found nothing. But when he searched Justin's boots, he found the pick.

The warden lit a cigar and blew the smoke towards Justin. "As I said before, gringos are stupid, and they believe me to be stupid, also." He held up the pick and shook his head as he made a clicking noise with his tongue.

Turning to one of the guards, the warden said, "Strip them down to their bare skin. I want them searched, completely. Even Senor Jeremiah."

"Why do I need ta be searched, I ain't done nuthin?" Jeremiah protested.

The warden walked out of the cell before turning back to speak to Jeremiah. "You are a gringo and a member of the Hacker family. Neither can be trusted."

Later, when they were finally alone and the humiliation of the strip search was over, Jeremiah looked down at his brother, who was stretched out on his bunk like nothing at all had happened, "Well, so much for the great escape plan, big brother. Got any more brilliant ideas?"

Ben, who had been looking through the bars, turned and nodded at Jeremiah. "Don't be in such ah rush ta give up, cousin."

Jeremiah looked back and forth between Ben and Justin as Justin swung his feet over the side of the bunk and stood up. "As long as he thinks he's smarter than we are, we have the upper hand," Justin said as he walked back to the far corner of the cell where he'd sat when they first entered the cell. Justin bent down and brushed the dirt off a second pick he'd hidden there without anyone noticing. "I wanted him to find that pick in my boot. Now he thinks he's ah smart man."

Jeremiah shook head. "Well, I'll be damned."

"We may all be, before this is over, little brother," Justin said as he slipped the long, thin piece of metal into his boot.

The three men spent a long while getting to know one another again. Both Ben and Jeremiah wanted to hear about all of Justin's adventures during the years he'd been gone, while Ben wanted to know about this woman Jeremiah had gotten himself involved with.

Justin also wanted news of his long lost sweetheart, Julie, but neither one knew much other than what they'd heard. Shortly after Justin left, Julie had gone up north and got married. Jeremiah thought she'd kept in touch with their mother, but he wasn't sure.

Justin lay back on his bunk and lit a cigarette, thinking about what might have been if his father hadn't run him out of town on the end of a shotgun. Maybe, it would have been him Julie married. And maybe they'd have a nice little horse ranch, with a son to help take care of the place.

Justin remembered this little valley northwest of Nogales that he'd had his eye on. There was a spring there with good water and plenty of grass. Of course, that was all water under the bridge now, he thought as he snubbed out his cigarette and rolled over and closed his eyes.

CHAPTER SIXTEEN

Even though the trip had only been around forty miles, it was forty miles more than Ephram Hacker was used to riding and to make matters worse, something had spooked his horse in the darkness and the cursed thing had run until It was all lathered up and blowing hard, and he had come close to being thrown from the saddle.

Ephram had been able to guide his winded steed into a small arroyo where he could water the poor beast and let it rest while he grabbed a bit of sleep and respite from being in the saddle too long.

It was early morning when Ephram, dirty and tired, came riding into Nogales. The town was just waking up as he rode slowly down the main street, and then turned onto the street that led to the blacksmith shop and his brother's home. He knew he wouldn't get a greeting of welcome, but this was business and somehow he would make his brother listen to him.

Elizabeth Hacker was standing at the kitchen sink, pumping water into a pan when she glanced out the window and saw her brother in law riding slowly toward their house. She did a double take to make sure it was him before she ran into the dining room where Elijah sat drinking a cup of coffee. It was to be his last before returning to the blacksmith shop where he'd already put in two hours of labor, tending to the horses he boarded for several of the town folk.

Elijah Hacker looked up and saw his wife dancing around like a skittish colt as she hurried into the room. "What in tar-nation's wrong with you, woman? Ya look like you've seen ah ghost."

Elizabeth rung her hands on her apron. She was a nervous wreck, not quite sure how to break the news, so she plunged right in. "Elijah Hacker, now ye'll just be ah stayin' calm. Yer brother is ah comin' down the street and I think he's comin' here."

"What? You must be seein' things, woman. Ephram comin' here? Can't be," Elijah yelled as he jumped up from the table and rushed over to the window and peeked out between the curtains.

Elizabeth fidgeted back and forth. "That's what I was ah thinkin' at first. But I saw him through the kitchen window, clear as the sun comin' over the horizon. And where else would he be goin', comin' down this street?"

Elijah spun on his heel and headed for the front door, with Elizabeth right behind him.

Elijah opened the front door just a crack, but enough to see Ephram ride up and climb wearily out of the saddle. As Ephram tied his horse to the hitch rail, Elijah closed the door and tuned to his wife. "I don't know why he's here, but he ain't ah comin' inta this house."

Elizabeth Hacker was not about to take any nonsense from either one of these crazy ole fools, fighting over god only knew what for the past twenty years. "Now ye'll be keepin' ah civil tongue in yer mouth, Elijah Hacker. And there'll be no fightin' in the front yard, where ye'll be tearin' up me flower bed and embarrass me in front of our neighbors."

With nothing more than a scowl at her, Elijah opened the front door and stormed out onto the front porch and planted himself right in front of Ephram, just as Ephram was about to start up the front steps. Elizabeth stepped into the doorway and just stood there.

Elijah glared at his brother. "I don't know why yer here and I don't care. Yer not welcome, so just get back on thet horse of your'n and ride back ta where ya come from."

It was still early morning and he'd been riding all night. He was tired, dirty and hungry, and not in any mood to put up with his brother's stupid feud. "Ya danged ole fool, do ya really believe I'd be here if it weren't important? Our sons are about ta meet their maker at the hands of some damn fool Mexican hangman, and yer still ah frettin' about some damn fool twenty year old feud thet only you know the answer to."

He looked up at Elizabeth. "Elizabeth, may I come in? It's important."

The look in Ephram's eyes caused Elizabeth to raise her hands to her face. As she reached up and brushed a wisp of hair out of her face, she said, "Please come in and welcome. Wipe yer feet and mind yer swearin'." With that she stepped back into the house.

Ephram climbed the steps and walked past his brother. At the door, he wiped his boots on the mat that was there for that purpose, then took off his hat and entered the house.

Elijah followed, protesting. "Ephram Hacker, you come back here! Elizabeth, don't you let him inta my house!"

Elizabeth was tempted to close the door on her husband, but that would only cause more problems.

Once Elijah got inside his house, he continued his dialogue from the porch. "If'n you think you can jest come ah waltzin' inta my house as pretty as ya please, without even ah by yer leave, after what ya did ta me!"

Ephram bristled up like a fighting cock about to go into battle. "Now you see here you stubborn ole fool. I ain't got the slightest idee what yer ah talkin' about."

That was as far as either of them got before Elizabeth stepped between them, pushing them apart. "That's enough! Jest stop this petty bickering and try ta get along for at least five minutes, both of ya."

Immediately, Ephram stepped back and shook his head as he looked around. "Yer right, Elizabeth, and I'm right sorry fer my behavior. Well now, ain't you done some real nice things ta this place. It looks real good."

Flattered with his praise, Elizabeth smiled and said, "Why, thank ya, Ephram. It's nice ta see ah man that appreciates ah woman's touch." She turned and gave Elijah a stare.

Elijah glared right back at her, as Elizabeth took Ephram by the arm and escorted him into the dining room.

Ephram reached out and rubbed the table, then sniffed the air. He got a sad look on his face and then took out a handkerchief and blew his nose. He looked around the room. "Sure makes me miss my Bessie - gone ten years this comin' October."

Being a woman, Elizabeth was touched by his words and reached out and patted his hand, which set Elijah off, again. "You ain't here ta talk about no woman ya drove ta an early grave."

Ephram whirled around with his fist drawn, ready to smash his younger brother in the face.

Not to be outdone, Elijah drew back his own fist and squared off, ready to fight.

Knowing that neither one of them really wanted to be the one to take the first swing, Elizabeth stepped in between them and pushed them apart. "Both of ya sit down and have some coffee and cool down while I fix some breakfast. And if I hear even one bad word outta either one of ya, I'll be feedin' yer breakfast to the hogs."

Still glaring at each other, they sat down at the table. Elijah poured himself a cup of coffee, and then sat the pot down some distance down the table, causing Ephram to have to get up to retrieve the pot.

During this same time, the boys had just finished breakfast, and were filing out for the day's work detail. As they walked along, Justin said, "They don't need ta hang ya, the food will kill ya quick enough."

One of the guards slammed Justin in the middle of the back with the butt of his rifle. "No talking," he yelled.

Justin was driven to the ground but came up swinging, surprising the guard with a solid right to the jaw. The guard flew unceremoniously into the air and came down hard on his back. His eyes were wide with shock. His rifle lay several feet away.

Suddenly, guards surrounded them. Four guards pointed their rifles at Ben and Jeremiah to hold them at bay, while six others beat Justin with their rifles and continued when he went down again, by taking turns kicking him. When Justin could no longer put up a fight, two guards hauled him to his feet.

At that point, the captain of the guard turned to one of his men and said, "Report this incident to the warden, now!"

Everything came to a halt. The prisoners stood in silence, waiting to see what was going to happen, no one daring to say anything. Ben looked at Jeremiah and said, "What now?"

Jeremiah thought for a moment, "My guess would be that the warden won't hang him for this because he wants ta hang the three of us together. What he probably will do is give him ah whippin'. That's one of his favorite punishments. He likes ta hear ah man scream for mercy."

The guard returned from the warden's office and Jeremiah's prediction became a reality when Justin was dragged to the whipping post and his hands tied well above his head so that his toes were barely touching the ground.

After giving Justin twenty lashes, they left him there to bake in the sun while the rest of the prisoners went about their daily work.

The day dragged on slowly for Justin as sweat crept into his wounds and sent fire burning signals to his brain. He was given no water and his arms and hands had gone numb from lack of blood. By mid-morning, he was drifting in and out of awareness.

Several times he thought this was all just a dream and that he would wake up and find himself lying on his bunk. At other times, he was cognizant of where he was and why. And at those times, he would resolve to himself to be strong and not let the warden or the guards know of his pain. He would not be broken and that was his final thought on the matter as the sun grew hotter and hotter, and his tongue began to swell.

When the sun reached its peak, the prisoners were herded back inside the prison walls and ordered to line up, facing the whipping post where Justin hung, limp and unconscious.

After a few minutes, the warden appeared and walked up to Justin, lifting his head up by placing his fingers under Justin's chin. Then, without ceremony, the warden dropped his head, and turned to one of the guards. "Get a bucket of water and pour it over this miserable gringos head. I want him awake so he can feel his punishment."

After only a moment, a guard ran up with a bucket of water and poured it over Justin's head.

Justin's eyes opened and he greedily licked the water from his lips, then reached out with his foot and kicked the guard squarely in the groin, causing the man to drop the bucket and fall to his knees, groaning. "Thanks for the drink," Justin said in a muffled voice because his tongue was still too swollen for him to speak clearly.

"Bravo, Senor Hacker. You may yet be a worthy adversary after all," the warden said, clapping his hands together as he backed away to a safe distance out of Justin's kicking range.

The warden had a contemptuous look as he turned and faced the prisoners. "But we shall see how smug he is after more punishment." And with that, he nodded towards the prisoner holding a blacksnake whip in his hand. "Let's see how much he will enjoy another twenty lashes."

The whipping was brutal and with each lash Justin gritted his teeth, vowing to himself not to cry out. By the time the prisoner gave Justin the last lash, his back was covered with bloody streaks, but he had uttered no more than a slight groan throughout the two whippings.

The warden had two distinct emotions going on inside him. First, he was more than disappointed that Justin had not cried out for mercy as every man under the whip had so far done. But, his second emotion was admiration. This Justin Hacker would be a challenge. How long could he last before breaking? It would be interesting to see.

The warden felt he must be careful. He did not want Senor Hacker to die before he had the pleasure of watching him dance at the end of the hangman's rope. He just wanted to know that he had broken this gringo to the point where he preferred dying rather than have more punishment.

The warden took his time lighting a cigar before he spoke to the prisoners. "Let this be an example to anyone who thinks he would like to attack one of my guards."

The warden turned to the captain of the guards and said, "When the prisoners have finished eating their noon meal, untie Senor Hacker and send him to the fields with the others, there is still half a days work to be done."

With no shirt to protect his cuts from the burning sun, Justin tried hard not to think about the burning pain his salty sweat gave him as it mixed with the blood in the slashes across his back.

Slowed by the shackles he wore, Justin hoed weeds in the prison garden as Ben eased up next to him. "How are ya holdin' up?"

"Ah, tis floatin' in ah cool bath, with ah beautiful maiden bathin' me and pourin' good whiskey down me throat ta smooth away the pain is what I'm dreamin' of, but I don't suppose that will be ah happenin' anytime soon. So, other than that me bucko, I won't let the bastards know of me grevins. I'll not be givin' them the satisfaction."

A guard saw them close together and started in their direction. Ben moved on up the row, just as one of the prisoners came up to Justin and offered him a drink of water.

Justin stopped and stared at the bucket for just a moment before he reached for the gourd filled with cool water. The gourd had almost reached his lips when the guard knocked it out of his hand.

"Ah, Senor Hacker, how clumsy you are. You have spilled your daily water ration."

The guard reached down and picked up the gourd, which was now covered with dirt and sand and tossed it into the water bucket. "No more water for this one."

The prisoner nodded, then hurried on down the row to where Ben and Jeremiah were standing, hatred embedded on their faces. As the prisoner came near, Jeremiah's anger got the better of him and he raised his hoe and would have attacked the guard if Ben and the prisoner hadn't grabbed hold of his arm. "Later, cousin," Ben said in a quiet voice.

The prisoner put in his two cents worth. "Si, you would only make things worse. The warden wants you to get into trouble so he can give all of you punishment before he hangs you. It is his way. He is the devil."

The rest of the afternoon went without incident as the sun bore down on them all, especially Justin, who was ready to collapse by the time they were called back inside the prison walls.

Both Jeremiah and Ben were angered even more when they weren't allowed to help Justin walk.

With great effort and will power, Justin kept on his feet until he was finally able to sit down at a long table in the mess hall where beans and tortillas were served. Justin wolfed down his meal and asked for more. The prison cook filled Justin's tin pan to the brim, and watched as the gringo ate his second plate of food with the same flourish. Justin knew he needed food inside him to help regain his strength, nutrition that would help his body to heal. He was determined not to let the warden beat him down.

The prisoner sitting next to Ben whispered, "There is something on the bench between us. Please take it and do not ask questions. You need this more than I do."

Ben let his hand drop casually between them and scratched his leg. In doing so his hand ran over the shape of the long, slender weapon that lay there. But he didn't pick it up. Instead, he nudged it under his leg where it wouldn't be seen. Later, when the meal was over and the men were standing up and moving around, he would hide it under his shirt.

A guard had noticed the old man speaking to one of the gringo Hackers, but did not see the knife being transferred, although he had a suspicion something had taken place. He would mention it to his superior, but that was all. It was close to the time for his duty to end and he had a bottle of tequila hidden in his bunk.

Back in the cell, Jeremiah and Ben helped Justin to his bunk, where they laid him face down. By now, he could hardly walk of his own accord. Ben turned to Jeremiah and said, "Get a clean rag and some water from that bucket in the corner. We need to clean these wounds."

Jeremiah waited until Ben had cleaned Justin's wounds before asking him the question that had been nagging him since they left the mess hall. "Did that old man give you somethin' while we were eatin' supper?"

Ben nodded his head and reached under his shirt and pulled out the homemade knife. It was just a long, slender piece of steel that had been sharpened and had a short corncob handle. Ben handed it to Jeremiah, who stuffed it under his mattress.

Before going off duty, the guard from the mess hall told his sergeant about his suspicions. The sergeant told the captain and the captain, knowing the wardens wrath, decided not to take any chances and headed for the warden's office.

A short time later, the warden and three guards with rifles stopped in front of the cell, where for the moment, the Hacker boys called home. The warden ordered the cell door to be unlocked, after which he went inside. "Stand up and face the far wall," he ordered.

Ben and Jeremiah helped Justin to his feet and did as they were told, while the guard searched the cell and found the knife.

"Who's knife is this?" the warden asked.

Before either one of the others could speak, Ben turned around and looked at the warden. "It's mine."

"Where did you get it? I know you didn't have it when you came in. Who gave it to you?" the warden asked.

By now, Justin and Jeremiah had turned around and the three of them looked at each other. Ben grinned and said, "The good fairy left it under my pillow."

The warden shook his head as he walked out of the cell. "As you wish. We will play your little game."

He looked at the guards. "Take him down to the whipping post and have Morales give him twenty lashes."

The warden started to leave, then changed his mind and walked back to the cell door. "You Hackers may yet cheat the hangman. You may all die at the whipping post."

A few minutes later, Justin, Jeremiah and all the other prisoners were staring at the whipping post. They watched as Ben was stripped of his shirt, and then tied with his hands above his head, just as Justin had been. One of the prisoners emerged from the darkness with a whip in his hand and began carrying out the warden's sentence.

Benjamin was definitely of the Hacker bloodline, for no more than a slight groan emerged from his lips, even down to the last lash.

When it was over and the guards had untied him, Ben shook off their attempts to help him stand on his feet. Ben lifted his head and walked, under his own power, back to the cell where Justin and Jeremiah helped him to a bunk. When they were alone, Justin and Jeremiah tended to Ben's wounds with the help of a small tin of salve that was tossed into their cell from the cell next to them. After they treated Ben, Jeremiah rubbed some on Justin's back.

Before they went to sleep, Jeremiah uttered a single word, softly through the bars to no one in particular, "Thanks."

In the other cells, all was quiet. Down to the last one, every prisoner was in awe of these gringos who defied the warden, even in the face of death.

The rest of the night passed quietly, but when morning came and they left for the day's work, most of the prisoners lowered their eyes and made the sign of the cross as he passed the gallows. Not a one of them wanted to stare into the unseeing eyes of the old man who had given Ben the knife.

Sometime during the night, they had hanged him.

As Justin stumbled past the gallows and saw the old man hanging there, it struck him just how mean this warden could be and he began to understand whom and what he was up against.

The whole picture played out in Justin's mind as he trudged along. The warden loved to play mind games. The prisoners were his pawns with the final end to the game, death. And of course, the warden had no worries because the power was all on his side.

Well, somehow, the game was going to change, Justin thought to himself. How, he didn't know, but it would happen if he could just stay alive long enough.

Justin saw Jeremiah and Ben waiting for him outside the gate, and just as he caught up to them, a guard prodded him in the back and motioned for them to move along. It was going to be another long, agonizing day.

CHAPTER SEVENTEEN

After making his early rounds, the sheriff hurried down the sidewalk, the morning heat already making wet spots under his armpits and down his spine. Reaching his office, he rushed in and closed the door behind him, giving a sigh of relief, not because he was inside and out of the glaring sun, but because he had not had to deal with Elijah Hacker yet today.

He walked over and poured himself a cup of coffee from the pot that seemed to always be on the stove these days. Then he walked over and sat behind his desk and took a sip. Frowning, the sheriff reached into the lower right-hand desk drawer and lifted out a bottle of whiskey and poured a short measure into his cup took a long sip and then added just a small dollop more to his coffee. He knew this peaceful day would not last much longer and a bit of fortification wouldn't hurt.

As luck would have it, he'd only gotten through half his cup of whiskey-laced coffee when Elijah and Ephram came busting in the front door.

"Oh God, what did I do ta deserve two of 'em?" the sheriff whispered as he sat up and explained to both of them before either one of them could ask a question, that early this very morning he'd sent a telegram to try and to get some information, but there had been no reply so far, so they might as well go home and he'd get word to them as soon as he heard something.

But, instead of leaving, Ephram poured himself a cup of coffee and sat down in one of the chairs, while Elijah paced the floor.

After his third sip of coffee, Ephram looked over at the sheriff and said, "Sheriff, I'm not ah waitin' much longer."

The sheriff longed for a big gulp of whiskey, straight from the bottle. "Just keep yer shirt on. It won't be much longer," he said through gritted teeth.

Ephram stood up and placed his empty coffee cup on the sheriff's desk. "Actual, I don't know why we're ah wastin' time around here. If'n we'd ah done it my way we'd. . ."

Elijah spun around and glared at his brother. "Well, we ain't doin' it yer way. I ain't ah goin' off on no wild goose chase!"

Ephram took the two steps that put him directly in front of his brother, his fists balled up, ready to fight.

Elijah swelled himself up to his full height and drew back his fist.

For just a moment, the sheriff was ready to let these two fools punch each other's brains out. Except that it wouldn't have solved anything and they might tear up his office and get blood all over the floor. So, before they actually started throwing punches, he stepped in between them and pushed them apart.

"Alright, both of ya hold on just ah gall-derned minute. If you two ole buzzards really want ta fight then go out in the street and have at it. I won't try stopping ya."

Elijah and Ephram stared at each other for no more than a moment, then as though they'd been given a command, turned and headed for the door. As Elijah opened the door they collided with the telegraph operator as he came stumbling in from the outside.

For no more than the blink of an eye, they stared at each other with surprised looks, then the telegraph operator rushed over to the sheriff's desk and dropped a piece of paper down in front of him. "Here's the information you been waiting for. I brought it right over as soon as it came in."

He was beaming from ear to ear on his efficiency as Ephram and Elijah hustled up to the desk, their fight forgotten.

The sheriff handed the operator a coin and said, "Thanks."

The telegraph operator smiled and nodded his head as he pocketed the coin, but when he turned to leave, he found his way blocked by the two old men. Pushing them aside, he muscled his way between them, mumbling something under his breath about old codgers as he left.

The sheriff held the telegram up to the light to be able to read it better but was having trouble because Elijah and Ephram had, by now, crowded around him and were leaning over both his shoulders, also trying to read the telegram.

The sheriff gave them each a shove backwards. "Will you give ah man ah little room?"

Begrudgingly, Elijah and Ephram each took a step backwards, but close enough to read the telegram if the sheriff held it up to the light again.

With a stern look and a wave of his hand, he motioned them around to the front of the desk.

When they were finally at a proper distance, he held the telegram up to the light and read it, then tossed it across the desk for them to read, after which he stood up and walked over and poured himself more coffee.

The sheriff was standing outside his office, sipping his coffee and enjoying a bit of fresh air, contemplating the information in the telegram, when Elijah and Ephram came stomping out onto the sidewalk. The sheriff turned and looked at them. "Well, now that we know for sure that all three of'em are in that Mexican prison, what's the plan?"

Ephram looked at Elijah, then back at the sheriff. "Same plan as we had when we come in here. Me and Elijah are ah goin' down there and get'em out."

The sheriff tossed what was left of his coffee into the street. "Now boys, don't go off half-cocked. Breakin' inta that place is nye on-ta impossible. It jest can't be done."

Elijah stepped up next to Ephram. "The sheriff's right." Elijah turned towards the sheriff. "I been ah sayin' thet same thing all along. I hear they got armed guards both inside and outside'a thet place."

"Since when did you start side'n with the sheriff?" Ephram said as he stepped off the sidewalk and headed across the street. "Sides, none ah thet makes no never mind. We're goin' after'em and thet's all they is to it."

Elijah chased after his brother, leaving the sheriff standing on the sidewalk, shaking his head as the two old men hustled down the other side of the street, trading insults.

Elijah and Ephram were still going at it when they stomped into Elijah's house.

Elizabeth had seen and heard them coming down the street and opened the oven door and lifted out a large platter, holding it by a rag with both hands. She entered from the kitchen with their breakfast just as they planted themselves at the table.

Elijah, not even acknowledging Elizabeth, dragged a large piece of ham; three eggs and some fried potatoes onto his plate and began to eat. "I still say that's the dumbest idea you ever had."

"And I still say it's the only chance we got of getting' them boys outta thet Mex prison." He looked up at Elizabeth and smiled. "Thank ya kindly fer the vittles," then turned back to Elijah. "And unless you can explain ta me ah better plan." He let the sentence trail off, waiting for a reply from his younger brother.

Elizabeth was fed up with their constant bickering and said so as she slammed her fist down on the table. "Stop it! There'll be no more arguin' about it! Now, eat yer breakfast and then go down there and bring them boys home. I don't care how it's done, just do it!"

After swallowing a large mouthful of ham, eggs and potatoes, Elijah glared at Elizabeth and said, "I ain't ah gonna get Justin out, and nobody can make me!"

"Elijah Hacker, either ya bring all three of them boys home or don't ya bother comin' back, yerself."

Elijah slammed his knife and fork down onto the table and almost tipped over his chair as he stood up and stormed out of the house, mumbling something under his breath.

Elizabeth turned to look at Ephram just in time to see him slide Elijah's plate over next to his and dump what was left onto his plate and begin to eat. Before he could get more than a mouthful, she reached over and picked up his and Elijah's plates and gave him one of those looks a woman can give a man that makes him want to retreat in a fast hurry.

Ephram stood up and grabbed several biscuits and stuffed them into his pockets before she could stop him, then ran out of the room.

Elizabeth smiled as she watched Ephram hurry out the front door. He must like my biscuits, she thought to herself as she watched him go. She was still smiling as she walked into the kitchen.

The townspeople stopped and stared at what could only be considered a miracle, Elijah and Ephram Hacker riding side by side down the street, trailing three saddled horses. Elijah and Ephram sat upright and stared straight ahead, neither looking left or right, ignoring all of the gawkers as they rode toward the Mexican border.

For the past twenty years, they had barely spoken to each other, let alone do anything together. It would be a day to be talked about for some time to come.

Among those who stopped to stare, was a very pretty young woman and a small boy. When she saw the two men riding down the street together, she stopped and put her hand to her chest. She watched until they had passed to make sure her eyes were not playing tricks on her, then took the boy by the hand and hurried on down the street.

At the far end of town, the young woman and boy stopped in front of the Hacker house and hesitated a moment before opening the front gate and walking up to the door where she took a deep breath, then knocked.

When Elizabeth opened the front door, her eyes went wide and she looked from side to side to make sure the street was clear, then hurried the young woman and the boy into the house.

Once inside, she pulled the young woman into a warm embrace. "Oh Julie, tis so good ta see ya."

She then turned and lifted the young boy into her arms. "Well now, Patrick me boy, would ya be havin' ah big hug fer yer grandma?"

Patrick liked hearing his grandma talk with her Irish accent. He grinned and threw his arms around her neck and gave her his best hug as she hugged him back and gave him a big kiss on the cheek.

"Is it true? Is Justin back in town?" Julie asked.

Elizabeth looked at Julie and said, "Well it is and it ain't. Come inta the kitchen and we'll have a bite ta eat and some coffee, and I'll do me best ta try and explain it to ya."

During their breakfast, Elizabeth did her best to explain about Jeremiah and the woman south of the border and about how he'd gotten himself thrown into prison and how Justin had come back to help rescue him with Ben's help. She left nothing out.

With breakfast over, Patrick ran off to play while Julie and Elizabeth cleared the table and Elizabeth finished her story. "Elijah and Ephram left just ah few minutes ago ta go down ta Mexico ta try ta get the boys out and bring 'em home."

Julie sipped her coffee. "Do you really think they'll be able to get them out? I hear no one has ever escaped from there."

Elizabeth had a worried look on her face as she poured more coffee. "I don't know. And you're right, I don't think anybody has ever gotten outta that place alive. And let's face it, Elijah and Ephram ain't the young men they use'ta be. And they can't seem ta agree on anything. I wish I had the knowin' of the future, but I don't."

Both Julie and Elizabeth sat quietly sipping their coffee, each deep within their own thoughts.

The gray hawk that had earlier soared over the prison, searching for breakfast, now rode the high winds with a full stomach, idly watching two men riding silently across the desert, leading three saddled horses. She screeched at these new intruders, and then angled off in the direction of her nest hidden deep within the trees to the north.

CHAPTER EIGHTEEN

The prison graveyard was located on both sides of the road that lead into the prison. Sticks with small pieces of wood marked the graves of over a hundred prisoners, who had for one reason or another, never been released, even when their sentence was over. As a matter of fact, very few had ever lived long enough to serve out his entire sentence. The warden always seemed to find some reason to hang them, starve them, or beat them to death at the whipping post. Each piece of wood had a mark on it to indicate what was buried below, and only the warden knew what each mark meant.

Justin, Ben and Jeremiah had been ordered to dig a grave for the old man who had given them the knife. Would his marker carry a mark of what treasure was buried here, they wondered?

As far as the warden was concerned, it was fitting.

The day was, as was every day, hot and dry. Even with their shirts on, sweat ran down their backs, causing searing pain in the tracks left by the whippings. They were allowed no hats to help shade their heads, nor were they allowed any water to drink or pour over themselves to cool down their sun-dried bodies. And with every shovel full of dirt, their energy was waning fast.

An older guard who was at least thirty pounds overweight, with several wide spaces between his yellow teeth, stood nearby with a rifle in the crook of his arm. He made a big show of taking a long drink of water, then pouring some over his head, after which he pulled a small bottle from the inside of his tunic and took a pull of some clear looking liquid, which made him shake his head and make a wooooo noise.

A slight breeze brought the foul smell of body odor and tequila to the noses of Justin, Jeremiah and Ben, who were standing shoulder high in the hole they were digging. They looked at the guard with contempt. Jeremiah shook his head. "Have you figured a way outta here, yet?"

Justin reached down and picked up several small rocks. "I have an idea, but I need to check it out, tonight. Fill yer pockets with ah bunch of these small pebbles."

Before either Jeremiah or Ben could ask why they would need rocks of any size, the smelly, overweight guard ordered them out of the hole.

As they climbed out of the hole, they saw two other prisoners digging in an existing grave.

Ben punched Jeremiah in the arm with his elbow. "What'er they doin', stackin' people on top of each other?"

"No, they're hidin' loot."

Justin looked at his younger brother and asked, "They're doin' what?"

"The word was, the bandit, Snake-eye and his boys would steal gold, money, or whatever, up north and take it to his brother, Manuel, who would bring it here to the warden for safe keepin'."

Ben grinned. "And the warden hides the loot in the graves, safe and sound where nobody can get to it." Ben looked over at Justin. "No wonder the warden hates you so much, you killed the goose that laid the golden egg."

"Well, they musta' got themselves ah new goose," Jeremiah said, "cause I saw Manuel come rollin' in this mornin'. He was drivin' ah buckboard with somethin' in the back. And whatever it is, was covered with ah piece of canvas."

Justin wiped sweat out of his eyes and turned his face away from the blazing sun. "The only thing that concerns me right now is for us ta get outta here and back across the border. Did you collect them rocks like I asked ya to?"

Both Jeremiah and Ben nodded their heads, yes, but Ben couldn't hold back any longer. "What'er we gonna do with rocks, throw'em at the guards?"

"In a way, you might say that," Justin said as all three of them turned at the sound of a wagon coming through the front gates.

The buckboard with the canvas-covered cargo came out of the gates, driven by Manuel and next to him sat the warden. Manuel drove the buckboard up next to the hole the prisoners had just dug and stopped. The men on the ground unloaded a chest and dropped it into the hole, then began filling it up again.

Manuel turned the horse and drove up next to the hole Justin, Ben and Jeremiah had just finished digging. Justin whispered, "I think he brought somethin' more than loot, this time."

The guard pulled the canvas back to reveal the old man, along with Snake-eye and his two companions. Manuel looked directly at Justin. "I think it is fitting that the man who murdered my poor brother and his friends, is the one who digs his grave and buries him and his friends."

The boys just stood there, staring at the warden, Manuel, the guard and the four dead bodies.

"Bury them," the warden said in a quiet, no nonsense tone of voice.

Justin directed his attention toward the warden. "All of'em. In one grave?"

A little sterner this time, the warden said, "All of them."

Justin looked at his brother and Ben, then back at the warden and Manuel. "Sure ain't gonna leave much room fer no stolen loot."

From the look on the warden's face, Justin wasn't sure the warden wasn't about to order the guard to shoot him. But the seething seemed to drop down to a calculated anger. Then, after a pregnant pause, the warden cleared his throat and said, "So, Senor Hacker, you think you have things all figured out. And maybe you do, but it will do you no good because very soon, the only things you Hackers will be able to talk to are the worms and other flesh eaters that consume your bodies."

The warden nodded to the guard, who gestured with his rifle. The boys lifted the dead bodies out of the buckboard and dropped them, none too ceremoniously into the hole. They lowered the old man into the hole last, with a bit of reverence.

The warden watched the way they treated the body of the old man and had to bite his lower lip to not react to their contempt. Let them have their fun for now. Soon it would be his turn.

The scorching sun dropped toward the horizon as Justin, Jeremiah and Ben wearily began to fill in the hole. Manuel flicked the reins and the horse headed back towards the shade inside the walls of the prison. The wagon pulled away to the sound of the warden laughing like he'd just heard some outrageous joke.

Justin looked at the warden's back and said to himself in a low voice, "You may think this is funny, mister warden man, but the game ain't over yet. No sir, not by a long shot."

"What?" Jeremiah asked.

"Nothin', little brother. Nothin' at all. Jest talkin' ta the wind."

Ben looked around as he wiped sweat from his eyes. "What wind?"

They looked at each other for a moment, and then began laughing, hysterically.

The prisoners looked up from their work and stared in awe at these three loco gringos who continually laughed in the face of death.

With their arms over each other's shoulders, Justin, Jeremiah and Ben walked toward the open prison gateway, chatting away like three lost friends who hadn't seen each other in a long time.

CHAPTER NINETEEN

It was early evening when Ephram and Elijah reached their destination and eased their horses in among the clump of trees that stood atop a small rise just beyond the road leading to the warden's house. From here they could observe the house and anyone coming or going. It was a good spot. There was shade to protect them from the blistering sun, and grass for the horses to eat. Even their fire, for coffee, if properly done would give off very little smoke that would disappear into the tops of the trees and could not be seen from a distance.

With an abundant amount of free labor and stolen money, the warden had built himself a home to be envied by the wealthiest of men. It was of Spanish design with a wall ten feet high and three feet thick enclosing the entire housing area, barns and out buildings, which covered more than an acre of land. There was a wide front and back opening for coming and going, which had strong wooden gates that could be closed in case of an attack. The house was attached to one of the sidewalls and wrapped around onto the back wall. The walls and house were made of adobe brick, with red flagstone covering most of the courtyard. A covered walkway, with the same red flagstone ran along the entire length of the house. A large, ornate well stood in the center of the courtyard with benches all around for relaxing. There were also tables with benches in an area beyond the well that were shaded, where food and drinks could be served during the cool of the evening.

It was said the interior was decorated from the finest stores in Mexico City and Europe.

The opposite wall housed the Arabian horses he was fond of. The stables were of ample size and the horses were groomed and exercised daily.

Outside the back wall was another well and a large garden where they grew a wide variety of vegetables. And beyond that was an area where cattle, pigs, chickens and goats were raised, well away from the house so there would be no animal smells.

The warden's wife was from an aristocratic family in Spain and cared nothing of her husband's affairs, nor did she pry. Her duties were to run her husband's home.

She had never been to the prison, nor had she ever talked to the workers. That would have been below her station in life. She was not really a snob, but if they didn't work in the house as cooks or housemaids, then they had nothing to talk about. And the warden himself had warned the prisoners about speaking or bothering his wife for any reason. If there was an emergency, they were to take care of it themselves or speak to Juanita, maid to the mistress. Juanita took her instructions from the warden's wife and made sure they were carried out.

Although her love life was not what she had hoped and dreamed of, she made herself content with her home and the freedom to run it as she saw fit.

Each day, selected prisoners and guards would come and do whatever work was needed to be done, and then return to the prison before dark.

"Sure is mighty fancy digs," Elijah said as he and Ephram belly crawled up to the top of the ridge and peered down into the warden's hacienda.

"Yea, well, it's ah mite fancy fer my likin's." Ephram wasn't impressed with the warden's home. He had a mission and that was all he cared to think about right now. "Sides, we're here fer one reason and one reason only, and thet reason don't include no sightseein'."

Elijah was about to say something nasty when Ephram pointed toward the far sidewall where a road led from the garden and livestock area to the front road, which lead back to the prison.

A prison guard was driving a wagon loaded with ten prisoners. Four armed guards accompanied the wagon, one on each side and two following the wagon.

Ephram and Elijah watched until they disappeared down the road, and then turned their attention back to the hacienda, where all was quiet. A small woman with bare feet came out to the well and got a bucket of water. Other than that, there seemed to be no other activity.

After a while, Ephram snaked his way back down the hill, stood up and headed to where the horses were tied. "Might as well go make camp. Can't do nothin' til mornin', anyway," he said, rubbing his sore back.

Elijah chased after his brother and when he got close, he said, "You ain't really gonna go through with this half-baked idee, are ya?"

Ephram stepped into the saddle and began to ride away. "It's the only way we have a snowball's chance, little brother, the only way."

As Elijah climbed aboard his horse, he looked at the sky. "Don't go ah holdin' none of this ah'gin' me, Lord. It weren't none of my doin'. It's all Ephram's idee."

A few miles from the warden's home, in the shadow of a deep ravine and under an overhang, Ephram found a pool with enough water seeping from the rock to afford them a campsite where they could water the horses, cook a meal and not be seen.

While Ephram may have stumbled onto the camp sight, he wasn't about to stand on ceremony when Elijah asked him, "How'd you know about this place? You ever been here afore?"

"Nope, I ain't never been in these parts afore. But I think I must have some injun blood in me somewheres, cause I can smell water ah mile off. I'm what ya call. . . ah natural tracker."

"What you are is ah natural liar. Unfortunately, we got the same blood and I ain't got no injun blood in me. You jest happened ta stumble onta this place and we both know it. But I reckon it don't make no never mind. We got ourselves ah decent place ta camp and I can't argue that."

While Elijah and Ephram were settling down to a meal at their campsite, Justin was busy picking the lock on the cell door. "Once I'm outta here, take them rocks we brought in from the graveyard and create ah disturbance in the horse corral. I want them horses makin' ah lot of noise."

Staying in the shadow, Justin slipped out of the cell and made his way slowly toward the corner of the prison and the room where the guards kept a coffee pot and extra guns and other things.

While Justin was sneaking along in the shadow as best he could, Ben and Jeremiah began throwing rocks at the horses, who didn't like getting pelted by falling objects and began to whinny and kick up their heels, running around inside the corral, making a big disturbance.

The prisoners on the far wall saw Justin moving along the catwalk and without being told, began to yell and bang tin cups against the bars, to draw the attention of the guards away from where Justin was hiding, crouched in the shadow just beyond the door to the guard room, not daring to move, or even breathe.

The first guard came out and stopped very near to where Justin was hiding. Justin balled his fists, ready to strike should the guard see him. What he was going to do about the other one, he wasn't sure, but this one would go down.

Fortunately, he didn't have to find out because the second guard ran toward the prisoners making the banging noise. One of them pointed below. When the guard looked down into the corral and saw the horses jumping around, he whispered to the other guard, "Juan, I think someone is in the corral with the horses."

Both guards crept slowly down the stairs, taking their time, trying to see into the corral and who might be there. It made no sense to rush into anything, especially if there was someone in the corral with a weapon. They figured trying to rush someone you could not see was foolish and could get you killed, so they continued to move with great caution.

The other guards were also moving down the stairs and across the prison ground at a snail's pace, rifles at the ready.

Justin made sure all the guard's attentions were directed at the corral before he slipped quietly into the guardroom and began searching the far walls and floor. In the far corner of the room, he found what he was looking for – a trap door, with a steel ring for lifting, under a small rug.

As quietly as he could, Justin lifted the trap door and peered into the dark shaft below. The shaft was approximately four feet square with a ladder on the near wall that lead downward. There was no light and the hole smelled musty. He climbed onto the ladder, testing each rung as he began his decent, closing the door as he disappeared into the shaft. Once the door was closed, it was pitch black and he could see nothing. Fear of a step breaking made his decent that much slower which made him uneasy. He, for sure, didn't want to find himself trapped in the shaft when the guards came back.

Even though the shaft was cool, he was sweating profusely by the time he reached the bottom. Turning to where the outside portion of the wall should be, he could see a bit of light coming in from around the crack between the door and the prison wall. Smiling, he let his hands search for a door latch. He was sure he'd noticed a door on this back corner of the wall, while they had been working outside, and he'd been right.

When his hand rubbed over the door latch, his smile faded. There was a padlock in the hasp, and it was locked!

Disgusted, Justin turned back to the ladder and hurried back up to the trap door, easing it open just a crack so he could see the inside of the guard room. Good fortune was still smiling on him because the room was empty.

After climbing out of the shaft, and leaving the trap door open, Justin went over to the side of the door and peeked out. The guards were milling around, looking into the corral where horses would jump and kick their back feet into the air from time to time. In the darkness, none of them seemed to notice a stone hitting a horse now and then.

Justin rushed over to the desk and searched the drawers until he found a large ring with a single key on it. The key looked to be about the right size and since he was running out of time and had no one he could ask, he hurried back over to the shaft and once more descended into the darkness, closing the trap door as he disappeared below the floor.

Jeremiah had just tossed his last rock into the horse corral and pushed his face against the bars, trying to see down the catwalk. "What's takin' him so long?"

Ben, who was equally as worried, shook his head as he lit a cigarette. "I don't know. But if he ain't here before them guards start comin' back, we gotta think of somethin' ta stall'em or we'll all be in more trouble than we want to think about."

"Well, we can't do nuthin' ta draw attention to ourselves, cause then they would discover the cell door is unlocked and Justin is missin'."

"Yea, I know. Let's just hope he gets back before they start up them stairs."

The smile came back to Justin's face as the key turned and the lock dropped open. After removing the lock, Justin tried the door and with a bit of effort, it began to swing open. He closed it again and hurried back up the ladder.

The room was still empty as he climbed out of the shaft and closed the trap door. After returning the key to the desk drawer, Justin headed for the exit door, and was almost to it when he heard the guards returning.

He stepped behind the door and pressed his back against the wall, balling his fists into knots. He wasn't sure just how it would happen, but he wasn't about to go down without a fight. He took a deep breath and waited.

As the two guards are about to re-enter the guardroom, the prisoners begin to yell that they think they see someone in the corral. The horses are beginning to jump around again from being bombarded by all kinds of objects, tin cups, or anything else a prisoner might have to throw.

The guards turned back, and this time rush down the stairs, just as the sergeant of the guards came stumbling into the prison yard, dressed only in his nightshirt. "What is going on out here? And why are the horses making such a racket?"

By now, there are several guards inside the corral, and they find rocks, tin cups and other assorted items lying on the ground, which they show the sergeant.

While the sergeant is trying to figure things out, Justin belly-crawled along the catwalk in the direction of his cell.

When Justin is once again safely back in his cell, the prisoners stop their yelling and suddenly everything is deathly quiet.

The sergeant stared at the cells for a moment then yelled, "Check each cell! I want every prisoner accounted for!"

The guards lighted lanterns and paired off to begin checking each cell. First, they tried the door of each cell to make sure it is locked, then they yelled for the prisoners to stand up and be counted.

The guards are not happy about this extra duty and let the prisoners know about it by yelling and cursing at them.

When they came to the Hacker's cell, Justin swung his feet over the side of his bunk and sat up, pretending to be annoyed by the light. "What's goin' on? And who's makin' all that racket? Is this another one of the warden's stupid little games?"

The guard grumbled something under his breath as he counted heads and then moved on.

Justin waited until the guard disappeared down the catwalk before he opened his shirt and began to pick splinters out of his stomach and chest. Even though the catwalk was worn smooth by all the traffic the prisoners made, there were still rough spots and Justin felt sure he'd found every one of them.

Ben and Jeremiah moved over and sat next to Justin.

Ben whispered, "That was close."

Jeremiah felt the need to talk as he watched Justin removing the splinters from his chest and stomach. "It's ah good thing the other prisoners had sense enough ta make ah racket when them guards started comin' back too soon. Are you alright?"

Justin pulled one last splinter from his stomach area. It was the longest one so far. "I am now," he said with a sigh of relief as he reached for the can of healing salve.

Ben leaned in close. "Did ya find ah way out?"

Justin nodded his head as he slipped his tattered shirt back on. "There's a trap door in the floor of the guardhouse over ah shaft down to the ground and there's ah door at the bottom that opens ta the outside."

Jeremiah gave a chuckle. "What'a we gonna do once we get outside, jest walk away? I'm sure the guards won't notice us as we go strollin' across the desert. It ain't more'n twenty-five or twenty-six miles ta the border."

Justin rolled and lit a cigarette. "Hell, I don't know. Maybe the good fairy will be waitin' outside the door with three fast horses. One thing at a time, little brother. At least I found a way outta here. You got an escape plan we don't know about?"

Jeremiah got up and walked over and laid down on his bunk. He was ashamed to admit that he really hadn't tried very hard to find a way to escape. He would have acted on it if somethin' had come up, but nothing had presented itself. Besides, somewhere inside himself he'd known that when his big brother found out the predicament he was in, he would come ta break him out.

Ben patted Justin on the shoulder. "Get some rest, cousin, you've done enough for tonight.

Justin stretched out on the bunk with his hands behind his head, wonderin' how they could have some fast horses waitin' on them once they were on the outside. And a gun or two might come in handy.

Ben grinned when he looked over toward Justin's bunk. Justin was already asleep and his snoring was blending in with the sounds coming from the other cells.

CHAPTER TWENTY

The small campfire was no more than hot coals glowing in the night. Elijah and Ephram were wrapped in their blankets, trying to see who could snore the loudest, while the moon watched the warden drive his buggy up the road and through the front gate to his house.

After the incident with the horses, he'd been restless, and since he had things to attend to at home this morning, he'd decided to leave the prison early in order to get his business done with and hopefully be back in his office before there were any more mysterious goings on. Those Hackers were up to something, he was sure of it. And no doubt, escape was at the bottom of it, but last night was still a mystery. Why had the prisoners stirred up the horses? Especially with no one missing when the guards did their counting. Could it have just been a ruse to put them off guard? Or was it a trial run? What about the next time? Or the next? It was that Justin Hacker who was behind it all, he was sure. Yes, he would have to keep a close eye on that one.

One of the peons who worked in the stables woke up when he heard the horse and buggy approaching and rushed out to take charge of the warden's horse. "I will require my buggy here at sunrise, with a fresh horse," the warden advised as he stepped down.

"Si, Patron," the old Mexican man said as he led the horse toward the barn.

Inside his home, the warden lit a cigar and poured himself a glass of dark, red wine from his own vineyard as he talked to himself. "Yes, it will be amusing to have someone like this Justin Hacker to match wits with, for a change."

"Were you speaking to me?" his wife asked as she walked into the warden's study, dressed in her night robe. "I heard you arrive and thought I would come down to greet you. Do you require breakfast before we leave?"

The warden jumped, not expecting anyone to be up. "No. What I was saying was of no importance. It is too early to eat. We can get something when we arrive. Are you packed?"

The warden's wife smiled and kissed him on the cheek. "No, but it won't take long."

With that, she turned and walked out of the room, calling out, "Juanita, get up and come to my bedroom. We must pack my bags, now!"

While Elijah and Ephram slept a short distance away, the warden puffed lazily on his cigar and sipped his wine, thinking of how long he would allow this game to be played before he stretched their necks on the gallows. Maybe his wife's birthday would be too soon he thought, as the sounds of his wife giving instructions filtered through the house.

After finishing his glass of wine, it occurred to him that he would need the horse and buggy sooner than he had told Pedro. So he stood up, stretched, went to the doorway of his study and called out, "Paco, get up, you lazy little beggar. I have an errand for you."

The warden was pouring a second glass of wine when Paco came stumbling into the study. "Si, Patron, que quieres?"

Since they were trying to teach the boy a second language, the warden decided to communicate in English. "Speak English," he said to the young sleepy headed boy whose hair looked like a bird's nest after a windstorm.

"Yes Patron. What is it you want?"

"I want you to go down to the stables and tell Pedro I need the buggy and a fresh horse, now."

"Si, Patron. . . I mean, yes, Patron."

The warden grinned as Paco hurried off to do his bidding. The boy would do well. He was intelligent.

Within an hour, while the moon was low in the western sky, the warden drove through the gate in his buggy, his wife sitting next to him and her luggage tied down in the back.

Rolled up in their blankets, Ephram and Elijah saw and heard nothing.

By now, Ephram had left the horses and walked up to where Elijah and the woman were standing.

Elijah leaned in close to Ephram and whispered, "I ain't never kidnapped ah woman afore."

Ephram gave a snort. "You ain't never kidnapped no man afore, either, have ya?"

Elijah scratched his head before answering his brother. "Not thet I can recollect."

"Well, let's get'er done," Ephram said as he stepped up next to the woman and tipped his hat. "Beggin' yer pardon, ma'am, but you'll have ta be comin' with us."

The woman gave him a blank stare. "No comprende', Senor. No habla English."

"See, what'ad I tell ya," Elijah butted in, "she don't speak no English."

Ephram's face twisted up in frustration as he slammed his hat back on his head. "Jest shut yer trap and grab her so's we can get outta here afore somebody shows up and wants ta know what we're ah doin'."

Elijah was dumbfounded. "Grab her? Where?"

Ephram looked at the woman for a moment and then said, "You take one arm and I'll take the other. How's that?"

They grabbed the woman by her arms and had to force her down the path. She fought like a wildcat. She screamed and kicked. Then suddenly she reached up and bit Elijah on the shoulder, which caused him to let go of her arm. She then kicked Ephram in the shins. He yelped and let go of her, grabbing his leg.

She hadn't quite made it back to the house when Elijah threw his arms around her from behind and lifted her off the ground as she continued to try her best to get away by kicking him with her heels and head butting him. Elijah had his hands full and felt like he was fighting a losing battle.

"Don't jest stand there, do somethin'!" Elijah screamed at his brother, who was in shock at what was going on. He had thought she might give them a little resistance, but nothing like this. She was a holy terror. No wonder the warden had left early ta go to the prison, Ephram thought to himself.

After collecting his wits about him, Ephram drew his pistol and pointed it into the air and pulled the trigger. The roar of his six-shooter was enough to get her attention. She stopped fighting and when Elijah released her; she smoothed out her dress, rubbed her hand over her hair and then walked calmly to the horses, where she waited for one of them to assist her in mounting.

Less than a minute later, as the sun climbed into the sky, promising to be another scorcher, they passed through the gate of the hacienda. Ephram led the way with a lead rope attached to the bridle of the woman's horse as she sat rigid in the saddle with her hands tied to the saddle horn and her ankles bound by a rope leading beneath the horse's belly. They did this so she couldn't jump off.

Elijah followed, leading the other two horses, mumbling something under his breath about wildcats as he rubbed his shoulder where the woman had bitten him.

Hearing the gunshot, the peons had come running into the courtyard just in time to see two old gringos riding away with the housemaid.

Old Pedro looked at the others and asked, "Why do these two gringos ride away with Juanita tied to the saddle?"

Everyone looked at each other and shrugged, then turned and headed back towards the fields and jobs they were doing. They didn't want the warden yelling at them for not doing their work, after all, Juanita was just a housemaid and therefore of no real importance.

There was no talking as Ephram and Elijah escorted the woman down the dusty road that would take them to the prison. There were no shade trees in sight and the desert sun beat down on them without mercy. Several times they had to stop to water the horses from their canteens, then the woman, and finally, themselves. At one point, Juanita indicated she needed to go off, alone. So they untied her and since there were no bushes or trees to hide behind they turned their backs.

When some time had gone by and she hadn't returned, Ephram ventured a peek and saw her running across the desert. Juanita was nearly a quarter of a mile away. "Damn deceitful woman," he yelled and stepped into his saddle, shaking out a loop of his lariat, then kicked his horse into a lope, as he pursued the maid.

The loop swung wide in the air and dropped over Juanita's shoulders and jerked her to a stop, dumping her on her rear in the hot sand. Not allowing her time to get up, Ephram turned his horse and urged it into a fast walk as he dragged the woman back to the road.

Once there, the woman stood up, lifted the rope from her shoulders, then dusted herself off and climbed onto the horse that Elijah was holding. She placed her hands on the saddle horn and waited for Ephram to retie her.

After she was secure, they mounted their horses and resumed their traveling, with neither one of them knowing if she'd done her business or not.

CHAPTER TWENTY-TWO

While all of this was going on, the warden was entering the front gate of the prison, alone. He handed over the reins to one of the guards and started for his office to get in out of the heat. Even though he'd been born and raised in Mexico, he'd never cared for its climate. He would have preferred to live on the coast where there would be a cool breeze from the ocean. Maybe, now that Snake-eye was dead and no more treasure would be coming in, he could retire. Maybe he would sell his ranch and take all his money and move to the west coast. Of course, his aristocratic wife would not be able to accompany him. He would have to decide what should be done with her. She was not a bad wife, but he didn't think she would approve of all the beautiful, young senoritas he was envisioning his money could buy. That would be a problem he would have to give serious consideration. She loved Mexico City, maybe a shop of some kind.

Lost in thoughts of cool breezes and lovely senoritas, the warden almost didn't see our boys cleaning the horse corral. In fact, they were about to give a sigh of relief when the warden turned back and stood with his hands on his hips. Then he raised his arm and pointed at them, speaking loudly so that not only the guards, but also any prisoner working inside the walls could hear him.

"These gringos, they do not work hard enough. I think these gringos are lazy and try to anger me. That is not good. It sets a bad example for the other prisoners. I cannot stand lazy prisoners!"

The warden turned to the guard nearest him. "A week in the sweat box for these three!"

As the guard hurried to do the warden's bidding, the warden smiled and looked around at the other prisoners. The effect was exactly what he had hoped for, as each one seemed to work a little faster. He watched until the three Hacker boys were locked into the small sweatbox, and then turned and resumed his walk towards his office. He loved seeing fear in the faces of the prisoners.

As he opened the door to his office, he realized he'd never seen that look on any of the Hacker's faces. But, that too, would soon change, he mused to himself.

After closing the door, the warden walked over and poured himself a small glass of tequila, and sat at his desk, envisioning the different punishments he could use to put fear on the faces of these arrogant gringos.

His daydreaming was interrupted by a knock on the door. "Come," he called out.

The sergeant of the guards stepped just inside the door and snapped to attention. "Your pardon warden, but you did say to keep the gringos in the sweat box for a week, Si? They will be too crowded to move, I think." It was evident he didn't like putting all three men in the sweatbox at the same time. It was also evident that the sergeant hadn't wanted to come here. He feared the warden almost as much as the prisoners did.

The warden took his time, lighting a cigar, blowing the smoke into the room and taking another sip from his tequila. "Do not worry about them. Every morning you may take them out and change their positions. In the meantime, they are to have bread and water only."

"As you wish." The sergeant saluted, then backed out the door.

When the warden was alone again, he smiled broadly. Even the guards showed fear when they were in his presence. He liked this. It made him feel like one of those roman gods he'd read about.

While the warden was enjoying his tequila and cigar, the boys were acquainting themselves with their new quarters – the sweatbox. The box, as it was called by the prisoners, was eight feet in length, four feet in width and four feet in height, so the boys had to hunker down, just to get inside. The only place for air or light to come in was the door, which had small spaces between the boards.

In the past, the sweatbox had been used to house only one prisoner at a time, but with the warden trying to devise ways to break the spirits of the Hacker boys, this seemed like an ideal situation.

Being the smallest of the three, Jeremiah crawled in last and the guard had to wait while they situated themselves before he could close the door. Three bodies in a space that was designed for one, was not an easy feat.

When all three men were finally inside, the guard closed the door and dropped the padlock into position on the hasp, but before he could snap it closed there was a commotion at the front gate and he turned and hurried to see what the ruckus was all about, leaving the lock hanging in the hasp, unlocked.

Ben and Justin had gotten themselves into workable positions, and if not comfortable ones, at least they weren't on top of each other. But with the addition of a third body in the personage of Jeremiah, they were pressed together like ten pounds of meat pushed into a five-pound bag. It was a tight fit.

As the guard who had forgotten to snap the lock ran to see what the ruckus was all about, he saw the guards were lined up on the top wall of the prison, looking down and pointing their rifles at something or someone. He hurried up the steps and looked down. He was astonished to see two old gringos and a Mexican woman, sitting on saddled horses.

The trio looked back at the guards for a moment, then Elijah slowly pulled his pistol and pointed it at the woman's head as Ephram called out, "Tell yer warden we wanna talk to'im. Now go get'im, pronto. Tell'im we been ridin' all day in this infernal heat and we ain't in the best of moods. Now get!"

Ben, who was the farthest from the door, asked, "Who's doin' all thet yellin'?"

Jeremiah looked down at the far end of the box where he could just make out the outline of Ben's face protruding over Justin's feet. "Well now, if I was out there where them guards are, instead of in here, socializin' with you fine gentlemen, I might be able ta tell ya. But, since I'm not. . ."

"I didn't mean it that way. Is it just me, or did that voice sound familiar? Did either one of you notice that?"

Both, Jeremiah and Justin shook their heads, 'no.'

Suddenly, Jeremiah got all excited. As he was trying to look through the spaces between the boards he noticed the lock hadn't been closed.

Justin punched Jeremiah in the back. "Quit squrimin' around."

"You'd squirm too, if you could see what I see. The guard done run off and left the lock unlocked. Look around and see if you can find ah stick I can use ta lift the lock off the hasp so we can get outta here. Hurry afore one of them guards comes back."

While the boys were searching for a stick in hopes of getting out of the sweatbox, one of the guards had gone to inform the warden of the two old gringos who wanted to talk to him and a Mexican woman they had with them.

The warden hurried along the catwalk to the front of the prison, where his guards were still pointing their rifles at the people below.

The warden studied them for a moment, then smiled. "I am the warden of this prison and you must be the fathers of the gringos I have in my custody, who will hang for the many crimes they have committed against our country. And now, you come to my prison, uninvited. For what? To rescue your sons? I think you must be as loco as your young men. Well, speak up. Tell me, what is it you want? I do not have all day."

Elijah and Ephram looked up at the man dressed in a suit, standing between two Mexican guards. Both, Elijah and Ephram, were flabbergasted to see how short the warden was. Ephram was the first to recover and said, "I reckon you're ah reasonable man. Figured we might do ah little tradin', yer wife fer our boys. What'ya say?"

As the warden stared down at Ephram, his smile widened ever further. These old men were even dumber than their sons. "I see," he said. "And just what have you done with my wife. I must warn you, if you have you harmed her."

This was brilliant, he thought. All the guards had heard him. So, if something should actually happen to her he would have his guards as witnesses that he wanted no harm to come to her.

Ephram and Elijah looked at each other, then at the woman sitting between them.

Ephram looked back up towards the warden." What's the matter? Don't you see none too good? She's ah sittin' right here between us," Ephram said, pointing at the woman.

"And if'n you don't haul them boys out here pronto, I'm gonna shoot her."

The warden took his time taking a cigar from the inside breast pocket of his suit jacket, retrieving a stick match from his pants pocket, then lighting the cigar and blowing a long stream of smoke into the air. "Ah, such foolish gringos. Like your sons, you are truly stupid. Early this very morning, I put my wife on the train to Mexico City. She has family there. This woman sitting between you is my wife's maid. Go ahead and shoot her. She means nothing to me." He took another long pull from his cigar and blew a smoke ring into the air once again. "Then I will hang you for kidnapping and murder." He flicked the ashes from his cigar, over the edge of the wall. "But it really makes no difference because I am going to hang you anyway for kidnapping a citizen of Mexico."

The warden's mood changed back to business as he turned and headed back in the direction of his office. "Take their weapons and then bring them to me."

At a nod from the sergeant, six guards rushed through the front gate, pointing rifles at Elijah and Ephram, while two other guards took their weapons.

The captain of the guards stepped forward. "You will follow me."

As Elijah and Ephram stepped down from their horses and followed the captain of the guards toward the gate, Elijah could stand it no longer. "Well, mister know-it all, what are we gonna do, now?"

"Don't go ah layin' no blame on me. You was the one thet said she was his wife," Ephram said in a smug tone.

"Oh yea, well you as the one who said ta take her with us," Elijah said, shaking his finger at his brother.

The captain of the guards shook his head from side to side as he led the still arguing old gringos through the gate and up the front set of steps that led to the catwalk and the warden's office. They reminded him of a wife he once had before he escaped to the quiet of the prison.

One of the guards led the five horses inside the prison and tied their reins to the railing of the corral, then escorted Juanita to the captain's office where she would wait until someone could return her to the warden's hacienda.

The boys had manipulated themselves around so that Justin was now trying to lift the lock out of the hasp with a stick they'd found. Jeremiah was trying to lean over and look between the cracks in the boards. "What's all the fuss out there?" he asked.

Justin shoved him back with his elbow. "I don't know. Can't ya see that I'm busy? Now, don't bother me. If I can just. . . damnit!"

"Now, what's wrong?" Ben asked.

"The stick broke just as I almost had the lock outta the hasp. We need a bigger stick."

Ben reached under his leg and pulled out a good-sized stick. "Here, let me give it a try."

So, after more manipulating, Ben took over the task of trying to set them free from the infamous sweatbox. He peeked through the opening between the boards to make sure no guards were close, and then preceded to concentrate his efforts on the lock. Fortunately, this stick was longer and stronger than the other two had been and without a lot of effort, Ben lifted the lock out of the hasp and allowed it to drop onto the ground.

For a moment, there was silence. Then, Ben slowly pushed the door open just enough to stick his head out and look around. Except for the guards on the walls, the yard was empty. It was still a workday and everyone was outside. Even the front gates were standing wide open, and like a miracle, five saddled horses were standing, tied to the railing of the corral.

Quickly, but quietly, they made their way to the corral unnoticed, and untied three horses, turning them around so they were facing the open gates.

"Mighty big of'em ta leave horses, saddled and ready ta go for us," Jeremiah said as they stepped into the saddles and began walking them slowly toward the gates.

They were trying not to alert the guards too soon and give them the opportunity to close the gates before they could make their escape. Their nerves were on edge and their hearts were pounding as fast as a rabbit scratching his ear, but none of them even dared to cough or breath hard.

This was very quickly becoming quite a turn of events. The boys were about to escape from a prison that no one had ever escaped before, astride horses their fathers had brought into the prison for just that reason. And, without realizing it, they were in turn leaving their fathers in their places as captives of a maniacal warden whose plan it would be to put them through hell and a great deal of pain before finally killing them.

At this point, one might wonder how things might have turned out if any one of them had paid attention to the horses they were about to escape on and possibly realize who they belonged to. Instead, they were so intent breaking out of the prison they took absolutely no notice. Like a gift from heaven, there were horses available and that was all that mattered.

Inside his office, the warden was sitting in his chair, puffing a cigar and studying the two old men while they stood in front of his desk, fidgeting from one foot to the other. Two large guards with rifles stood just inside the door to make sure Ephram and Elijah behaved themselves and did no harm to the warden.

Although, to be honest, Jose', one of the two guards was having private thoughts of his own. Last year the warden had given him a week in the sweatbox for nothing more than a minor infraction, falling asleep while on guard duty. There were five other guards on duty and there was no threat to the prison. Jose had never forgotten, and prayed for the day he might have his revenge. At that moment, a thought leaped into his mind. What if he shot the warden and claimed the old men had overpowered him, taken his rifle and shot the warden? Then, his fellow guard had shot and killed the old men before they could do any more harm. It seemed like the perfect plan to him. But when he whispered the plan to the other guard, the man's eyes grew wide with fear and he shook his head, 'no!'

Jose' sighed. He could only hope another opportunity would soon come along.

The warden's mind was whirling with excitement. This was definitely going to exceed anything he had ever hoped for. First, he would make the old men endure watching their sons being tortured; then he would reverse the situation and the sons would have to watch their fathers scream and beg for mercy. Ideas were racing through his brain like a herd of stampeding horses. But the big decision would be who should die first, the sons or the fathers? Then a new thought flashed in his head. Since there were more sons than fathers, why not mix it up - a son, a father, a son, a father, and leave Senor Justin as the last one to die, making him watch his entire family being tortured and then executed.

Like providence, another idea suddenly popped to the forefront of his brain. Why not leave Senor Justin unharmed throughout the entire process? Yes! That would make added torture for the man who thought he could outwit him. Yes, yes, yes, let him suffer with the guilt as the others were screaming with pain, while he went unharmed. Possibly he should put him in a separate cell where he could hear and see them suffer, but could not offer any help. Suddenly, he felt himself beginning to breath heavily. This excitement was almost more than he could bear. He willed himself to calm down.

CHAPTER TWENTY-THREE

As the boys neared the gates, sitting their saddles as quietly as they could, a guard heard the rattle of a bridle and the sound of shod horse's hoofs. He turned his head and saw the three Hacker boys astride saddled horses, heading for the open gates. As the boys neared the gates, sitting their saddles as quietly as they could, a guard heard

At the same time the guard yelled the alarm, Justin dug his heels into the ribs of the mount he'd chosen and the big gelding jumped into a full on run like a race horse at the sound of the gun, with Ben and Jeremiah close behind.

Before the guards realized what was happening and began shooting at the escaping prisoners, the boys were well through the gates and racing down the road towards freedom.

Within moments of the shooting and yelling, a guard came rushing into the warden's office. "The three Hackers, they are escaping on the horses these two brought!" he yelled, pointing his finger at Ephram and Elijah.

Outside, the sound of yelling and shooting continued to fill the air.

Chomping down hard on his cigar, the warden raced for the door, screaming at the top of his lungs. "How did they get out of the sweat box and who left the horses unguarded? Someone will suffer for this."

As he ran past the two guards standing by the door, he yelled, "Watch these two! I will handle those troublemakers, once and for all!"

The warden ran out the door and down the catwalk in the direction of the front gates.

Elijah nudged Ephram in the ribs and said, "Well, it weren't the way we planned it, but looks like we still gott'em outta here."

They looked at each other and began to laugh out loud as the two guards stood solemnly holding their rifles at port arms, ready should the old gringos try anything.

While he showed no emotion, Jose' was laughing on the inside. These gringos were driving the warden crazy. Maybe he would die of a heart attack. Secretly, he hoped the young gringos would get away.

The warden arrived at the front gate in time to see a wild melee going on. The Hacker boys were escaping on the horses the old men had arrived with, the guards were shooting but were having a hard time hitting the moving targets, and the prisoners were cheering the escapees along. It was pandemonium.

One of the rifle bullets from an unidentified guard hit Justin's big gelding in a vital spot and it pitched forward, throwing Justin to the ground.

Ben and Jeremiah turned their horses back to pick him up as a hail of lead filled the air, and when they got close to Justin, Ben took a bullet in the shoulder that knocked him from his horse.

The horse tried to bolt, but several of the prisoners working nearby ran in front of the horse and Jeremiah was able to grab its reins. With bullets kicking up all around him and the prisoners scattering to get out of the line of fire, Jeremiah held the horse still, as Justin mounted Ben's horse, and then helped Ben up behind him.

Somehow, no more bullets found their mark and the boys raced the horses down the road and out of rifle range, knowing there were still two guards along the road they would have to deal with.

By now, the warden was beside himself with frustration. Even a small child could shoot better than these stupid guards.

Of course, he had not taken one of the rifles to do any shooting himself because the truth was he had never shot a rifle before and didn't know if he could do any better. But none of that mattered. Guards were supposed to know how to hit what they shoot at.

He would have to set up a target practice with a prisoner riding a horse, and a somewhat decent chance to escape. And as an added incentive for the guards to shoot straight, if the prisoner should get away he would hang one of the guards.

Turning to the sergeant of the guards, the warden yelled, "Go after them! Kill all three of them, and bring them back to me, with their faces down across their saddles!"

Jeremiah led the way with Justin and Ben on the second horse as they raced toward the outpost guards, who were scared, half out of their wits. No one had ever tried to escape before, especially on horseback, screaming like wild Apache Indians. And, of course, the outpost guards had no way of knowing if these men were armed or not.

Neither of them had ever shot at another man before, and they didn't want to take any chances on being shot themselves. As the three men on horseback got close, the two outpost guards dropped their rifles and threw up their hands as the boys went racing past.

One of the two guards noticed the escapees had no weapons and suddenly found himself full of bravado. "Get your rifle," he bellowed. They have no guns to shoot back with!"

Both guards ran over and picked up their rifles, throwing the butts hastily to their shoulders and began firing. Just as the men and horses were reaching the crest of the sand hill that would put them out of sight and out of rifle range, a bullet found its mark.

This was the first time the younger of the two guards had ever fired a rifle, let alone shoot at someone and his bullet flew off into who knows where, to imbed itself in the sand. But the other guard's second shot found a victim.

This time it was Jeremiah's horse that took the slug and reared up on its hind legs and fell down the backside of the sand dune hill, rolling over and over. Jeremiah leaped from the saddle and landed wrong on the down-slope of the hill, which caused him to scream out, "Aheee!"

When the two guards heard the scream they jumped up and down, thinking they had killed one of the escapees. There was a loud noise behind them and when they looked back toward the prison, they saw a group of armed guards heading their way.

Justin swung Ben's horse back to pick up Jeremiah. Jeremiah was holding his arm. "Careful, I think I dislocated my shoulder," he called out.

It was not an easy feat, getting Jeremiah on the horse behind Ben. First of all, the horse was still nervous from all the shooting and yelling, and next, he didn't seem too keen on carrying three men on his back. It was hard enough running in the sand with no weight on his back, but now with a saddle and three men?

Justin finally got the animal quieted down enough to let Ben help Jeremiah get up behind him. Once he was in place, Justin urged the horse into a slow gallop, saving the horse as much as he could, but still putting distance between them and the prison.

As the boys disappeared over yet another sand dune, the sergeant and several armed guards rode at a fast gallop, past the two outpost guards. The older of the two outpost guards yelled out, "I think I shot one of them!"

The sergeant nodded and spurred his horse on even faster. The two guards watched in awe as the armed guards disappeared over the sand dune.

What the posse of guards saw was a dead horse lying on the back slope of the hill.

The sergeant surveyed the situation and realized the outpost guard had shot one of the horses, not one of the escapees.

One of his men pointed at horse tracks leading off to the northeast. "They went in that direction, Sergeant. See how deep the tracks are? I think all three men are on one horse now. I believe we will catch up to them very soon. They cannot travel fast with three on one horse. Si?"

Like the outpost guards, the sergeant didn't know if the Hackers were armed or not. Since they had saddled horses, it stood to reason they might also have guns and he wasn't about to ride into an ambush.

The sergeant led off at a slow trot. It would not do to put himself or his men in peril by rushing in too fast. With so many sand dunes, a man could hide and have the advantage of ambush as you came over the ridge. Besides, with three on one horse they could not go far, nor travel fast in this heat.

By his reasoning, if they tried to push the horse too fast the horse would keel over from fatigue, and leave them on foot. He could not believe they would act so stupid. This gringo, Justin Hacker, was not one to be taken lightly.

Yes, he would take his time, allow his men to stay fresh, and let the sun do its work for them. After their last horse was dead, leaving them on foot, they would follow far enough behind so the gringos could see him and his men, but not close enough for the escapees to shoot at him or his men if they have weapons. And when they become exhausted and lying in the sand, begging for water, he would order his men to shoot them in the leg or shoulder so they would be in great pain and begging for mercy when he returned them to the prison, dragging them behind the horses for all to see.

It would be his revenge on them for making him come out in this miserable heat. Bringing them back wounded and in much pain, but still alive so the warden could vent his anger on them would raise him in the eyes of both, his captain and the patron. The patron would enjoy seeing they had suffered for their attempt to escape and he had no doubt the warden would be pleased, and maybe even reward him.

The mounted guards walked their horses slowly toward the crest of the next sand dune, rifles at the ready.

Since the Hacker boys had no weapons, their only hope for escaping was putting as much distance as they could between themselves and the armed guards they knew would be coming after them.

Justin pushed the horse as fast as he dared without killing their main means of escape by having it drop beneath them. Of course, with three riders this meant going only a little faster than they could walk.

Ben looked over his shoulder and saw nothing but empty sand behind them. He tapped Justin on the shoulder. "We'll never get away at this rate. Let us off and you go on. You could bring some help back," he said, even though he knew his words were falling on deaf ears.

"There'll be no leavin' anybody behind. Besides, I've got an idea I'll tell ya about as soon as we get over that next ridge, yonder," he said, pointing at the next sand dune.

Still moving at a snail's pace, they topped over the next sand dune and made their way to the bottom. As it leveled out to flat desert again, Justin pulled the horse to a halt and said, "Ever-body, off."

When they were all on the ground, Justin swatted the horse on the rear with his hat and watched it trot off in the direction of the border.

"Are you crazy?" Ben yelled. "There goes our only means of escape."

"Maybe, but I hope he runs clear to the border before they catch'em," Justin said in a low voice.

After a quick examination of Jeremiah's right shoulder, Justin took Jeremiah's right wrist in both hands and told Ben to grab Jeremiah's left wrist and hang on tight.

"You're right, little brother," Justin said. "It's dislocated and we gotta reset it. It's gonna hurt ah might and if'n you want ta yell real loud, that would be just fine. In fact, I'm hopin' ya do."

With that, Justin gave a quick, hard yank, on Jeremiah's right arm and heard the shoulder pop back into place.

Justin grinned from ear to ear when Jeremiah let out a blood-curdling scream, "Eeeeeeeeiiiiiiiiiiii!" which reverberated across the desert like thunder rolling across the sky.

Without their knowing for sure if anyone was following them, Jeremiah's loud screaming brought exactly the effect Justin wanted it to. If there were guards from the prison chasing after them, Jeremiah's cry of pain would not only slow the patrol down, but also give them time to implement the plan Justin had in mind.

The sergeant and his guards all pulled their horses to a stop when Jeremiah's scream assaulted their ears.

One of the guards rode up next to the sergeant and said, "Holy Mother of Christ, what was that?"

The sergeant looked at the next ridge and let his eyes slowly sweep the desert both and left and right. "I do not know. It may be a trap. Tell the men to go slow, and keep their eyes open for anything that moves. And I mean, anything. Do you understand me?"

"Si Sergeant," the man said as he saluted, and then turned back toward the other members of the patrol.

After receiving their instructions, the posse of guards moved forward at a snail's pace, rifles at the ready, their eyes darting in all directions, even to the rear.

A short time later, the patrol cautiously topped over the sand dune and stopped while the sergeant scanned the desert in front of them.

"There they are!" one of the guards yelled as he pointed towards a cloud of dust in the far distance.

The sergeant looked around and saw no evidence of the three escapees on foot. "After them!" he yelled and spurred his horse into a gallop, with the others following close behind.

The warden paced back and forth in front of the old gringos, blowing clouds of cigar smoke in their direction before he finally stopped and glared down at where they sat in chairs that had been placed there for them. "You and your sons have given me much aggravation. It will give me great pleasure to see your faces when my guards return with your sons face down across their saddles."

Ephram bristled up. "Don't you go ah countin' yer chickens afore they're hatched, Mister Warden. Those boys jest happen ta be Hackers, and Hackers don't die none too easy. Plus, you're assumin' them guards of your'n can catch our boys. That's another thing thet ain't gonna be none too easy."

The warden smiled at the old man's gumption. These Hackers were all alike, full of bravado and challenge. Even though they couldn't win, he enjoyed the game and would play it to the end. But in the end, they would all die a horrible death. He would make sure of it. At least he hoped that would be the outcome. These Hackers were turning out to be more of a problem than he had expected. They were not like any prisoners he had ever encountered. Inside, he hoped his guards would be able to capture the escapees, but he wasn't sure anymore. But to the old men he said, "I admire your courage, Senors. Like your sons, you are quick with the words, but we will see how brave you are when it comes time to die a slow, painful, death." For effect, he leaned back in his chair and propped his feet on his desk. "Yes, I believe watching each of you travel the road to hell and burning damnation will give me a great satisfaction."

The two old warhorses, as the warden thought of the old men, just sat there with no expressions on their faces, staring at him as though they hadn't heard a word he'd said, which proved to agitate the warden even more.

The warden stood and began his pacing again, speaking as he walked. "Hanging would be too quick. Maybe it will be all right for one of your sons to die on my gallows, while you watch him squirm and kick as he goes to hell for his crimes, but not for either of you. No, I have decided you will watch your sons die before it is your turn to face the slow, painful death that awaits each of you."

He had other plans, but this would give them something to worry about. He could always say he had changed his mind.

His only acknowledgment that he had said anything came after he stopped in front of them and blew a puff of cigar smoke into their faces.

While Ephram remained rigid and stared straight ahead, Elijah's temper got the best of him. "Yer an evil little man thet thinks orderin' men ta die makes you big. Well, I'm here ta tell ya it don't. No matter what you do, you'll still be jest ah evil little man who's gonna ride the devil's pitchfork for all eternity."

The warden returned to his chair and stared across his huge desk at the two men, in who he could not create fear. He was about to say something in his defense when Elijah seemed to get his second wind.

"I don't reckon you've ever read the good book, but it says an eye fer an eye and a tooth fer ah tooth. And with all the sinnin' you've done, I don't reckon the man up above would frown none too much on me if I took both yer eyes and all of yer teeth."

The warden smiled. It wasn't the response most men in their situation would have given, but at least it was a response. "Like I said, you Hackers are quick with the tongue." The warden turned his head and looked at the two guards standing just inside the door. "Take them down to the yard and tie them where they can see for themselves when the sergeant and his men return with their dead sons."

The two guards quickly hurried the old men out of the warden's office and down to the yard where they could, once again, be away from the patron's evil eye. While they tied the old men to the posts, each guard secretly prayed the young gringos would somehow make good their escape, and the patrol would never return.

The rumble across the desert announced that the guards had ridden off in pursuit of the exhausted horse headed for the border.

All three Hacker boys stayed where they were, as was Justin's order. It would not take the patrol long to catch up to the riderless mount and resume the search. Justin was certain the sergeant didn't want to return to face the warden empty-handed.

The horse that had been carrying the three Hacker boys was loping along at an easy pace, heading back to the place where he knew he would be fed and watered. He didn't know anything about borders or prisons, but he did know that he wanted to be away from all the loud noise and heavy weight he'd been forced to bear. But now that he was free, he was in no hurry. Instinctively he knew running too fast in this heat would not be good for him, so he kept himself to an easy pace.

Suddenly, he heard the sound of other horses coming up behind him and he lengthened his stride until he was running full out.

The sergeant raised his hand and called his patrol to a halt when he saw the riderless horse. Where did the three escapees disappear to? He wondered. There was no place for them to hide. There was nothing but sand as far as he could see. In front of them was a small clump of trees, but there was no way they could be there. Was not their horse still this side of the border?

The sergeant might not have been the shiniest apple on the tree, but he was far from being stupid. He knew that somewhere behind them the escapees had found a place to hide after releasing the horse, hoping to send them on a wild goose chase. And it had worked, and he was not happy about it.

The sergeant turned his horse around and let his eyes scan the barren desert, trying to spot a place the three men might be hiding, but he could see nothing. This was stupid, he thought to himself. They could not just vanish into thin air. And they were not birds with wings that could fly away. After a moment, he took off his hat and wiped the sweat from his eyes as best he could on his jacket sleeve. After replacing his hat, he squared his shoulders and spoke to his men.

"The gringos are somewhere between us and the last place we saw them. We will have to search the desert very carefully. I do not have to tell you what might happen if we return without the gringo prisoners."

The guards all nodded, knowing it would not be a good thing. A few of them even crossed themselves, thinking about what the warden might do.

One of the guards whispered to the man next to him, "Juan, do you think maybe the desert got hungry and swallowed them up?"

Juan gave him a look and said, "Do not talk loco, Cisco. You could wind up in the sweatbox for a week. You do not want that, do you?"

Cisco sat upright in his saddle and shook his head, no.

"Fan out, do not leave even a grain of sand unnoticed. We must find the gringos and return them to the warden," the sergeant said as he led out, retracing their back trail.

How the boys kept from being discovered by the guards will always be a mystery that will never be explained; except to say it was nothing short of a miracle, or just plain dumb luck.

Justin sat upright once he could no longer feel the earth vibrating or hear the guards talking. He was covered with desert sand. Keeping his hat over his face had allowed him to breath as long as he kept his breathing shallow.

Justin had covered his brother and cousin, and then covered himself, hoping he hadn't left any part of himself showing. Evidently, he had done a good job because they hadn't been found. Looking around, he could see horse tracks within a foot of where he had buried himself in the sand. He gave a low whistle as he realized how lucky they'd been. Not only would they have been discovered, but also one or more of them might have been trampled to death.

After checking to make sure the guards couldn't see them, Justin rolled over. Still keeping a low profile, he crawled closer to where the others were buried and called out, "Jeremiah, Ben, get up. We need ta get ah move-on."

Ben and Jeremiah sat up, breathing the fresh air and brushing the sand from their bodies.

"Keep low and no talkin' til we're beyond that next sand dune, yonder. No need takin' ah chance of one of the guards hearin' us, or catchin' ah glimpse of us."

After they had belly crawled over the crest of the next dune and started down the backside, they stood up and dusted themselves off. Justin checked behind them again to make sure the guards hadn't doubled back before he looked at his younger brother and asked, " How's the shoulder?"

"It's ah mite sore, but I do believe I'm gonna live ta squeeze me another senorita again when we get back," he said, grinning at his older brother.

Justin then turned to Ben. "How about you?"

"I guess I got lucky. The bullet went all the way through my shoulder. It pains me some and I can't use it, but it's my leg that's sore as hell because one of them horses stepped on it when they came back through. I can still walk on it if I take it easy, but I'm not up ta runnin', yet. Guess we're damn lucky they didn't find us."

Justin nodded at both of them and looked at the sun, which was by now on the far side of noon. "If we're gonna reach the border before night we'd best be on our way. Are you boys up to it?"

Ben grinned and started limping across the sand. "Do we have a choice?"

As the day wore on, the sun beat down relentlessly on Justin, Jeremiah and Ben as they trudged across the hot sand, scanning the far horizon for the clump of trees that would mean the border and safety. Several times Justin stopped, taking his time he scanned their back-trail to make sure the guards hadn't back tracked and might be at this very moment, heading' their way. So far, their luck had been good but he knew that it could go bad in the blink of an eye.

Elijah and Ephram found themselves facing the front gate with their backs to the posts that held up the gallows. They could see some distance out into the barren desert that surrounded the prison, but so far, they saw no horses returning with the dead bodies of their sons face down across their saddles. As time wore on, their hope began to rise. But in the end, their good spirits began to dwindle as the blistering heat did its damage. Not only did it drain what little bodily fluids they had by causing sweat to drench them from head to foot, but as time passed, their skin became clammy and their attitudes turned to grouchy.

"Well now, ain't this jest ah fine howdy-do," Elijah said as he shook his head to rid his eyes of the burning sweat that blurred his vision.

Ephram looked at his brother and said, "Don't be fussin' at me right now. I'm tryin' ta figure ah way outta this mess you got me inta."

"What'ya mean, thet I got ya inta? It weren't my idee ta come down here and it weren't my idee ta kidnap thet woman. And it fer sure weren't my idee ta come ridin' right up ta the front gate of this here prison, with the wrong woman!"

"It was yer son what got hisself throwed in here in the first place," Ephram snapped back at his brother.

"Well, yer son was in here, too!" Elijah retorted.

Not to be outdone, Ephram yelled, "But yer son was in here, first!"

By now, between what the hot sun was doing to his brain and the aggravation Ephram was causing him, Elijah was beside himself with rage. "Ephram Hacker, if'n I could get my hands on you right now I'd. . ." but before the argument could go any farther the sound of horses filtered through the front gate, causing both men to shut up and turn their heads in that direction to see if their sons were dead or alive.

The sergeant and the guards rode slowly through the front gates with their heads hanging down. They were sun beaten, tired and had no escaped prisoners to show for their efforts. They didn't even have the lone horse they had pursued.

The prison guards watched the patrol ride slowly through the gate without the Hacker boys, and, to the man, were glad he hadn't been chosen to go after the three gringos. Who knew what the warden would do when he found out they had not been caught.

As the guards rode past, Ephram and Elijah looked at the weary guards and knowing the warden, could almost feel sorry for them, but not quite. The sigh of relief from each of them was audible, and then slowly turned into a chuckle.

After no longer than the time it took to realize the boys had not been captured or shot, the low chuckle turned into hysterical laughter. The late afternoon sun no longer seemed to be of any consequence, or the fact that their very lives might be in danger once the crazy warden found out the boys had eluded capture and gotten away. For Ephram and Elijah Hacker, that relief outweighed anything else. The Hackers had once more beaten the warden at his own game.

The warden was sitting at his desk enjoying a glass of tequila when he heard the hysterical laughter and the sound of hoof-beats coming from the yard below. He took a final swallow that emptied the glass, then slammed the glass down on his desk as he got out of his chair and hurried to the door. Why should there be laughter coming from the yard? Are my guards returning with the Hackers in some form that everyone found to be funny? the warden wondered.

The warden opened the door and stepped out onto the landing and froze. He looked down into the yard and saw the guards, but no prisoners. Immediately, he felt anger welling up inside him and his blood pressure began to rise to a dangerous level. The two old gringos were staring up at him with wide grins on their stupid faces.

"Sergeant, I will see you in my office immediately! And bring your captain with you," he yelled at the top of his lungs.

As the warden turned to go back inside his office, he heard Ephram's voice filling the inside of the prison so everyone could hear. "Hey, Senor Warden, I reckon capturin' those stupid, gringo Hacker boys weren't as easy as ya thought, was it?"

The guards watched in total silence as the warden turned to stare down at the two old men tied to the gallows posts. There was murder in his eyes. "Senors, laugh while you can. The game is not yet over."

He spun around and strutted into his office so they could not see his frustration. These Hackers had the lives of ten cats.

He filled his glass with more tequila and drank it down, the alcohol burning his throat but calming his nerves.

After a moment, he felt the anger slowly drain from his body. He was beginning to think rationally again as he heard footsteps hurrying along the catwalk.

CHAPTER TWENTY-FOUR

Because of Ben and Jeremiah's injuries slowing them down, the boys hadn't been able to reach the border before nightfall, and had to endure a miserable night sleeping on the cold desert sand. Even though the day had been scorching hot, the night was just the opposite and the three men had to huddle together to try to stay warm.

When the sun came creeping over the horizon and they were still alive with no Mexican guards standing over them with guns, they climbed wearily to their feet and began walking once again in the direction of the border.

In less than an hour, they topped yet another sand dune and saw in the near distance the group of trees they'd been seeking.

"Boys, it's time ta put ah hitch in our get-along. When we get ta that clump of trees, yonder, we can rest on American soil," Justin said as he began to walk a little faster.

Jeremiah hurried up next to his brother. "If the warden sends out another bunch of guards, and I reckon he will, you can't really believe the border is gonna stop'em, do ya? As far as we know, some of'em might already be in thet clump of trees, waitin' fer us ta get there."

At that moment, Ben called out, "We're about ta find out. I count nine riders ah comin' our way," he said, pointing his finger in the direction of the trees.

With nowhere to go, the boys had no choice but to stand their ground and wait for the approaching riders. "Sure wish we had somethin' ta defend our selves with, like ah loaded pistol," Ben said with a sigh.

But, as it turned out, weapons were not needed. The sheriff and eight riders came loping into view and hauled up in front of them, creating a large cloud of dust, just as the gray hawk lifted from her hidden spot. As she climbed into the morning sky, she screeched loudly, wishing the humans had not come so close to her nest.

The sheriff spit out a stream of tobacco from the jaw-full he was working on. "You boys alright? We've been worried some about'cha."

As the unofficial leader of the group, Justin spoke up. "While we were escapin' from thet prison back yonder, Jeremiah got his shoulder jerked outta place, but we got it back in its socket, and Ben there, took ah bullet in the shoulder that went all the way through. He walks with ah limp cause a horse stepped on him, but other than that we're alive and still kickin'."

The sheriff nodded and spit out another stream of tobacco. "Glad ta hear that," he said, as he continued to look around, as a frown began to creep into his forehead.

Jeremiah smiled and said, "Sure glad it's you boys and not them Mexican guards that's been chasin' us."

"We ain't seen no Mexican prison guards out this way," the sheriff replied.

"If you don't mind my askin', what are you fellers doin' out this way? You chasin' some criminal?" Justin said with a bit of a grin.

The sheriff shook his head. "Actually, we're lookin' fer Elijah and Ephram. Kinda hoped they was with you boys. You wouldn't happen to know where they are, would ya?"

Overhead, the gray hawk let out another scream that caused everyone to look up and watched as the beautiful gray and white bird flapped her wings as she soared in a wide circle, then screeched a third time, telling them to leave her domain.

One of the posse riders grinned and said, "I think she wants us ta ride on. She must have ah nest and some young'uns somewheres in them trees."

They all agreed he was probably right, but Justin was more interested in the sheriff's last statement. "What'ya talkin' about, sheriff? Why do you think we would know the whereabouts of pa and uncle Ephram? We've been in the hoosegow. Remember? And come ta think about it, why would pa and uncle Ephram be together. They don't even speak ta each other."

The sheriff shook his head and spit a long stream of tobacco at a scorpion that was crawling across the sand. The large glob of tobacco spit landed squarely on the scorpion's back and pushed it down on its belly. After finally getting back to its feet, the scorpion continued on its way, trying to rid itself of the tobacco juice.

"You still got the eye, sheriff," one of the posse said.

The sheriff ignored the compliment and got right to Justin's question. "What am I talkin' about?" he said with slow deliberated words. "What am I talkin' about? I'm talkin' about two old men who put their feud aside and might be in danger of losin' their lives because they went off ta try and rescue three numbskull sons who got themselves in trouble down in Mexico and throwed inta that hell-hole of ah Mexican prison. That's what I'm talkin' about."

It took a moment for the sheriff's words to sink in, but when they finally did Ben stepped up next to the sheriff's horse. "Are you sayin' thet pa and uncle Elijah come down here ta Mexico, together, ta break us outta thet prison? Not separate like, but together?"

The sheriff looked down at Ben with a bewildered look on his face. "You lose yer hearin' while you was down there in that prison, Ben? Cause that's exactly what I said. They may've been arguin' ever step of the way, but that didn't stop'em. Yer ma laid the law down and told'em ta go down there and bring the three of ya back or don't bother comin' back themselves."

Justin took off his hat and wiped his forehead on his shirtsleeve. Along with this information, and the morning sun having its effect, he shook his head in amazement.

"Why'd ya let'em go? Why didn't ya stop'em?" Justin said as he put his hat back on.

"Let'em go?" the sheriff said. "Don't you think I tried ta talk'em out of it? I talked til I was blue in the face, but their minds was made up and that was that. No discussion in the world could'a changed their plans. You know how stubborn they are. Besides, I think they're both skeered of yer ma."

Justin, Jeremiah and Ben all shook their heads, knowing the sheriff was right.

The sheriff turned his horse back toward the border. "You boys find somebody ta climb up behind and let's get you back ta Nogales where the doctor can have ah look at ya. This is as far across the border as we can legally go."

As they rode towards the border all three boys looked over their shoulders in the direction of the prison, wondering if their fathers had actually replaced them, and if so, what would that crazy warden do to them.

That same morning, as the sun was still low in the eastern sky, the warden stood on the walkway just outside his office. The sergeant and twelve handpicked guards stood in the yard next to saddled horses, looking up at the warden, awaiting his final instructions.

The warden took a puff from his cigar and slowly exhaled a stream of smoke, after which he said, "The gringos who escaped your bungling attempt to capture them must be found and killed – and returned to me, even if you have to go across the border to do it. Do not come back without them. If you fail, I will have you tracked down and shot. Do I make myself clear?"

The sergeant stepped one step in front of his horse and came to attention. "Si. I understand, Patron, and I will not fail this time."

The warden nodded and watched as the guards mounted their horses and left the gate, following the sergeant two by two.

Before returning to his office, where a breakfast of eggs, beans, tortillas and black coffee awaited him, he turned to the captain of the guards who had been standing nearby. "Maybe you should pray that they succeed."

A cold shiver ran down the captain's spine as he watched the warden enter his office and close the door.

Could the warden possibly blame him if the sergeant should fail, again? After all, he would not be there. That is why he gave the job to the sergeant. It was the sergeant's responsibility now, not his. Sweat broke out on the captain's forehead as thoughts of what the warden might do to him raced through his brain.

As though the man could read his mind, the guard who stood just outside the warden's door, whispered, "Begging your pardon, mi capitan', I think the warden, he is maybe loco. I would not want to be in your boots if the sergeant fails."

Instead of reprimanding the guard for his insubordination, the captain turned and headed toward his office in the far corner guard tower. Maybe he should think about getting on his horse and riding away during the night. Maybe California, or Canada. Or, if he dug up one of the sacks of treasure buried in the graveyard, he could disappear in a foreign country. He'd always wanted to go to Spain. He had family there who would be glad to see him. If only he had more courage.

CHAPTER TWENTY-FIVE

Nogales sported only one doctor and with the town being a border town, his job was not an easy one. Fortunately, being in his early forties, he was still young enough to carry the load, and wealthy enough to have what amounted to a small hospital right in the center of town; even though it wasn't called one. It was just known as 'Doc's Place.' In fact, if a person were to ask anyone around Nogales what the doctor's name was, they would more than likely tell you Doctor James, or just plain Doc. It was doubtful if anyone in town knew that his first name was Fredrick, or that he came from a poor family background and had struggled just to get himself admitted to a top rated medical school back east.

He had worked at a hospital, sweeping and mopping floors and anything else they needed done to earn enough to pay his way, and in the end everything had paid off because Fredrick James, MD, graduated with honors.

The day Doctor Fredrick James landed in Nogales, he had his medical certificate proclaiming him to be a doctor of medicine, a small box of drugs, surgical instruments, his bag and forty dollars in his pocket.

Shortly after setting up his practice, Doctor Fredrick James came into a large sum of money, which was given to him by a wealthy rancher.

What had happened was, one stormy night the doctor was called out to help the rancher's wife during an extremely difficult delivery. According to the rancher, the doctor not only saved her life, but also helped her deliver a healthy male child into the world – a son whom the rancher proclaimed heir to the vast empire.

With this windfall and the money he made with his busy practice, the doctor was able to purchase what had once been a small, two-story hotel.

The former owner, being a man whose nervous system couldn't stand all the excitement a western border town had to offer, was glad to sell out to the doctor and go back to civilization where he belonged, Bangor, Maine. He had family there who were civilized.

The doctor converted the hotel into his home, his office, an operation room, and rooms where patients could spend time recovering from whatever it was they needed to recover from.

On the first floor, as you entered the front door, a couch, several easy chairs and a couple of tables were available in what became the waiting room. The register counter still stood where it always had and was used for a place where patients could sign in. Behind the counter, was a door that led to a storage room. Just to the right, between the stairs leading up to the patient's rooms and the front wall stood a large wooden desk, a chair with wheels, several filing cabinets, and six long shelves filled with medical books.

To the left of the waiting room where the dining room used to be, walls and doors had been added to divide the room into smaller rooms. The front half was now the doctor's examining and treatment room, which also doubled for an operation room, while the back half had been converted to the doctor's living quarters and kitchen, and up stairs there were six recovery rooms for those who needed them.

The doctor was very pleased with what he'd accomplished in such a short time in this rough and tumble town. And the best part was, the people liked and respected him. He even had a woman who assisted him from time to time when he needed her, but she was out of town at the moment, visiting relatives up in Phoenix, so he had to do all the doctoring himself.

The examination room was crowded with the doctor, Justin, Jeremiah, Ben and the sheriff. The doctor tended Jeremiah and Ben's wounds first as they were the most demanding. Justin's wounds also need tending, but they were older and already beginning to scab over and could wait until he was finished with Jeremiah and Ben.

The doctor wrapped Jeremiah's shoulder with a piece of cloth to hold it in place, then put his arm in a sling. The doctor told him, "It ain't absolutely necessary, but holdin' it in place and keepin' it inactive for a couple of days should make it heal ah mite quicker."

Justin found a chair along the wall, next to the sheriff and sat down.

Ben also had his arm in a sling and a patch on his shoulder, after the doctor put medicine on the in going and out going bullet holes. The medicine burned like hell and Ben was not reluctant to tell the doctor about it. Next, the doctor put salve on Ben's leg and wrapped it up, and told him to stay off it for a few days to let the swelling go down. Ben hobbled over and sat in a chair next to Jeremiah with his leg propped up on a stool.

When the doctor began working on Justin's wounds, Ben and Jeremiah watched with puckered grins as Justin gritted his teeth when the doctor began pulling off the old scabs on his back. Both Ben and Jeremiah were shirtless, but not uncomfortable, as the day, like most every day in Nogales, was hot.

To keep his mind off the pain caused by the stinging medicine the doctor was using to clean his wounds, Justin tried to make sense of what had taken place. "It stands ta reason that the horses we found tied ta the corral belonged ta Pa and uncle Ephram."

"So what you're sayin' is, instead of bustin' you boys out, they wound up takin' yer places," the sheriff said, grinning and shaking his head.

Jeremiah let out a long whoosh of air. "So now, Pa and uncle Ephram are at the mercy of that lunatic warden, which means we haf'ta go back down there and bust'em out."

"Kinda funny when ya think about it," Ben said, chuckling. "How things work out, I mean. First them two joinin' up after all this time, ta come down there ta rescue us and us escapin' at the same time they was gettin' captured. And then, we ride away on their horses. Ya gotta admit that's gotta be some kind of trick of fate."

"Don't matter," Justin said. "Like Jeremiah said, we haf'ta go back down there, bust'um out somehow, and bring'um back home, alive. Otherwise, Ma will have our hides."

The sheriff scratched the back of his neck as he said, "What makes you think they're still alive?"

Before anyone could debate whether or not Elijah and Ephram are still with the living, the door to the examination room opened and Elizabeth walked in. She stopped and smiled in Ben and Jeremiah's direction, but when her eyes caught sight of Justin, her smile grew even wider and her face took on that special glow when a mother comes in contact with a son she thought she might never see again.

When Justin looked up and saw his mother smiling at him, all he could think to say was, "Ma!"

All three boys jumped to their feet and grabbed for their shirts, trying to cover themselves as best they could.

Paying no attention to their nakedness, she gave both Ben and Jeremiah a big hug and kiss on the cheek, then turned to Justin, who was still trying to get his shirt on.

"Stop fussin' with that shirt and give yer ma ah hug," she announced as she wrapped her arms around him with an embrace that left no doubt about how happy she was to see him again, but also sent shock waves through Justin from the wounds on his back, which he bore without so much as a whimper.

When the embrace was over, Elizabeth stood back and looked at them. "Tis fine ta have you boys home."

Justin stepped forward. "About Pa and uncle Ephram. . ." he began to explain.

"We'll discuss that at home, over ah hot meal," Elizabeth said as she turned to the others. "Now, all of ya but Justin take yerselves out inta the waitin' room."

Before the doctor could complain that he wasn't finished treating Justin, Elizabeth ushered him and the others out the door, then turned back to her eldest son.

"Finish puttin' yer shirt on, and then stay right where ya are."

Justin did as he was told as he watched his mother follow the others out of the room, closing the door behind her.

Once his shirt was on, Justin sat down in one of the chairs, wondering what his mother was up to. It wasn't like her to be so coy. Fortunately, he had to wait only a few moments before he got his answer.

As the knob turned and the door slowly began to open, Justin stood up and when he saw who was entering the room his breathing became irregular and his heartbeat increased ten fold.

Justin stared at the one woman who would forever own his heart and soul. Julie McCoy was the girl he'd hoped to marry seven years ago. His plan had been to spend his life growing old with her, but that was before his father had run him out of town.

He'd meant to tell her what had happened before he'd left town, but she was up north - somewhere around Phoenix at the time and he couldn't wait for her to return.

He'd wanted to write to her, but with his wandering from here to there, never in any one place for too long, time had just gotten away from him.

Nearly a year later, a letter from Ben caught up to him, informing him Julie had gotten married. When his grieving was over, she became just a memory of what might have been, but never gone from his heart.

For a long moment after she closed the door, Justin stared from her to the small boy standing next to her, then back to the face that was imbedded in his brain forever.

It was only after swallowing several times that he was able to find his voice.

"Hello Julie, It's nice ta see you again," Justin said, drawing the words out very slowly.

She approached to within arms reach and smiled at him, causing his pulse to race even faster, if that was possible. "Hello, Justin. It's good to see you again, too."

Trying to find something to talk about, he said, "Good lookin' boy."

Julie's face lit up at the mention of the young boy standing next to her, looking up at Justin with interest. "His name is, Patrick."

Justin turned his attention back to the boy. "Hello, Patrick," he said, extending his hand.

The young man reached up and took Justin's hand, shaking it. "Hello, sir," Patrick said in a formal greeting.

Justin grinned. The boy had the makings of a gentleman and that was good, he thought. As he released Patrick's hand, Justin looked once again into Julie's radiant face. "Yours?" he asked.

"Ours."

It was the only word she spoke, but it created a silence inside the room like the inside of a tomb at midnight, along with a gigantic explosion inside his head.

After a long, pregnant pause, Justin found his voice again and stammered, "What do you mean, ours?"

Julie smiled and rubbed the top of Patrick's head. "Ours, as in yours and mine."

Justin's brain was erupting like a volcano in full blast. "How can that be? What are you tellin' me? That I've got ah son!"

"The apple of his grandma's eye," Julie said with pride.

"Ma knows?"

"Even before I did," Julie said.

"I heard you got married, about ah year after pa run me off."

"No. That was just a rumor that went around. I've never gotten married and more than likely never will, that is, unless Patrick's father wants to make an honest woman out of me," she said as she stepped even closer, allowing Justin to smell the soft fragrance of her that reminded him of lilacs.

It was taking Justin a few moments to put all of this into prospective, fit each piece of news into the pigeonholes of his brain so he could make sense of it all. The girl he loved but thought was lost to him had returned - informing him that she wasn't married and never had been, and was suggesting they get married.

To top it off, there was a young boy standing next to her, who she said was his son. How could that be? Well, he knew how it could happen, but when? It was all very confusing.

While Justin was trying to sort out the news about Julie and his new son, who wasn't so new to the rest of the world, the people sitting in the waiting room were staring at the door to the examination room, wondering what was going on.

When they heard Justin give out with a rebel yell, Ben, Jeremiah and the sheriff jumped out of their seats and headed for the door, only to be met by Elizabeth blocking the way.

Standing firmly in front of the door with both her hands held up, preventing them from going any further, they stopped short.

"What's goin' on in there, Ma?" Jeremiah demanded.

"Elizabeth Hacker, yer hidin' somthin' and I want ta know what it is," the sheriff said with a stern voice.

"You'll be knowin' soon enough I'm thinkin'," she said as a wide smile stretched across her face. "Now, all of ya, just sit down and wait. It shouldn't be long now."

As she followed Jeremiah, Ben and the sheriff, back to their respective chairs, she looked at the doctor who smiled back at her and gave her a wink.

For Justin, the room seemed to be spinning. Never in his wildest dreams could he have imagined this much joy. Not only was she standing right here in front of him, but also she had presented him with a son! And to make his happiness even greater, Julie wasn't married, but was talking like she wanted to be, and to him of all people!

It was all so overwhelming. He was having a whole passel of feelings he had never had before and he wasn't real sure how to deal with them. He drew in several large breaths of air, trying to calm himself.

Justin squatted down and looked at the young boy, his flesh and blood according to what Julie had just told him. The boy, Patrick, she'd called him, had her eyes, but his face and rusty colored hair. Justin reached over and brushed a strand of hair out of Patrick's face. "Hello again, son. I reckon I'm your father."

The boy smiled back at him and said, "I know. Mama told me. Hello again, sir."

Tears welled up in Justin's eyes as he reached out and drew the boy to him, wrapping his arms around him in a giant bear hug. He blinked back the tears that were about to over flow, because he didn't want the boy to see his father's weakness.

Patrick put his arms around Justin's neck and gave him a hug, causing Justin to almost burst with pride and happiness as he stood up, holding the boy in his arms.

Tears flowed down Julie's cheeks as she stepped closer and wrapped her arms around both of them.

At that moment, Elizabeth slipped into the room, quietly closing the door. What she saw made tears overflow and run down her cheeks as well. This was a sight she'd long prayed for.

Justin saw his mother come into the room and stop. She was just standing there, smiling like the cat that had caught a fat mouse and was bringing its prize home. Tears ran down her cheeks and dripped from her chin and her heart was overfilled with joy.

And like a flash, it all made sense to Justin. His mother had planned this whole thing. He stood Patrick back on his feet, and then took the few steps over to where his mother was standing.

They stared at each other for a moment before Justin reached out and kissed his mother on the cheek. "Thanks, ma."

Justin didn't know how it was possible, but the glow in his mother's eyes got even brighter.

Justin turned back and walked over to stand right in front of Julie as he took a deep breath, and then said, "I don't know how else ta say it, except I love you, Julie. Always have. And I would be the proudest man in the world if you'd agree ta be my wife. I promise I'll do my best ta take real good care of you and Patrick."

Julie had tears streaming down her cheeks as she pulled him close to her and kissed him passionately, right there in front of his ma and his son! "Yes, yes, yes," she said when she finally released him.

Patrick walked over and tugged on his grandmother's skirt. "Is he going to be my daddy for real now?"

Elizabeth reached down and lifted her grandson into her arms, hugging him tightly. "Yes, Patrick, I do believe he is and I'm going to be your grandma for real, too."

Looking at Justin and Julie, Elizabeth said, "Come on you two, there's some folks out in the waiting room who are dying to hear what's been goin' on in here, and I think they've waited long enough."

Elizabeth opened the door and ushered them into the room where a thousand questions awaited them.

Justin became so panicked that he almost turned and ran out the back door. For the first time in his life, he didn't know what to say. Having Julie back in his life was new to him. Plus, he was now the father of a fine looking son. Everything was happening so fast. He realized she'd just said she would marry him, and he guessed they would need a priest or a preacher. Jesus, he didn't even know what religion she was. His ma was Irish and she was Catholic, but his pa didn't go to church, and he hadn't been to ah church in over seven years, and that had only been to say a few words over his younger brother's dead body because he would be gone before the funeral took place. Plus, he knew his father would never have allowed him to attend the funeral.

It seemed to Justin that his heart was beating so loud everyone in the room could hear it. It was pounding faster than a racehorse at full stride. He stared at the faces of people he'd known most of his life. He knew he was supposed to say somethin', but what? Finally, after several gulps of air, Justin blurted out, "Julie and I are gonna get married and this here boy, Patrick, is my son."

Before anyone had a chance to ask questions or Justin had a chance to try and answer any, Elizabeth held up her hands and said, "I know ya all have ah million questions, and I'm tellin' ya, they'll all be answered tonight at supper, since ye'll all be ah comin' ta my house."

Everyone but the doctor, who was grinning like a Cheshire cat, began to protest, but Elizabeth ignored them and whisked Justin, Julie and Patrick out the door and down the sidewalk.

"Well, I'll be, "Jeremiah said. "Did he say he was the boy's father? How in the world could that be?"

The sheriff bit off a small bite of tobacco from the plug he carried in his shirt pocket and shoved it to the side of his jaw. "I wonder what we're havin' fer supper?" he said as he stood up and headed for the door.

CHAPTER TWENTY-SIX

The sun was blistering hot, raining down like sheets of fire, burning everything it could reach.

Vapors rose like steam coming out of the mouth of a volcano, in the corral where Elijah and Ephram were shoveling mounds of horse manure into a wooden cart that had large wooden wheels. Each time the cart got full, which seemed far too often, the two old men pushed the cart outside and dumped the manure on an ever-growing large pile, then pushed the empty cart back. When the corral was clean, they started on the barn. After each stall had been cleaned, by sweeping them with straw brooms, they carried large buckets of water from the well and washed down the wooden floors.

It was so hot and the ground was so dry that it sucked up the water almost as fast as it was swept from the boards to the ground of the corral. Both Elijah and Ephram shook their heads with amazement. The corral didn't get muddy, just damp for a few minutes. Then steam, mixed with the smell of horse manure, dissipated into the sky, and the ground was dry again.

Both men were soaked with sweat and to keep the smell of horse manure from gagging them, they covered their noses with their bandanas, which made them look like bandits. While this helped their breathing some, nothing could be done about the killer heat, which drained them of all fluids and energy.

Just before noontime, Ephram threw down his shovel and began rubbing his sore back with both hands. "Well, ya finally got yer wish. I'm shovelin' horse manure."

Elijah propped his shovel against the side of the stall and wiped his eyes on his shirt sleeve, while looking around to make sure there weren't any guards close by to yell at them. "Yea," he said, "but this ain't exactly how I pictured it."

Ephram wiped the sweat from his eyes and then looked at his brother. "Elijah, don't'cha think it's about time we ended this here feud and get back ta bein' brothers again? What'ya say?"

Ephram stuck out his hand and noticed his brother change back to his old self. Elijah spit into the dust, then turned his back on Ephram and without a word picked up his shovel and went back to slinging horse manure.

Ephram stood there for a few minutes, looking at his brother and wondering what had caused them to quit speaking. In all the years, Elijah had never actually said what the feud was about. Shortly after their folks had died, Elijah ordered him to stay away from him and then went on to tell him he wasn't welcome at his house, ever again. And since that day, there hadn't been ah civil word between them.

Ephram saw a guard coming in their direction and he grabbed his shovel and went back to work before the guard could get there.

The guard saw the old man's actions but decided not to yell at him. They were old men, and shoveling manure was hard on the backs of young men, so if none of the other guards were around he let them take short breaks. Even though he couldn't let anyone know it, he felt sorry for most of the prisoners. He didn't like his job much, especially when he had to discipline someone. At heart, he was a poet and would much rather be sitting under a shade tree, next to a small stream, writing his poetry. But his mother was not well and could not work, so he'd accepted this job when his cousin, the captain of the guards, had offered it to him.

He stepped into the shade of the upper walkway and lit a small cigarillo while keeping an eye on the prisoners. The air was hot and stung his nose, but standing in the shade was better than walking around in the scorching sun with that awful smell coming from the corrals.

The relentless scorching sun was not limited to the prison area. The small group of guards pursuing the Hackers also felt the sun's wrath as they rode into the blessed shade provided by the small stand of trees near the border. The same stand of trees where the Hacker boys had met up with the sheriff and his posse; the same stand of trees where the female gray hawk now sat her nest, watching yet another group of humans invade her domain, wishing they would move on. Humans made her nervous.

The sergeant stepped down from his horse and studied the ground. "Several men met them here and from the looks of it, took them in the direction of Nogales."

"What do we do now?" one of the guards asked.

The sergeant looked at his men. They were beat. "First, we take a short breather out of that wretched sun. You may step down and have a smoke while you rest your horses. After we have had a short rest and watered our horses from our canteens, we will go after them. I believe they went to Nogales. It is the only town close to here."

"But then we will no longer be in Mexico, " one of the guards complained.

The sergeant walked up next to the man's horse and with one hand, jerked him from his saddle and slapped his face. "The warden told us not to come back without them - even if we have to follow them all the way to Canada."

The sergeant released the guard and looked at the others. "Who of you will defy the warden's orders? Speak up now."

When no one said anything, the sergeant lit a cigarillo and smoked it slowly while he poured water from his canteen and offered it to his horse. When he was finished, he stepped aboard the big gelding and rode out in the direction of Nogales without a word. He hadn't gone far before the creaking of saddles filled the air behind him. All of his men were as afraid of the warden as he was.

Thoughts of defying the warden had crossed his mind before. But now, they were even stronger. Even if they went so far away as this Canada country he had heard about, which was said to be many weeks ride to the north, the warden would just send others after them. They would still come after them with orders to shoot them on sight. No, he thought, it would be easier to follow the gringos to Nogales and let it be them who were shot on sight.

Maybe, if the warden was pleased, he would get promoted to lieutenant. As an officer, he could consider asking Consuella for her hand in marriage.

With these thoughts filling his head, the sergeant lead his men toward Nogales in pursuit of the three gringos he was ordered to bring back dead or alive.

As the gray hawk watched the humans leave her domain, her nerves began to quiet down. Normal life would return and she could rest while she sat on her nest of three eggs. She would have a family soon and would need her strength.

She watched until the humans were almost out of sight before she took wing in search of something to eat.

CHAPTER TWENTY-SEVEN

Kerosene lamps glowed brightly in the dining room of the Hacker house as Justin, Ben and Jeremiah returned from the barn where they'd been tending the livestock in Elijah's absence. Through the windows they could see the sheriff, the priest, the doctor and Julie. The men were sitting around the long dining room table talking about everything that had happened lately, as Julie made her way around the table, filling cups with coffee.

Through the kitchen window, Elizabeth could be seen darting around the kitchen as she prepared a meal for her sons and other guests. A large smile seemed to be permanently etched into her face. Her sons were home, safe and sound.

But behind the smile, worry for her husband and brother-in-law haunted her. She didn't know if they were alive or dead; any more than she had known about her sons and nephew. But if prayers meant anything, they were still alive and she would see them home again. She had spent more than an hour at the church, talking to Father Sandy about that very subject. Father Sandy had told her to hold steadfast to her faith and had assured her that everything that could be done, would be done.

On her way home, Elizabeth allowed her mind to return to the day Father Sandy had arrived by stagecoach eight or nine years ago. No one knew who he was, only that a new priest had arrived. On that first Sunday, he walked up to the pulpit and introduced himself simply as Father Sandy. To this day, as far as she knew, his full name was still unknown. Everyone had just accepted that he was Father Sandy, and nothing more. One day she would have to ask him about it, but not today.

As the boys climbed the three steps to the front porch, Jeremiah patted Justin on the back and asked, "You sure about this, big brother? You realize what you're gettin' yerself into? I mean, marriage ain't somethin' ah man jest says okay to. There's all the responsibilities ta consider."

"I've never been more sure about anything in my life, little brother," Justin replied as he opened the front door and entered the house. As he walked into the dining room, his nostrils were greeted with the smell of fresh brewed coffee and aromatic food scents coming from the kitchen.

"I can hardly wait ta taste ma's cookin' again," Justin called over his shoulder to Ben and Jeremiah.

Both men nodded their heads in agreement as the three of them entered the dining room and took seats at the table.

Julie poured coffee for Jeremiah and Ben, and then sashayed up next to Justin. "And what can I get for you, handsome?"

"Hot, black coffee for now, wench. And be quick about it," Justin said with as much bravado as he could muster.

She curtsied, poured his coffee, then waltzed away toward the kitchen, her hips swinging from side to side.

Ben slapped Justin on the back. "Yer gonna have yer hands full with that'un."

"And I'm lookin' forward to it," Justin said, grinning from ear to ear.

Before anyone could start bombarding the boys with questions, Elizabeth and Julie arrived with platters filled with steaks, potatoes, and fresh cooked vegetables that had come from Elizabeth's garden, along with two loaves of fresh baked bread and two bowls of fresh churned butter.

For the time being, all talk was forgotten as the men competed to see who could pile the most food on their plates. To the man, they attacked the food like a bunch of starving wolves, with Justin holding his own with Father Sandy, who was now known for his appetite.

The two women, along with Patrick, took their places at the far end of the table and marveled at how much food the men could consume. Julie ate quickly, and then took her plate to the kitchen and returned with the large coffee pot and began refilling everyone's cups.

The men finished eating and reached for their coffee cups, while at the far end of the table, Elizabeth finished her supper and then began gathering the empty plates, which would be washed and put away later. There were more important things on her agenda at the moment and she wanted to miss nothing.

Coming back into the room, she said, "Now that ye've filled yer faces, we can get down ta talkin' about what's goin' on. Justin would you mind bringin' us up ta date."

Justin put his elbows on the table, clasping his hands together. "I'll make things brief. As you all know, seven years ago, pa ordered me ta leave town and not ta come back. But ah few weeks ago, I got ah telegram from Ben, here," he said, indicating Ben, "that Jeremiah was in ah Mexican prison, waitin' ta be hung fer some crimes he didn't commit. So, I came back and Ben and me went down there and broke him out. After we got back, we found out pa and uncle Ephram went down ta rescue us and the best we can figure, they must'a got themselves captured 'bout the same time as we was breakin' out."

Justin took a long sip of coffee. He hated what he called "speechifying." After a moment, he continued. "And when we got back here, ma brought Julie ta see me ta let me know she's still interested in us bein' together as man and wife, and ta let me know I have ah son. I'd wanted ta ask her ta marry me afore I left all those years ago, but didn't get ah chance ta. So, now I've asked her and she said, yes. And that's about it, except," and here he turned to Father Sandy and said, "Father, me and Julie, we talked about it and we'd like you ta say the words over us, if'n you wouldn't mind."

Father Sandy clasped his hands together and gave a nod, yes, as a grin began to spread across his face. This was followed by a multitude of questions from everyone else at the table, to fill in all the blank spots.

Elizabeth held Patrick on her lap, enjoying all the camaraderie. It was good to have people in the house again.

Father Sandy stood up, waving his hands for everyone to quiet down. "First things first," he said, the wide grin embracing his face. He looked at Justin and Julie, who were by now sitting next to each other. Patrick walked over and climbed onto his father's lap.

"Tis honored I would be ta marry the two of ya. And tis high time the boy got ta know his father, not to mention I'll finally be getting' ya inta the church." Looking upward he said, "The Almighty does work in mysterious ways."

There were jeers and finger pointing from all around the table, until Father Sandy raised his hands again. Looking straight at Justin, he said, "And you, Justin

Hacker, tis glad I am ya finally decided ta come back ta take over yer fatherly duties, and of course, bein' ah husband ta poor little Julie here. Raisin' ah son all alone these past years has not been easy for her. Of course, she did have ah wee bit of help from the likes of me, the doctor and yer ma. Tis a good thing you have friends, young man."

"But Father, I didn't know," Justin pleaded, holding up his hands.

Father Sandy folded his hands over his ample belly. "I know ya didn't, me boy, I know the whole story. Yer sainted mother and young Julie come ta me about three months after ya went away, right after Miss Julie had gone ta see the doctor, here," he said, indicating Doctor James, "and knew fer sure she was with child. And I admit, twas my idea ta keep things ah secret until we could figure out what ta do. It was unlikely that yer pa was gonna change his mind and allow ya to come home, and with you ah moving around so much, Miss Julie couldn't chance tryin' ta go where you were."

"But didn't people notice? It's kinda hard not ta," Justin said with a puzzled look on his face.

"Aye, tis ah problem I gave ah lot of thought to. With you not here ta do yer duty, and yer ma and me and the doctor not want'in ta see Miss Julie embarrassed, I came up with ah plan. We sent her up north to ah convent ta birth the child. And when she returned, she tole everybody she'd gotten married and her husband had gotten himself killed."

The sheriff sat his coffee mug down on the table and turned to look at Father Sandy. "So yer the one who perpetrated the lie? And you our priest. Well, all I can say about that is, good for you." He then looked at the rest of the people sitting around the table. "Oh yea, I heard the story, but I also knowed about Justin and Julie seein' ah lot of each other afore his pa sent him skee-daddlin'. And after seein' the boy, somethin' didn't settle right in my mind. Look at the boy, and then look at Justin. Ya got ta admit, it's ah-nuff ta make ah body think."

For the rest of them, it was like the first time they'd taken notice and they each one had a comment to make.

Justin looked at his mother. "Does pa know?"

"Many was the time I wanted ta tell him," Elizabeth said, "but the good father thought it best ta keep the secret, so as not ta give him more ta grieve about."

A consensus of head nods went around the table.

Justin shook his head. "I still think ya should'a somehow let me know. I would'a sent for you and Patrick," he said, looking at Julie.

Julie smiled and placed her hand on his shoulder. "I know, and thank you. There were many times I thought about doing just that, but I wasn't sure what you'd think about havin' ah son ta take care of. I was so mixed up. But you're home now and what's done is done. I know you'll get things straightened out with your father. He's become very fond of Patrick and I just know he'll be glad to find out he has ah grandson. If not, well, I guess we can. . ." and here her words trailed off as she glanced at the floor.

Before Julie could go any further, Justin stood up and walked to the window and stared out into the growing darkness. After a moment, he turned back and looked at his mother. "Ma, I'm gonna get this mess with pa straightened out once and fer all. If we're gonna live in this town or anywhere close to it, I don't want ta have ta keep looking over my shoulder fer him, or duckin' buckshot ever time I come around ah corner."

Tears welled up in Elizabeth's eyes as laughter filled the room. Justin looked around, confused at first, then saw the humor in what he'd said and joined in.

Back at the prison, an unexpected conversation was about to take place. Elijah was laying on the same bunk his son had occupied a short time earlier, while Ephram paced back and forth, deep in thought. After awhile, Ephram stopped directly adjacent to where Elijah was stretched out, on the verge of dozing off.

When Elijah heard the footsteps stop, he opened one eye.

Ephram saw his brother's eye open and realized he wasn't asleep. "Elijah," he said, "I got somethin' ta say and I want ya ta keep quiet til I get it said."

He took a moment to get his words straight in his mind. "It jest might be these are our last days and I aim ta get this thing between us settled. I think I got it figured out. You was put out when the folks died and left the store to me and the black-shop ta you. And you been grindin' yer teeth on it ever since. But you can't blame me fer that. It weren't my doin'."

"They knowed I wanted the store," Elijah said, rolling over to face the wall.

Ephram threw up his hands. "That still don't give ya no cause ta blame me all these years."

Elijah rolled back over and sat up on his bunk, facing his brother. "You jest don't understand, do ya? You was always the favorite. You always had it so easy. You did all thet book learnin', so's you could read and write and cipher. I knew I could never keep up with you, so I didn't even try. And you with all yer smarts, never knew what it was like ta be second best."

Ephram started to speak, but Elijah raised his hand. "Nobody looks up ta ah blacksmith, but everbody looks up ta ah store owner. Up in Tubac, yer somebody. You own the general store thet supplies the mine. And the way I figure it, yer getting' rich in the doin'."

Ephram sat down next to his brother. "If'n you was so dad-blamed unhappy, why didn't ya sell the blacksmith shop and buy yerself ah store of some kind, right there in Nogales, or where-ever ya wanted ta live? It could'a been somethin' you and Lizabeth worked at together. You know she's almighty good with people and figures. She can read and cipher right along with the best off'em."

Elijah turned and looked at his brother like this kind of thinking was completely new to him. Before he could say anything, Ephram continued.

"Instead, ya let yer anger fester inside ya and grow out of control all these years, jest like yer anger at Justin. It weren't his fault Joshua got hisself killed. Joshua was jest like you. He was hot headed and stubborn as ah Missouri mule. Hell, Justin pulled Joshua outta ah dozen fights thet I know about and probably ah bunch I don't know about. He jest didn't happen ta be around thet one time. The fact is, Joshua let hisself get inta trouble he couldn't get hisself out of. Now thet's the dad-blamed truth of the matter."

With that said, Ephram stood up and walked over and stared through the bars of the cell overlooking the horse corral.

It took Elijah several minutes of mulling things over in his brain before he came to a conclusion. Finally he nodded his head, stood up, walked over and stood next to his brother.

"Reckon I've been ah danged fool, fer ah long time. I was so busy feelin' sorry fer myself I couldn't see how it was affectin' everbody else. I reckon I drove folks crazy with all thet rantin' and ravin' and carrin' on."

Elijah laid a hand on Ephram's shoulder and took a deep breath. What he was about to say did not come easy. "I'm sorry," he said with a cracked voice. "Maybe, if'n we get outta this mess, I can try ta make it up ta everbody, especially, you, Justin and Elizabeth."

Ephram turned and opened his arms wide, allowing Elijah to step closer. The two old men finally came to terms with their feud and became brothers again as they held each other in a brotherly hug.

CHAPTER TWENTY-EIGHT

Stars were lighting the sky by the time the guards rode up to the outskirts of Nogales, on the Mexican side of the border. They hadn't eaten all day and they were tired and hungry. The sergeant led the way to the stable, where an old man with a limp came out.

"Feed and water our horses while we get something to eat," the sergeant said as he stepped from his saddle.

"Si, Senor," the night watchman said as he took the reins of the horses.

"How much for all?" the sergeant asked.

"Quattro pesos," the man with a bent back and crippled leg said, bowing his head.

The sergeant reached into his pocket and counted out four pesos and handed them to him.

As the old man led the horses away, the sergeant and his men walked toward the open doors of a place where the smell of food and the sound of music welcomed them.

As he watched them enter the cantina, the night watchman of the stable shook his head and crossed himself, wondering what poor soul they were after. They were guards from that prison with its crazy warden who killed people for no reason.

Inside the cantina, the smell of liquor out-weighed the smell of food. The music was loud and there was a large abundance of young women looking to take your hard earned money for services promised to be beyond your wildest dreams.

"We are here to eat and have one tequila, but that is all. Maybe, when this mess is all over," the sergeant said over his shoulder to his men who were eyeing the whores like starving wolves. He let his words trail off, their meaning understood.

After they'd seated themselves at a table, the sergeant spoke to his men. "One of you will go across the border and find where the escaped prisoners are hiding. When you have found them, you will come back here and report to me so we can make a plan. We will be down near the stables, waiting."

As if it would make a difference, each of the men slumped down in his chair, just a little bit. The sergeant rose and walked to the bar and spoke to the bartender. The bartender reached beneath the bar and handed a pencil and a piece of paper to the sergeant. The sergeant stood at the bar for a moment before he returned and sat down.

"I have written a number between one and twenty on a piece of paper. Each of you will guess, and the one who comes the closest to the number I have on this piece of paper will go in search of the gringos.

Pablo lost, and as soon as he had downed his tequila, a plate of beans and several tortillas, he returned to the stable and retrieved his horse.

Knowing he could not go parading around a gringo town in his uniform, Pablo rode up behind a small house that had several garments hanging from pegs next to the back door. Keeping his horse well away from the house, Pablo crept up next to the side of the hut and quietly made his way to where the garments were hanging. He chose a poncho that looked the right size, and found a sombrero that fit him, then crept back into the darkness and dressed himself as a common peasant. From there he rode into the American side of Nogales. He allowed his horse to walk at a slow pace, up and down the streets. From under the wide brim of his sombrero, Pablo eyed everyone he saw and was about to think he would not find them when he looked down a street on the far side of town and saw a large house with many lights burning brightly.

After supper and a hardy discussion about Justin and Julie, the men wandered outside to smoke their pipes, cigarettes and cigars while the women finished clearing the table.

Jeremiah and Ben sat in the two big rockers on the front porch that Elizabeth set such store by. "Pa sure is gonna be in fer ah big surprise when he gets home. I sure do hope him and Justin can patch things up. I'd like ta see Justin stay around fer awhile," Jeremiah said with conviction.

Ben lit a cigarette and blew a smoke ring that drifted into the front yard. "I just hope they're alive ta bring home," he said as he stared off into the night sky.

Jeremiah leaned forward in the rocker, causing it to squeak. "Com'on, Ben, don't talk like that! Pa and uncle Ephram are two of the toughest men I know. Hell, they've probably got that warden wishin' he'd never heard of us Hackers."

Still looking at the starry night, Ben shook his head and chuckled. "You sure got that last part right. That warden ain't never met the likes of pa and uncle Elijah."

Doc lumbered over and sat down on the porch close to where Ben and Jeremiah were sitting. "What are you two plottin now?" he asked.

"We was just wonderin' bout pa and uncle Ephram," Jeremiah said.

Doc rubbed his chin as he looked out across the yard. "I've been meaning to talk to you boys about that very subject."

Ben began to rock back and forth slowly in the rocking chair, the runners causing a squeaking noise against the wooden floor of the porch. "Can't see that there's much ta talk about, doc. We're goin' down there and if they're still alive, we're gonna get'em out and bring'em home, or die ah tryin'."

From the look on the doctor's face, this was the kind of answer he'd expected, but didn't want to hear. "When are you boys ever gonna learn, you can't go around takin' the law inta your own hands. There's got to be something legal we can do."

Ben stopped his rocking and looked the doctor in the eyes. "It' ain't so much thet we want ta take the law inta our own hands, or even break the law. And from what I understand, thet there prison is south of the border and outta the sheriff's jurisdiction. Besides, we ain't never been much on askin' fer help about family matters. We take care of our own."

While all of this palavering was going on, the guard from the prison rode slowly down the street and passed by the Hacker house. His stolen poncho covered the upper part of his uniform, while the large sombrero shaded his face in the growing darkness.

Everyone standing in the front yard of the Hacker house saw a man riding down the street, but they were concerned with their own problems and took no notice of the man or his clothing. A Mexican riding down the street was so commonplace in Nogales they paid him no attention.

Having never been to Nogales before, Pablo didn't know what was normal and what was not, so the palms of his hands were clammy with perspiration and his nerves were on edge as he peeked beneath the wide brim of his hat.

Pablo was not what you would call a highly educated young man, so his body went rigid when he saw Justin standing in the front yard, calmly talking to a man with a star pinned on his vest. This is not good, he thought to himself. Senor Justin is a wanted criminal and this, this sheriff, is doing nothing.

Senors Jeremiah and Ben were sitting in rocking chairs on the front porch and seemed to be in a heavy discussion with a man who looked to be someone important.

Willing himself to stay calm, Pablo continued riding down the street at a slow pace until he was able to disappear down a different street. It was only then that he urged his horse into a gallop, wanting to be back across the border as quickly as he could. Criminals who could stand and talk with sheriffs made him nervous.

The sergeant would decide what they would do with this information. In his heart, he hoped they would return to Mexico and tell the warden the prisoners had disappeared, but he knew that was just a foolish dream. The sergeant had his orders.

Meanwhile, night had descended on the prison, and after a long, hard day of working in the corrals and the emotional drain of resolving a twenty year old feud, Elijah and Ephram welcomed the rough mattresses of their bunks. In no time at all, they were competing in a snoring contest.

While the two old men succumbed to the deep slumber their bodies pulled them into, the rest of the prisoners did not fare so well. Some paced their cells, cursing the two old gringos in their rural tongue, while others banged on the bars with tin cups and yelled at the old men to shut up. Finally, one of the guards came to investigate the racket and when he realized who was at fault, went down to the well and drew a bucket of water, which he doused the two snoring culprits with.

Screaming like they'd been attacked by a band of Apaches, Elijah and Ephram
    jumped out of their beds and yelled obscenities at the guard with the bucket standing in

front of their cell. To the applause of the prisoners, the guard grinned a toothless grin as

he headed back to the guardhouse.

"You were snoring," he called over his shoulder.

Elijah and Ephram dried themselves as best they could, and then turned their mattresses over before lying down again. It would be some time before either of them would get back to sleep, and by the time they did, the other prisoners were creating their own wall shaking noises, which didn't seem to bother the two reunited brothers.

After hearing Pablo's report, the sergeant allowed each man one drink before they boarded their horses and headed toward Nogales, with Pablo leading the way.

Jeremiah, Ben and the doctor were still on the front porch debating the merits of the plan to rescue Elijah and Ephram when Father Sandy came out of the house.

Jeremiah looked up. "Where's ma and Julie?"

He nodded his head back toward the inside of the house. "Mistress Julie would be puttin' little Patrick down fer the night, and yer sainted mother shooed me right outta the house, she did, without ah reason why. But in her ladyship's defense, she did say she'd be along in ah minute with ah nice surprise."

Father Sandy joined the conversation on the porch, while Justin and the sheriff and some of the towns men continued talking in the front yard.

Justin stood looking at the stars. Smoke from his cigarette drifted off into the darkness.

"It's been quite ah day," the sheriff said, lighting up a cigarillo.

Without looking around, Justin nodded his head up and down. "Yea, quite ah day."

As he stood there looking at the night sky, a thousand thoughts and questions ran rampant through his brain. What was he gonna do to make ah livin' for his new family? He still had the money from his hat. Maybe he could buy ah ranch? How was he gonna get his pa and uncle out of that hell hole of ah prison and bring them home? Could there be ah way ta make his pa understand Joshua's death hadn't been his fault? On and on the questions and thoughts bounced around inside his head, until the sheriff spoke.

"Ah lot of new responsibilities are ah headin' yer way, now. Havin' ah wife and young'un makes ah man do some thinking."

Justin didn't like the sheriff's tone and knew he should just drop it and keep his mouth shut, but the Irish flared up in him and he found himself looking straight into the sheriff's eyes. "If you're tryin' ta say somethin', don't beat around the bush. Jest spit it out."

The sheriff broke eye contact and looked down at the ground.

"I reckon what I'm tryin' ta say is, don't go off half-cocked and do somethin' you'll regret later, that is if ya don't get yerself killed first, I mean."

"Like goin' off half-cocked and doin' what?" Justin asked.

"Like goin' down there and shootin' up the place and maybe getin' Elijah and Ephram killed. Lord knows them two's probably got that warden talkin' ta himself by now. Maybe, if we could jest talk ta the warden and explain this whole sicheation."

Justin had heard enough and butted in. "Sheriff, you ain't got no idea who or what yer talkin' about. If you'd ever had ta deal with that warden, you wouldn't be talkin' such foolishness."

Their conversation was interrupted by the sound of Julie's voice floating out across the yard. "Come and get it."

The sheriff and Justin turned to look in the direction of the house. They saw Julie standing on the porch, just beyond the doorway, with Elizabeth standing behind her in the middle of the doorway. Both had trays with coffee pots and steaming cups of Irish coffee, waiting to be served. "Tis fine Irish coffee, I've made fer ya," Elizabeth said with a wide smile on her face.

A small cheer went up from the men, for they had tasted her Irish coffee before and it was not something to be turned down.

Suddenly, a cloud passed in front of the moon and the sound of running horses filled the air as the Mexican guards rode up at a high gallop with pistols drawn. Before anyone had a chance to react, the guards began yelling and firing their pistols into the small crowd of people, both in the front yard and on the porch.

Instantly and without thinking, the men in the yard grabbed for their guns and began shooting at the prison guards. Justin dove to his left with the sheriff headed in the opposite direction. Doc stepped behind a porch column, pulled a pistol from his jacket pocket and shot one of the guards, while Jeremiah and Ben leaped from the porch to the yard, dropped to one knee and commenced firing.

Before the guards passed the house completely, several had taken bullets and were lying dead in the street.

Just beyond the house, the sergeant turned his horse around and headed back for a second go at the gringos, with the remaining guards following. The cloud passed by the moon and the night sky lit up the yard and street almost like day.

The sergeant's first shot caught Elizabeth in the chest and drove her back into the front entryway of the house. She was dead before she landed on the floor, the cups of Irish coffee thrown off to the side.

Julie screamed and dropped the tray of coffee she was holding. And, as she ran to help the woman she thought of as her mother, she caught a slug in the middle of her back from one of the many bullets flying helter-skelter through the air. The slug drove her forward, pitching her face down on top of Elizabeth. Both women were dead.

The doctor had just taken a step away from the post to go to the women when a bullet smashed against his left shoulder, spinning him around, driving him backward through the front window. Glass shattered and covered the porch and the inside of the room.

In the meantime, Justin, the sheriff, Jeremiah and Ben had been making every shot count, knocking the rest of the guards from their horses to join their comrades lying dead in the street.

The sergeant looked around and saw only one guard left. With the odds no longer in his favor, he spun his horse around and dug his spurs into the horses' ribs.

The last remaining guard saw the sergeant making a retreat and whirled his horse at the same time, riding hard to also get away from the air that seemed to be filled with flying lead. Then came the short-lived pain in the middle of his back. Driven out of the saddle, the last thing he saw was the sergeant falling toward the ground with blood gushing from the back of his head.

As quick as it had started, it was over. Jeremiah and Ben stood up, reloading their pistols in case there were more, as townspeople came running from their houses, staring at the Mexican prison guards filling the street in front of the Hacker house.

Justin and the sheriff climbed to their feet just as the sound of Patrick's voice filled the now quiet night air.

"Mommy, mommy! Please wake up, mommy!"

Justin was already running for the porch, calling over his shoulder. "Somethin's happened ta Julie."

Justin and Jeremiah hit the top of the steps at the same time, with Ben and the sheriff close behind, but it was Justin who entered the house first and saw Julie laying face down on top of his mother. Patrick was on his knees next to them, his little hand on his mothers shoulder, shaking her.

"She won't wake up," Patrick said, looking up as Justin knelt down next to him.

As gently as he could, and with shaking hands, Justin lifted his son into his arms and held him for a moment, then looked up and saw the room was crowded with people. A woman stepped closer and Justin stood Patrick on his feet. "You go with this nice lady and I'll see ta your mother."

When Patrick hesitated, Justin's voice became a little stronger. "You go on now, like I told ya."

He looked at the woman and nodded, and she led him away.

Turning back, tears clouded his eyes as he rolled Julie off his mother. He didn't need the doctor to tell him they were both dead. The red spot on Julie's back was nothing in comparison to the bloody mess on both their fronts. He knew they'd both died instantly.

Movement next to him caused Justin to look up in time to see Ben helping the doc through the horde of people. And as the doc dropped down on one knee, Justin noticed the wad of cloth stuffed inside his coat, next to his shoulder. Justin realized the doctor had taken one of their bullets.

Doc reached out and checked both Elizabeth and Julie, then shook his head.

Father Sandy was also on his knees, praying over the two women, repeating the last rites, as the people stood about in silence.

To say that Justin Hacker felt numb would be stating it lightly. Suddenly, he felt closed in, his throat constricting, making it hard to breath. He wanted to scream, but he couldn't. He wanted to cry like a baby, but something inside held him back. Justin stood up slowly, his eyes staring blankly as he made his way through the people and out into the darkness of the night.

Ben started after him, but the sheriff grabbed his arm. "He needs some alone time right now."

Ben nodded as Jeremiah rushed past them and headed around to the side of the house, where shortly, gagging noises were heard as Jeremiah emptied his stomach.

As Jeremiah came walking slowly back to the front of the house, he stopped by the front steps and watched as Doc and a few of the townsmen carried the bodies of Elizabeth and Julie out to the undertaker's wagon that had just pulled up.

Jeremiah re-entered the house and watched two of the townswomen on their knees, cleaning up the bloody mess left behind. He just stood there, mesmerized by it all. He knew his mother and Julie had been killed in the shootout, but somehow it didn't make sense yet. He was still standing there when the sheriff and Ben walked up next to him.

The sheriff placed his hand on Jeremiah's shoulder. "I think we should go sit down and stay out of the way. Maybe there's some coffee left."

With that, the three men walked into the dining room and sat down at the table.

Three women were already in the kitchen, making coffee and sandwiches for the rest of the people who had pushed their way into the house. In the dining room, they all surrounded the table, inundating Ben and Jeremiah with questions.

The two men stared at each other, not knowing which question to answer first.

"Where's Doc and Father Sandy?" Ben asked the sheriff. "Me and Jeremiah only know what Justin tole all of us earlier."

The sheriff looked around for someplace to deposit some of the tobacco juice that was filling the inside of his mouth. Sam Billingsgate had given him a bite from his plug just before he came into the house, and now he needed to spit.

When he couldn't find a spittoon, or anyplace else to get rid of it, he swallowed it and said, "Doc went down ta his office ta patch up thet bullet wound he took in the shoulder. And since Father Sandy knows ah bit about patch'in folks up, the doc took him along ta help, cause his regular nurse, Carolyn, is off visitin' some of her kin."

Sarah Burton came in from the kitchen with three cups of coffee and a tray filled with sandwiches. She ignored the dull roar that filled the room, caused by the horde of people asking questions all at the same time. The words mingled together so much that it prevented Jeremiah or Ben from understanding what was being said.

"Coffee and something to eat. That's what you need right now," the woman said as she sat the coffee and sandwiches in front of them. "I put a little something extra in the coffee. Thought it might help."

The sheriff lifted his cup up in a salute to her. "Thank ya kindly, Sarah."

As the woman made her way back to the kitchen, the sheriff wolfed down one of the sandwiches, followed by a long sip of the whiskey laced coffee. It helped quell the grumbling feeling he was having in his stomach caused by the tobacco juice.

The sheriff could see that Ben and Jeremiah were on the verge of bolting. They were not liking all these questions. "Take it easy," he said. "I'll handle this."

After another drink of coffee that burned it's way into his stomach, the sheriff stood up and raised his hands to quiet the small crowd.

Since the sheriff was the authority in Nogales, the room went quiet. They stood in silence, waiting to hear what the sheriff had to say.

"Ben and Jeremiah here ain't in no mood ta answer ah bunch of fool questions, so I'll try ta answer'em best I can. And when I've answered all I can, I want all of ya who ain't doin' somethin' perductive ta go home."

During the time the sheriff was fielding questions as best he could, Justin had other things to tend to as he made his way into his father's barn. There, he selected one of his father's horses, saddled it, stepped into the saddle and rode away. Tears were running freely down his cheeks as he disappeared into the darkness.

Sendin' those guards after him, Jeremiah and Ben was one thing, but killin' innocent folks like they did was more than he would tolerate. Thoughts of revenge were building in his mind as he rode at a high lope, heading northeast from Nogales.

Fortunately, the temperature had dropped considerably, making the journey easier on both him and the long legged gelding he'd selected. Back in the barn, the horse had looked like it had sand, and that was what was needed right now. The sky was filled with brilliant stars to help guide the way.

Justin looked to the heavens and spoke as though he were speaking directly to his mother and Julie. "Thet warden won't get away with this, I promise. And if they're still alive, I'll bring pa and uncle Ephram home with me, when I come. And, Julie, don't you worry none, I'll take good care of our son."

The big gelding stretched its legs, happy to be out of that tiny stall.

CHAPTER TWENTY-NINE

The mess hall was filled with prisoners, eating their breakfast before lining up for their work details. It was already proving to be another scorcher and the men were taking their time. No one wanted to face the day any sooner than he was forced to.

Ephram dropped his spoon into his bowl, making a ker-plop sound. "Mush. Every mornin' we have mush. Ain't they got nothin' decent ta eat fer breakfast around here?"

"The warden and the guards get the good stuff," Elijah replied, as several nearby heads nodded in agreement.

"Wonder how long it'll be afore the boys come after us?" Ephram mumbled.

Elijah shook his head from side to side. "Thet warden will probably hang us afore they can get back here, if'in they even bother ta come a'tall."

Knowing he had to keep up his strength, Ephram swallowed another mouthful of mush. "I thought you was gonna put thet kind of bitterness behind ya."

Elijah cleaned the last spoonful of mush from his plate, lifted the spoon to his mouth and swallowed the tasteless glob of food as he stared at the ceiling. "It's kinda hard ta believe thet anybody would care after the way I've treated folks all these years, especially, Justin."

Ephram got a soft look on his face as he stared at his brother. "Hell, yer still his pa. I can't believe he's fergot thet. Asides, there's still Ben and Jeremiah. They'll talk some sense inta his head, if'in they need to. Don't you fret. They'll all come, cause they's Hackers and ah Hacker don't let family hang out ta dry."

"I'm hopin' yer right," Elijah said as he stood up and carried his wooden plate and wooden spoon to the tub filled with dishwater sitting next to the doorway. He dropped them into the gray water, then walked outside and got in line to receive his instructions for the days work.

Elijah was soon joined by Ephram who patted him on the back. "It's gonna be okay, little brother, it's gonna be okay. You jest wait and see."

A short time later the two old men found themselves back in the corral, scooping manure.

"Ya know, I'm beginnin' ta get the hang of this," Ephram said with a chuckle as he tossed another shovel filled with manure into the waiting cart.

"Well, don't get too used to it. I'm ah hopin' ye'll be back tendin' yer store real soon like," Elijah said with as much conviction as he could muster.

The following morning the mayor and a few of the towns leading people, along with the doctor, Father Sandy, the sheriff, Ben and Jeremiah sat around the dining room table, talking while the womenfolk served up coffee and a breakfast consisting of eggs, large slices of ham, biscuits, thick gravy, fried potatoes and large slices of bread one of the ladies had baked the night before. Another woman brought several bowls of fresh churned butter.

Over the rim of his coffee cup, doc asked, "Has anybody seen Justin?"

"I heard Jake Brewer say he saw Justin riding north out of town last night about the same time Elizabeth and Miss Julie was being loaded onto the undertaker's wagon," the mayor said.

"Well he ain't come back yet, cause I been askin' everbody I met as I come down here this mornin'. Ain't nobody seen hide nor hair of 'im," the doctor said as he filled his mouth with a large piece of ham.

Ben swallowed a bite of egg and ham and said, "Me and Jeremiah scouted around some this mornin' too, and I can guarantee he ain't nowhere in town."

"Do ya reckon he headed fer Mexico?" Jeremiah threw out for discussion.

There was a long moment of silence as they mulled over the possibility that Justin had gone off on his own to try and rescue his father and uncle Ephram.

Finally the sheriff asked the question that was on everyone's mind. "He wouldn't ah gone off by hisself, would he? I mean, it's plumb loco goin' down there in the first place. But goin' by yer self would be the same thing as commitin' suicide. And I caint' never remember Justin bein' on the stupid side."

The doctor nodded his head in agreement with the sheriff, but his words said something else. "I don't know. He was hurtin' pretty bad the last time I saw him. With both his ma and his sweetheart killed and all, it's hard ta say what ah person might do when they're grievin' like that. Ah man might not be in his right mind."

Ben wiped up the last of his breakfast with a piece of bread, flushed it down with a long swig of coffee, then stood up. "Maybe we should go have ah look-see."

To the surprise of everyone, the sheriff stood up and said, "We'll meet in front of my office in thirty minutes. Bring ever man who can ride."

Like mice following the pied piper, everyone followed Ben, Jeremiah and the sheriff out the front door.

The sun was already threatening another scorching day of a hundred degrees or better. Even so, the men merged onto the walk leading to the front gate of the Hacker house.

"Look," Father Sandy said, pointing his finger down the road to his left.

To a man, they stopped and stared in the direction Father Sandy was pointing.

Through weary eyes Justin saw the men came out of his parent's house and head for the front gate as if they were in a hurry, then stop when Father Sandy pointed in his direction. Justin drove the team of four weary, lathered horses up to the front gate and pulled back on the reins.

The horses gave no resistance and stopped, glad for a chance to rest. Like the horses, Justin was spent. They'd been up all night.

Jeremiah was the first one to run up to him. "Where in the hell have you been? We were about ta go lookin' fer ya. Are you alright? You had us worried sick."

Justin was able to eek out a small grin. "I'm fine. Just ah mite tired. I rode over ta uncle Ephram's store and picked up ah few supplies."

Ben and the rest of the men crowded around.

Ben looked at the canvas, covering it's hidden contents. "What kind of supplies?" he asked.

Justin was dead on his feet and felt compelled to answer their questions, but just not quite yet. "Jest hold on. I'll answer all yer questions. But first, I need some coffee."

Maude Butterworth had recently been widowed at the ripe old age of eighteen when a horse kicked her husband, Jake Simpson, in the head, causing instant death.

Two years prior, when Maude's mother Clara had died from exhaustion, Maude was forced to take over her mother's duties at the tender age of sixteen, including the nightly ones when her father came home with a snoot full. Her father had gone to drinking more and more, and in a short time, what little savings there had been dwindled down to almost nothing.

Then one night, her father came home with a rough looking man who stank of whiskey and needed a bath. His clothes were dirty and he had tobacco stained teeth. Her pa introduced him as Jake Simpson and Maude was informed that this man was the new owner of both the horse ranch and her. Her father had lost her into bondage in a game of poker.

The next day a pastor of some dubious religion showed up, and Maude was imposed upon to marry Jake Simpson, legalizing the arrangement. An hour after the ceremony, her father left with the so-called minister and she never saw either of them again.

Since her marriage had been prearranged by her father, to an older man, for a sum of money and definitely not based on love or the assurance that it was a legal joining, his passing had been a blessing of sorts.

The man had been demanding and rough in his lovemaking, if that's what you wanted to call it, along with being abusive in every other way.

During their short married life she had been careful, with the doctor's help, to make sure she didn't allow herself to get in a family way and when the horse killed her so called husband, it was like a giant weight had been lifted from her shoulders.

Maude happened to be in town when she heard the commotion down at the Hacker place. Like many others, she had gone to see what the ruckus was about, and her heart nearly broke when she saw both Elizabeth and Julie lying dead in a pool of blood. She had been close to both of them, and out of reverence, she stayed to do what she could to help. Besides, Jeremiah would be there.

Maude was on her way back to the kitchen with the last of the dirty coffee cups when she happened to look out of the window and saw Justin drive up in the wagon and stop. Her heart went out to him as he climbed down and the crowd of men surrounded him. Why couldn't they leave him alone? The poor man had just lost his mother and his bride to be.

He looked so haggard, like he hadn't slept all night. And he probably hadn't had a bite to eat, either.

So, when she saw them start toward the house, the female in her took over and by the time the men walked into the dining room, Maude was sitting a plate filled with food on the table, along with a steaming pot of coffee.

She stepped back and folded her hands in front of her, waiting to see if there was anything else he might want..

Justin saw the food and coffee and knew it had been put there for him. He lifted his hat and hung it on the corner of the chair. "Thanks, Maude," Justin said in a quiet voice.

"You look like you haven't had your breakfast, yet. Just being neighborly, that's all."

All the while she was speaking to Justin, her eyes were on Jeremiah, who blushed at her stare and quickly sat down and poured himself a cup of coffee.

"We're much obliged," Jeremiah said, lifting his hat.

Maude smiled and for Jeremiah's benefit, sashayed back into to the kitchen.

Ben gave Justin a couple of minutes to get some breakfast into his stomach and take a few sips of coffee before resuming the conversation. "So, Justin, what kind of supplies did you get from pa's store? And is that one of his wagons?"

Justin wiped some egg yoke from his mouth with the napkin provided with his breakfast. "Yea, that's uncle Ephram's wagon. When I left last night, I jest wanted ta get away, so I saddled thet big gelding from pa's barn and rode off. After ah few miles down the road, the anger begun ta swell up inside of me and I had me ah thought or two. And since I wasn't fer from Tubac and had this idea forming up' in my brain, I went on over ta yer pa's place and picked up ah few things I figured I mite be needin'. Jest ah few items like guns, ammo, dynamite and such."

The sheriff jumped in. "What'er you up to, boy?"

Justin's eyes, as tired as they were, gave the sheriff a stare that would melt an iceberg. "Don't start with me, sheriff."

"Don't start with you? Don't start with you! Now you listen ta me." He said with authority in his voice and shaking his finger at Justin.

Before the sheriff could say more, Justin shoved his chair back and stood up, his fists trembling. "Ma and Julie are dead because of thet crazy warden. Pa and uncle Ephram come lookin' ta bust our dumb asses outta thet prison and might be dead too fer all I know. But I do know thet I'm goin' down there and find out. And if they ain't dead, I'm gonna do everthing I can ta get'em out and bring'um home. And not you or anybody else is gonna stop me. In fact, I plan on lett'in all them men loose cause I doubt there is even one of'em thet deserves ta be there."

Everyone was silent as Justin paused and took a sip of coffee to help calm his nerves. "Now, I can use all the help I can get. That's why I got all thet stuff out there in the wagon. But if nobody wants ta come along, I'll understand and there'll be no hard feelin's, but I'm goin', so don't even think about tryin' ta change my mind."

The sheriff looked at Justin for what seemed an eternity before he spoke. "I ain't gonna try and stop you no more, son. In fact, I plan on goin' with ya."

The sheriff took off his badge and handed it to Father Sandy. "If I don't make it back, see ta findin' ah new sheriff. I figure my deputy should fit the bill. He's ah good man."

Father Sandy was the only man in the room who hadn't vowed to go along. He felt he needed to stay behind. Besides, he wasn't sure he was cut out to do what they had in mind.

As he headed out to take care of his own business, the sheriff called over his shoulder, "Spread the word for every able-bodied man in town to meet in front of my office in thirty minutes."

He'd made his decision and knew in his head it was the right thing to do, even though he'd been preaching against it from the start.

The woman earlier charged with Patrick's care, told Justin she would be glad to watch over him as long as need be. Father Sandy also said he would check on the boy.

Satisfied that Patrick would be looked after, Justin joined the others out near the wagon.

For some reason he couldn't understand, Jeremiah found himself last to leave, and when he reached to open the front door, he heard his name called.

"Jeremiah."

Jeremiah turned and saw Maude standing a few feet behind him. He pulled off his hat and said, "What can I do for ya, Maude?"

She stepped closer, gathering all her strength. With a slight tremble in her voice, she said, "I couldn't help overhearing what you men said." Suddenly, she found it difficult to speak.

"And?" Jeremiah asked.

Maude sighed and looked Jeremiah in the eyes. "Well, you might say I was hoping; I mean I was going to say. . ." but once again she found herself unable to speak.

"What is it you want ta say, Maude?" Jeremiah said with a roguish grin. He had an idea what might be, and was hoping he was right, but he wanted to hear her ask it.

"Oh alright," she said, determined to finish this time. "When you get back, what would you say if I asked you to come out to my place some evening for supper?"

Jeremiah smiled his best smile and said, "I'd like thet real fine, Maude. Real fine."

Her young heart was beating like a child on Christmas morning as his reply reached her ears. And then, bold as brass, she reached up and kissed Jeremiah right on the mouth.

It was everything she thought it would be as she released him and ran for the safety of the kitchen before he saw the blush on her cheeks.

Jeremiah felt his own cheeks turn red, and when he turned to leave the house he could hear the sound of female giggles, which greatly hurried his departure. He couldn't believe his good fortune. He'd had a thing for Maude for the past four years and when he'd heard she was married, he'd been crushed. But now that she was available again, and knowing the circumstances, his hopes were soaring.

An hour later, practically every man or boy old enough to ride and carry a gun showed up in front of the sheriff's office. The Hackers were well liked and most of the men owed at least one of the Hacker boys a favor or two.

The sheriff retold the story of what had transpired to the Hackers and when he finished, he lit a cigarillo, thinking on how his own views had changed. Every man there, stood quietly, waiting. Finally, he blew out a stream of smoke and said, "Well sir, that's jest about where she stands, boys. Now, as ah peace officer, I ain't allowed ta go down there or take part in this here shindig. So I'm takin' ah leave of absence from bein' the sheriff and turnin' my duties over ta my deputy. And as ah private citizen, I'm ah loanin' my gun hand ta the Hackers."

There was a huge roar and the sheriff raised his hands for them to quiet down and when they did, he said, "Now, how many of ya are with me?"

To the man, or boy in some cases, they stepped forward. Justin Hacker had his army, such as it was, and he felt pride as he nodded to them and shook the sheriff's hand.

Boys turned into men at a young age in this part of the country and there were several in this bunch who would never be the same again.

Justin leaned in close to the sheriff and said, "They'll do ta ride the river with."

An hour later, Justin, Jeremiah and Ben led the way south into Mexico, with the sheriff heading up the small army of friends and neighbors following close behind.

It was hot and they moved slowly to conserve the energy of the horses. There was no laughing or loud talking. This was a volunteer mission where each one of them knew he might not be coming back. But two of their own were down there in a Mexican hellhole of a prison for no good reason, and they needed to be brought home.

If there had been any thoughts otherwise, the raid on the Hacker house and the deaths of Elizabeth and Julie had made it clear what needed to be done.

Sometimes determination makes the difference when fighting a larger or stronger opponent. In years past, other determined men had ridden off to do battle with the odds stacked against them, but they would have been hard pressed to be more committed than this bunch of men.

CHAPTER THIRTY

There was only one window in the warden's office. It was shuttered and closed to keep out as much of the intense heat as possible. During this time of year, the window was only opened at night to let in the cool air, and then only when the warden stayed late or spent the night. Otherwise, the shutters covering the window had a large lock on them and the only key was in one of the desk drawers.

The warden's suit coat hung on a peg on the wall just beyond the window. The warden sat at his desk with his shirtsleeves rolled up to the elbows as he went over the figures written in his private ledger. Said ledger contained information about the amount of stolen money on hand, both in his safe and what was hidden in the graves in front of the prison. With every delivery, a certain portion made its way to the warden's private stash in a safe that only he knew about. Should there ever be an accounting, this money would not be included with what was hidden in the graves. It was a small fee he secretly charged for hiding the stolen loot.

He smiled to himself. Even though Snake-eye was dead and would be supplying no more riches, there was enough in the safe to keep him in style for the rest of his life.

"But what if Manuel was also out of the way?" a little voice in his head said.

There was a knock on the door. The warden looked up and said, "come," as Manuel entered and approached his desk.

"Why have you sent for me?" Manuel asked when he stood in front of the desk.

"I have nothing to deliver. My brother is dead so we will have no more stolen goods to hide, unless you have a new plan, or a new bandito."

The warden folded his fingers under his chin and smiled at Manuel. "Ah, Manuel," he said with just a touch of malice in his voice. "It is true. Since the gringo, Justin Hacker, killed your brother there has been no more treasure for me to hide and I fail to see how you will have anything to deliver to me, now or in the future. And to answer your question, no, I do not have a new bandito to bring us stolen treasures. So, Manuel, without your brother, or a new bandito, what good are you to me?"

Manuel knew the tactics the warden used to intimidate people, and on the way out here he had decided he would not allow himself to be threatened by this little man who thought so highly of himself.

Standing up straight and squaring his shoulders, Manuel looked the warden in the eyes. "So, what are you trying to tell me, that you mean to cast me aside just like that?" Manuel said, snapping his fingers. "Do not forget my friend, now that my brother is dead, I am entitled to his share, so half of the treasure buried in those graves belongs to me. And do not think you can scare me, little man. I am not afraid of you."

The warden scooted his chair back from the desk. "I am glad that you are not afraid of me, which has given me much to think about. I too have decided it is time to settle the account, and that is why I have asked you to come here today."

"You want to split the money and go our separate ways? Is that it? Well, I agree. It is time," Manuel said, wondering how rich he would soon be.

"Not exactly," the warden said, reaching into his desk drawer and pulling out two pistols and aiming them at Manuel.

Manuel's eyes grew wide when the warden walked around the desk and stood in front of him. He felt the urge to run, but before he could actually muster up the courage to do so, he heard the report of one of the pistols as it sent a large piece of lead into his chest. There was time for only one sharp pain, and then there was nothing.

The warden dropped the other pistol next to Manuel's dead corpse just before a guard came rushing into the room.

"He drew a pistol and was going to kill me!" the warden yelled. "I had to defend myself."

The guard knew better than to say anything, no matter what he thought as he looked down at the dead body of Manuel. He had frisked the man himself just before allowing him to go into the warden's office, and had found no weapon of any kind. But if the warden said the man had tried to kill him, then that is what he would say if anyone asked. If one valued his life, it was not in his best interest to disagree with the warden.

"Get the two old gringos to take him to the graveyard and bury him in a new spot. I do not want him near the special graves."

The guard turned to do the warden's bidding, but before he reached the door the warden called after him. "And send someone in to clean up this blood splattered on my floor. I do not like things to be messy."

The guard hurried out and closed the door behind him. The warden returned to his desk and after reloading the fired pistol, he dropped the guns back into the drawer, then went back to work on his ledger as if nothing had happened. It was all his now.

Some time later, the warden looked up and noticed that the prisoner who had come in earlier to do the cleaning had done a good job. The floor was clean and shiny. He retrieved a gold watch from his vest pocket and checked the time. All this work and the shooting of Manuel had made him hungry. He would order lunch.

Outside, under a relentless sun, Elijah and Ephram finished digging a grave for Manuel and just as they reached to drag his body into the hole, Manuel let out a groan which caused both of the old men to jump back.

"We cain't bury him, he ain't dead!" Elijah whispered to Ephram. "Ya cain't jest throw somebody inta ah hole when he's still breathin'."

Ephram took a closer look and turned to Elijah. "Looks like he's tryin' ta say somethin'."

When Elijah and Ephram bent down close to Manuel, the dying man spoke in a ragged whisper. "Which one of you is the father of Senor Jeremiah?"

"I am," Elijah whispered back.

With what strength he had left, Manuel tried to say what was on his mind. "Not that it will do me any good, but I want to confess to someone. I have done many bad things in my life and I am sorry."

Elijah nodded his head and said, "I can understand thet."

Manuel reached out and put his hand on Elijah's arm and squeezed it as hard as he could, which wasn't much. "I want you to know that your son did not kill Maria. He loved her and she loved him. They were going to run away together, but I told my brother, Snake-eye, to kill her because I did not want to give her up, especially to a gringo. It was also my brother who raped her. I hope you can. . ." but before he could finish what he was saying his eyes went wide. Manuel drew in a last breath and went limp, his hand sliding off Elijah's arm.

Manuel Gonzales was buried in an unmarked grave with no words said over him.

"Could almost feel sorry fer him," Elijah said. "But since it was on account of him thet our boys was in here, and now us too, I reckon I won't go down thet road."

"Men have been knowed ta do some funny things when it comes to ah woman," Ephram said as he shoveled dirt into the grave.

"You can say what ya want, but I don 't see nuthin' funny about it."

"Ah com'on, Elijah, you know what I mean," Ephram said, shaking his head.

The old men continued to talk as they shoveled dirt into Manuel's grave, never realizing what was taking place out on the desert, or what fate was about to bestow on them by the ever-scheming warden.

CHAPTER THIRTY-ONE

As the sun was fading in the west, somewhere in the neighborhood of fifty men rode across the desert in silence, the creaking and jingling of saddles the only sounds to be heard. They were about to go to war and no one felt much like talking.

The gray hawk, once again, soared overhead, wondering how many more times these humans would come to disturb her hunting grounds. She veered off toward the south in hopes of finding something there. She would soon be a mother and needed to know the best places to find food for her young ones. If only these humans would stop coming here and scaring all the food away.

Elijah and Ephram had just finished throwing the last bit of dirt on the grave and was patting it down when the warden and two guards came walking up.

"Ephram, you smell somethin'?" Elijah said, nodding his head in the direction of the warden and the two guards.

"Ya know somethin', I do. Smells like dead skunk."

Both men burst into laughter as the warden's eyes glazed over and he gnashed his teeth together.

After regaining his composure, the warden spoke in an even tone. "You Hackers do have a way of trying my patience, but we'll see how quick your tongues are when you have finished digging two more holes."

The warden turned to face the two guards. "Make sure they dig them exactly as I told you. And give them no water. Do you understand?"

The guards lowered their heads and nodded that they understood.

The look on the warden's face told the whole story. Ephram put his hand up to shield his eyes against the sun and said, "If'n yure talkin' bout us diggin' our own graves you can ferget it, we ain't gonna do it."

The warden had already started walking back toward the prison to get out of the wretched heat but stopped. Turning around slowly, he spoke to the guards with a measured voice. "If they refuse, take them out into the desert and beat them until they are near death. Make sure they are very bloody so the buzzards and other meat eaters will be attracted to their smell. It shouldn't take long before we hear them begging to be shot to take away their pain."

A smirk spread across his face as he again turned and walked away, this time at a leisurely pace. As he entered the gates of the prison, the two old men had already started digging two new holes.

These were not typical grave holes, long enough for a body to lie in, but round holes, ones like a man might stand in.

It was late in the afternoon when Justin called a halt and told the men to take a break. They needed something to eat and their horses needed tending.

They were out in the middle of the desert. There were no trees for shade, no water from rivers, lakes or ponds. Nothing.

The two men who had volunteered to do the cooking stopped the wagon and began to unload the things they needed to prepare the meal. Some of the men went about staking out the horses, while others removed saddles and did quick rubdowns. Two of the men filled buckets with water from the barrel in the wagon and were going from horse to horse, allowing each one a short drink so as not to make them sick in this heat. This was followed up by two men strapping feedbags filled with grain over the horses' noses.

The cook started a fire and set a metal frame across it so he could hang a large cast iron kettle filled with stew makings over the flames to cook. Next, he hung two coffee pots over the fire to brew, one on either side of the stew pot. Next, the two cooks attached the corners and middle of a large piece of canvas to the side of the wagon, facing away from the sun as much as possible, then stretched it to some poles that had been stabbed into the sand. This made a feasible shade where the men could eat and have a smoke. They carried no tables or chairs, so they had to sit on the hot sand. To keep from burning themselves, each man sat on his horse blanket.

With their mission being such as it was, talking was held to a minimum until after the meals were finished and they began lighting up whatever each man carried to smoke, or in some cases, chew.

Justin finished his meal and carried the spoon and tin plate over and dumped it into the water in the small wooden tub used for washing dishes. Bill Wendell offered him a cigarillo and Justin nodded his appreciation. He lit the small cigar with a piece of wood sticking out of the fire, put there just for just that purpose. Justin smoked, drank coffee and made small talk with Bill until all of the men had finished their meals.

When he was sure he could get everyone's full attention, he raised his hands for quiet. When they were all staring at him, he commenced. "Men, me, Jeremiah and our cousin Ben, want to thank ya for coming along. It's fer sure gonna be dangerous. Some of us might die. And the truth be told, it might all be fer naught."

He looked straight at the sheriff, then said, "Some might even say it's ah fool's errand, but I can assure ya, if pa and uncle Ephram are still alive, and we can get'em out and safe back across the border, each one of'em will be behold'en to ya."

All the men just nodded their heads and waited for Justin to continue. None of them were looking for favors for doing what a man did when his neighbor was in trouble. You might say it was a code they lived by, so no favors would be asked for. It would be for the Hackers to decide somewhere down the road when to lend help, if and when, help was needed.

"Men, we've got ah long night ahead of us, so when we've finished our smokes and the wagon is ready ta go, we'll be headin' out. In the meantime, just ta make sure there's no slip-us, I'd like ta go over the plan one last time."

When Justin finished, they got up and saddled their horses. By now, the sun had dipped below the horizon and the temperature began to drop, making the rest of the ride a bit more comfortable.

When Justin saw that the wagon was loaded and the driver sitting on the bench with the reins in his hands, Justin stepped into the saddle. The rest of the men followed his lead, and they started off across the desert once again. Jeremiah, Ben and the sheriff fell in with Justin as the others made a column behind, with the wagon taking the drag position.

The moon shined brightly on the prison, the graveyard and the bleak desert surrounding it. Tombstones dotted the graveyard. Where two tombstones should have been, there were instead, two heads. One was Ephram and the other was Elijah. The two old men were buried up to their necks, facing each other. Since being buried, neither one of them had spoken a word. Night critters climbed over their heads and the only thing they could do was to blow at them, hoping it would make them go away. So far, nothing had bitten them, but the night was young.

Ephram finally sighed and said, "Well, at least we ain't ah layin' somewheres out there in the desert, heavy with pain, slowly bleedin' ta death, waitin' fer the buzzards ta come and finish us off."

"Thet's ah real comfort ta know," Elijah offered. "Know what makes me mad? If'n one of them idiots starts ta shootin', I can't duck."

After a moment, they looked at each other, then broke out in laughter. The guards standing on the walls looked down at the two crazy old men whose uproarious outburst filled the night.

"Loco gringos. Do they not realize they are about to die?" one of the guards said as another guard nodded in agreement.

"I say it is bravery to laugh in the face of death," another guard said.

Just beyond a tall desert knoll, Justin raised his arm. With hand signals, he told the men to silently step down from their saddles. Justin, Jeremiah, Ben and the sheriff, handed the reins of their horses to one of the nearby men, then Justin took a pair of binoculars from his saddlebag and headed up the side of the knoll, with Ben, Jeremiah and the sheriff right on his heels.

Near the top, they dropped to their stomachs and belly crawled the rest of the way. Justin lifted the binoculars to his eyes and studied the terrain ahead. The moonlight made it easy for him to see what he needed to see.

"There's one guard standin' next ta the road about ah hundred yards from here, and another one ah bit further on," he whispered to the sheriff. "Are the men ready?"

"They're chewin' at the bit ta get inta action," he whispered back.

Justin grinned, then said, "Well then, let's not keep'em waitin."

And with that, they scooted back down the hill far enough for them to stand up without being seen, and then in a whispered voice, Justin started the dance.

Near the top of the knoll, two of the townsmen covered themselves with pieces of canvas and dropped down on their bellies. In the moonlight, they very much resembled small humps of sand. Then with great stealth, crawling very slowly, they inched their way in the direction of the two guards standing next to the road.

While this was taking place, the man driving the wagon headed slowly and quietly further south so he could approach the road leading to the prison without being seen. After pulling the wagon onto the road some distance away, he stopped and let the horses rest while he took a rifle and went to the back of the wagon. His job was to guard the road behind them. They didn't want anyone disturbing their raid.

A slight breeze came up that made the guards relax even more than they already were. Plus, the sound of the wind helped cover any noise made by the two mounds of sand that were inching their way closer and closer.

The sheriff, who was observing through the binoculars from the top of the knoll, made sure both of the townsmen were in place before making a soft whistling sound that somewhat resembled a dove cooing.

The guards were not used to the sound of doves cooing. They seemed bewildered and became nervous, looking around for whatever was making the unusual noise.

Both townsmen heard the cooing sound and went into action by lifting the canvas from their heads and saying, "Psssst, hey, down here."

Before either of the guards could react, they were jerked off their feet and fell to the sand, where they were quickly rendered unconscious by sharp blows to the head.

Hats and uniform coats were quickly donned, and in less than a minute two new guards stood watching the road.

Also under the cover of sand looking canvas, Justin and Jeremiah had been crawling at a rapid pace alongside the road in the direction of the prison. When they saw the gates open and a wagon come through with two relief guards, they stopped and stayed perfectly still until the wagon was well beyond where they lay. The guards were talking and laughing about something and paid no attention to the two small lumps of sand on the side of the road. Why should they? After all, they had no idea what was about to happen.

Once the relief guards had driven past, Justin and Jeremiah, who were by now just at the outer edge of the graveyard in front of the prison, crawled slowly between the existing graves to cut down their chances of being seen.

Shortly, they reached the front wall of the prison and each one gave a short sigh of relief. It was a clear night, but clouds passing in front of the moon made objects on the ground temporarily almost invisible. They shucked off their canvas coverings and got to their feet, flattening themselves against the wall. Each one carried a half filled burlap sack.

The small cloud passed by the moon and just for an instant, both men were in plain view of the guards standing at the top of the wall. But Irish luck was still with them. None of the guards were looking downward. Within three heartbeats, a large cloudbank moved in and once more blanked out the moon, throwing the entire area into darkness. When there were no shouts from above, they knew they hadn't been seen.

Justin whispered, "Give me ah couple of minutes ta get in place. I'll wait fer yer signal."

Jeremiah nodded and waited as Justin moved out, inching his way toward the far corner of the prison. Only a few moments had passed before he turned the corner and disappeared around the wall.

Elijah, whose head was facing the prison, saw some movement up near the wall, but couldn't make out who or what it is.

Ephram, having keen ears, heard someone whispering, but couldn't make out what was being said. He asked in a low voice, "What the hell's goin' on? Who's thet talkin'?"

Elijah blew an ant off his lip and said, "I don't rightly know. Looks like two fellers ah movin' real sneaky like up next ta the wall. Now be quiet til I find out who it is," he whispered as he squinted his eyes to try and see better in the darkness.

Beyond the knoll, just a short distance from the road leading to the prison, about fifty well-armed men sat their horses, quietly waiting to be called into action. Some were dressed in a mixture of old military uniforms of Rebel gray and Yankee blue. Some wore blue jeans, chaps and work shirts. The rest, being respectable shopkeepers, bankers and such, wore suits with ties.

Ben and the sheriff stood beside their horses at the front of the small army. They too were anxiously awaiting the signal.

Ben nodded toward the group of men. "Do ya really think we'll fool them guards inta believin' we're the Cavalry?"

The sheriff glanced over his shoulder and grinned. "Why not? It's dark and by the time they figure out we ain't, it'll be too late."

Ben gave that some thought, and then replied, "Yea, I reckon you're right. We should confuse the hell out of'em. At least fer awhile."

Once he was on the far sidewall of the prison, Justin moved quickly and quietly down to the door at the corner, beneath the guardroom, the one he'd unlocked earlier when they were still incarcerated and the prisoners had created the diversion in the horse corral.

Justin opened the door just wide enough to slip inside, then pulled it closed. He was in total darkness and used his hands to find the ladder that led up to the trap door, which would allow him access to the guardroom. He climbed the ladder very slowly so as to not make any noise. It would not do to be found out at this point.

Just below the trap door, Justin stopped, and waited. He could hear the guards talking, but paid little attention to what they were saying. He was waiting for his signal from Jeremiah.

In the far distance, Jeremiah could make out the silhouette of a wagon with two men in it coming slowly down the road and knew it was time to implement the next part of their plan. He opened the burlap bag and was about to reach inside when he heard whispered voices coming from the graveyard that sounded a lot like his pa and uncle Ephram.

What in the world would they be doin' out in the middle of the graveyard at this time of night? he wondered. Jeremiah decided he had to make sure before he did anything else. If they were, for some strange reason, out in the middle of the graveyard, he had to find out why, and then make sure they would be safe before he went any farther. The raid couldn't be stopped now, there was more to it than just rescuin' two contrary old men.

Once more, Jeremiah pulled the canvas over himself and slowly crawled toward where he'd heard the voices coming from. Time was of the essence. The men in the wagon were coming and timing was crucial. Justin, along with the men beyond the knoll, were all waiting for his signal. But he had to know before he did anything else. He could only hope the two men in the wagon would drive slow until his signal told them it was time to start the party.

The cloud was still covering the moon and it made it difficult to see anything with much clarity, but he thought he could make out two small, round objects in an area between a couple of the graves that shouldn't be there. When he got close, Jeremiah called out softly, "Pa, uncle Ephram?"

One of the objects that sounded just like his pa, turned slightly toward him and said, "Psssst, over here."

The other round object whispered, "Shhhhh, not so loud!"

Jeremiah snaked his way up next to Ephram and Elijah and was astonished to find them buried up to their necks in the sand. He didn't have time to listen to explanations or to go into details about what he was doing there, so he would have to keep it short. They would have an interesting story to tell, later, but only when they were back home.

"What'er you doin' out here?" Ephram asked.

"Did ya come ta bust us out?" Elijah wanted to know.

"I ain't got time ta explain right now," Jeremiah whispered. "Things are about ta start happenin' thet I can't stop and you two bein' out here sure does complicate things."

"If'n you boys start somethin', the warden has ordered his guards ta shoot us first," Ephram informed him.

It took Jeremiah no more than a moment to decide on what to do. "They can't shoot what they can't see," he said and pulled the canvas off his body and covered their heads with it. "I'll be back as soon as I can. When the shootin' starts, just try and stay quiet."

Jeremiah then turned and crawled back to the front wall of the prison, hoping the cloud would continue to hide him until he could get his job done. The wagon was getting dangerously close by now, and he knew Justin would be getting impatient.

Indeed, Jeremiah's thoughts about his brother were true. Justin was chewing on his bottom lip, wondering what was taking Jeremiah so long. Had something gone wrong? Had they spotted him? He was at his wits end. Waiting was not Justin's strong suit. He would wait a few more minutes, then make a decision whether to burst through the trap door and take his chances, or go back down and find out what had happened.

While Justin was stewing, Jeremiah made it back to the wall and inched his way over to the front gate, which was still closed. He reached into the burlap bag and pulled out several sticks of dynamite with very short fuses, stuck them into the cracks of both gates and took a deep breath.

At this hour, the guards were half asleep, but the one leaning against the guardhouse door heard the creak of the wagon as it got close and called out to the guard down below, "They are returning. Open the gate," which caused the guard down below to stir.

At that point, Jeremiah struck a Lucifer and lit the short fuses, then dove for cover along the wall.

The guard down below was lifting the bar from the gates when he saw a bright light and heard the sizzling of the fuses. He dropped the bar and dove to the side, just before the dynamite exploded, turning the front gates into small chunks of splinters and flying debris.

Jeremiah jumped to his feet and waved to the wagon coming down the road, but the driver of the wagon needed no signal. He was already slapping the reins against the horses hindquarters and yelling, "Yaaaa!"

Ben heard the dynamite explode. It was the signal he'd been waiting for. He turned in his saddle and yelled. "This is it, boys! Sound the bugle!" As the bugle sounded, Ben yelled as loud as he could, "Charge!"

The sentries saw the team react, running hard toward the prison, but they thought it was just the returning guards hurrying to get back inside. They were more concerned with the army of men racing down the road with one of the men blaring loudly on a bugle.

"We are being attacked by the Americano army!" one of the guards shouted. Another guard began ringing a bell to alert the others that the prison was under attack. Guards, still in their long johns, came rushing out of their sleeping quarters with rifles in hand.

As the relief wagon came racing through the open hole, the driver jerked back on the reins and pulled the wagon to a quick halt. The townsmen lying in the back threw the canvas aside and jumped out of the wagon, pointing their weapons at the prison guards.

One of the guards from the upper walkway started the fracus by firing at the men from the wagon. That was all it took to get the ball rolling. The townsmen were spoiling for a fight because of what had happened at the Hacker house and they had ridden a long way to even the score.

The rag-tag army made up of townsmen and cowboys came charging down the road with the bugle blowing like Sherman marching through Georgia to join the fight. Lead flew through the air thicker than a flock of ducks lifting off a pond, with the guards getting the worst of it.

Smoke from the gunfire filled the area making it hard to see as the townsmen inside the prison sought sheltered places to shoot from.

As planned, the guards were caught off guard and in a crossfire. And like Justin had figured, there would be a lot of confusion among the guards, giving the American army the advantage.

The warden had fallen asleep in his chair with his feet propped up on the desk. When the shooting started, he jerked awake so hard that his chair overturned. On the way to the floor, he banged his head on the side of his desk so hard that he was almost knocked unconscious.

He was dazed for a moment or two. Then it came to him that the noise was gunfire. Was his prison under attack? Impossible, he thought. Suddenly, the realization came to him. It had to be those Hackers! As quickly as he could, he climbed to his feet and opened the desk drawer where he kept his pistols.

When he opened the door to his office, smoke filled the doorway causing him to cough. He put a handkerchief to his nose and stepped onto the catwalk, cocking the hammer back on the Smith & Wesson six-shooter he'd gotten as part of the stolen loot Snake-eye had taken from the gringos north of the border. He leaned on the rail trying to see below. The warden pointed his pistol down into the yard in hopes he could get a clear shot at one of the Hackers.

The prisoners were yelling and screaming to be set free. Their shouts were almost as loud as the gunfire filling the air. Stray bullets ricocheting off the bars and walls of the cells, wounded nine prisoners. Two prisoners were killed outright.

The loud noise and rancid smell of gun smoke caused the horses in the corral to jump around and kick up their heels in terror as bullets grazed their skin and found a home in two of them - one in the shoulder and the other in the rump.

Below the trap door, Justin heard the two guards run to see what was going on. When he heard them stop and begin to fire their pistols, he lit the fuse in the stick of dynamite he'd brought with him and waited until it had burned down very short. When there wasn't much left, he raised the trap door and tossed the dynamite into the room near where the two guards were standing.

As he slammed down the trap door, he knew that some of the men killed would not deserve to die, and for that he felt bad, but war was war and they were shooting at his people.

The explosion shook the room, blowing part of the wall away. When Justin opened the trap door and climbed out, the room was full of smoke and burnt gunpowder. The two guards were lying dead on the catwalk and he was beginning to feel bad for them.

Then Justin noticed one of the dead guards lying on his back and saw that it was the one who had taken pleasure in torturing him and any prisoner who committed even the slightest infraction. At that point, Justin's conscience bothered him no longer.

He knelt down next to the other dead guard and pulled a ring of keys from his belt. After standing up, he looked around and handed them to the nearest prisoner who was eagerly reaching his arm through the bars. "See that all the cells are unlocked and the prisoners released," Justin told him.

"Si, Senor," the burly Mexican prisoner said as he began unlocking his cell door.

Justin didn't wait. He was already moving down the catwalk in search of the warden.

Ben was crouched behind a wagon near the corral when he saw six guards exit the   sleeping quarters. They immediately lined up and dropped to their knees and raised their rifles, aiming them at the men coming through the hole where the front gate had been. Ben reached into a sack slung over his shoulder and pulled out a long stick of dynamite, then lit the fuse with the glowing end of his cigar. He waited until the burning fuse got very short before he heaved it at the guards who where about to start firing at his fellow townsmen. The dynamite landed a foot in front of the guards and one of them yelled. As one, they turned and tried to get away but the fuse was too short.

Seeing the bodies flying through the air from the explosion, Justin looked down into the prison yard to see who had thrown the dynamite.

Ben looked up grinning, and raised a thumb.

Justin returned the thumbs up, before hurrying on toward the warden's office. He was searching for a man for whom his hatred had grown to epic proportions. During his time here, he, his brother and his cousin had personally felt the man's evil. Plus, they had witnessed the atrocities he commanded his guards to do to the prisoners. The man was like a wild beast that needed to be put down.

Normally Justin was slow to anger, for a Hacker. And he had been known to take a great deal of abuse to keep from having trouble. But when they hurt his family and the woman he was about to marry, they started a war they couldn't win. His son would never again know his mother's love, or would his grandmother be able to spoil him with cake and pie. And he had lost the only other woman besides his mother he'd ever loved. As he searched the catwalk, Justin vowed to himself to send the warden straight to hell where he belonged.

Outside the prison, men on horses were riding around, shooting and screaming. The man with the trumpet was still blaring away, and Elijah and Ephram were still buried up to their necks with a canvas over their heads.

"What the hell's goin' on out there? Ah war?" Ephram yelled.

"I can't see any morn' you can," Elijah screamed back. "I jest hope and pray some idiot don't come ah ridin' through here!"

"Help! Help!" they both yelled.

With the sound of the bugle, rifles and pistols going off, and men on each side shouting rebel yells, the two old men's cries for help were in vain. Bullets struck the sand all around them and when a bullet careened off of a tombstone and drove itself through the canvas right between their heads, both men became silent.

Little by little the battle began turning in favor of the townsmen and some of the guards had already thrown down their guns and were raising their hands in defeat.

Justin made his way along the catwalk in the direction of the warden's office and stopped short when he saw the warden come out carrying a gun. Justin raised his pistol and fired. But with the thick smoke, his aim was off and the bullet struck the wall near the warden's head.

The warden looked around and saw Justin raising his pistol for a second shot. Instinctively, he ducked, while at the same time, firing at Justin.

Justin saw the warden point his pistol and flung himself to his left and heard the bullet strike the back wall of the empty cell behind him.

Many of the newly liberated prisoners were picking up guns and joining in the war against the warden and his guards in the hopes of becoming free men again.

With this added firepower, the townsman and their new allies now outnumbered the guards. The guards seeing they were fighting a lost cause gathered themselves together in one corner of the catwalk for a last stand. Many wanted to surrender, but while the warden was still alive they were afraid to.

Justin stopped and spread his legs slightly for balance just as a second bullet ripped through his shirt, searing the skin on his right shoulder.

Out of instinct, Justin dropped to one knee and fired three shots as fast as he could pull the trigger. Justin watched as his first bullet buried itself in the warden's left shoulder. His second shot plowed its way into the warden's stomach, which pushed him back several steps, and his third and final shot tore its way into the warden's right shoulder, causing him to drop his pistol. The angle and impact spun the warden around with such force that he was thrust against the guard railing. He lost his balance and went screaming over the rail into the corral and the highly agitated horses below.

Justin looked over the railing and saw the warden's agonizing end, one that befit the death punishments he'd doled out.

The warden's screams were short. The horses were kicking and stepping on him, bouncing him around like a rag doll, until one of the horses stomped down on his head, ending any further pain he might have suffered.

Justin stood up and cupped his hands around his mouth and shouted, "Hold yer fire! The warden is dead! He was stomped ta death by the horse

The shooting stopped almost immediately. There was an excited cry that filled the inside of the prison, mainly from the prisoners but also from a few of the guards.

What few guards that were left put down their weapons and raised their hands over their heads.

The guards were not stood against the wall and shot, nor were they incarcerated. Instead, they were released and told they were free to go home to their families, or to wherever they chose to go.

Justin asked some of the guards to bury the warden in the graveyard out front. He didn't feel right about asking any of the prisoners to bury the warden; as far as he was concerned, they'd already dug too many graves.

Four of the guards gladly carried the warden's body away.

Justin gathered up the horses that belonged to them, leaving the rest to whoever claimed them.

Outside the prison, the sheriff and Ben dug Ephram out of his hole, while Justin and Jeremiah dug Elijah out of his.

Justin and his father stared at each other, but neither of them spoke.

The guards and prisoners who were now allies were retrieving boxes from the graves and setting them aside.

Once Ephram and Elijah had been pulled from their graves, the doctor came over and checked them for any outstanding wounds "You two look healthy enough to me," he said, and then turned away. "If you'll excuse me, there's some who do need my help," he said, heading toward several men with bullet wounds.

The moon was fully up now and shining brightly, giving the appearance of a cloudy day.

The sheriff turned to Justin and asked, "What's in them boxes the prisoners and guards are diggin' up?"

"Gold, money, jewelry, stuff like that," Justin said with a grin.

Elijah dusted himself off and looked directly at the sheriff. "You figure most of thet is stolen loot; come from up our way?"

The sheriff rubbed his whiskered chin and smiled. "Probably is, Elijah. Yea, it probably is. But I'm not ah law officer right this here very moment. Took ah leave of absence ta come down here and rescue you two old farts. Besides that, if I was ah peace officer, this here is out of my jurisdiction. And on top of that, I wouldn't know who ta give it back to. The way I see it, they're entitled ta whatever they can dig up after bein' in this place."

CHAPTER THIRTY-TWO

At the mention of stolen loot, Ben got an idea, and unbeknownst to the others went back inside the prison.

Once inside the walls of the prison, Ben quickly climbed the stairs to the catwalk and hurried down to the door that led to the warden's office. Inside, he began to search for what he believed might be the warden's secret stash – his emergency get away money. His gut told him the warden had been stealing from Snake-eye and his brother from the beginning.

He searched the warden's desk, but to no avail. He continued searching and as his eyes roamed around the room, they stopped on a boar's head hanging slightly askew on the wall. He hurried over and lifted the head from the nail it rested on.

Sure enough, hidden inside the wall were four sacks of gold coins. He hefted each sack and decided even sharing the gold five ways with his family, his share would be more money than he would earn in a lifetime. After what they'd been through, Ben figured they deserved every penny.

Near the coat rack next to the door, was a set of saddlebags hanging on a wooden peg. After stowing the money equally in the two bags, he hefted it over his shoulder and headed back outside.

Things were close to being wrapped up by the time he rejoined Justin and the others. The graves had all been emptied of their treasure and divided between the prisoners, the guards and townsmen. Some had already mounted horses and were riding away. Several were giving the doctor large amounts of gold coins for patching up their wounds.

The doctor accepted the money, thanking each man as he thought about the improvements he could make to his hospital. Hell, with this much money, he could build a regular hospital with plenty of medicine and all the latest equipment.

Ben walked over to his horse and slung the saddlebags up behind the saddle, tying them securely for the trip home. When he was satisfied, he walked over to where Justin, Jeremiah and the others were standing.

"Where you been?" Jeremiah asked as Ben sauntered up.

Ben took a moment, and then said, "Just wrappin' up some loose ends." He wanted to surprise them when they got back, in private.

The sheriff walked up, "I guess we're about ready ta leave. You boys ready?"

Justin turned to him and said, "Jeremiah and me got just one more thing ta do. The rest of ya go on ahead. We'll catch up."

It was like a parade. A string of wagons loaded with people and treasure and the rest on horseback making their trek down the road that would take them to the border, home and freedom.

As he watched them go, Justin lit a cigarillo and grinned. He was going to enjoy this last detail in his plan.

By the time he had smoked the cigarillo half way down, the line of people were far enough away for Jeremiah and him to get down to business. Justin removed several sticks of dynamite from his saddlebags and walked inside the prison where he placed the explosive pieces of black powder here and there in strategic places.

Jeremiah followed along behind with a long coil of fuse, attaching it to each stick of dynamite. Once this was done, he tied all the fuse lengths together into a single fuse that reached about a hundred feet beyond the prison.

Justin stood next to the horses, his cigar burning brightly as he watched Jeremiah finish his business.

"Well, I reckon that'll do it, big brother," Jeremiah said as he handed the end of the long fuse to Justin.

"Then get on your horse and ride," Justin said with a grin. "I'll be right behind ya."

Jeremiah stepped into the saddle and then put his spurs into the big sorrel's ribs.

Justin watched his younger brother race down the road in the direction of the others, then blew the ashes off the end of his cigar and placed the glowing end to the fuse. It sparked, then began to hiss as it burnt its way toward the strategically placed sticks of dynamite. Justin walked over to the big Appaloosa that stood waiting for him with its reins hanging down to the ground. He glanced over his shoulder to make sure the fuse was still burning and saw it racing toward the prison.

Satisfied, Justin placed the reins over the horse's head and climbed aboard. "Let's go home, big fella," he said as he turned the horse in the direction of the others.

Some distance from the prison the others stopped to wait for Jeremiah and Justin. Jeremiah was the first to reach them and when he did, he stepped down from his saddle and turned to look behind him.

Justin was riding hard in their direction, and when he had traveled nearly three fourths of the distance between them, the first stick of dynamite exploded, creating a chain reaction that lit up the sky like none of them had ever seen before.

Justin was bent over his horse, riding hard when the first stick of dynamite exploded and sent pieces of the prison flying off into the night. Flames blazed high into the air. The chain reaction that followed was even more than they had hoped for. But when the stick of dynamite in the armory went off, the explosion was deafening and the brightness lit up the sky like high noon and could be seen for several miles. The ground rumbled and shook for a quarter of a mile in all directions.

The gray hawk jumped off her nest and flew to the top of a nearby tree to see what was going on. In the far distance, she saw the bright sky, and heard the loud explosions. She let out a high-pitched screech and wondered once again why humans were allowed to come into her territory.

CHAPTER THIRTY-THREE

Justin brought the Appaloosa to a sliding stop just in front of Jeremiah, a wall of dust momentarily blocking their view. He turned his horse back in the direction of the prison and waited for the dust to clear. The explosions had stopped and the fire had begun to dwindle down to a slow, steady burn. The weight of the metal bars on the second floor collapsed onto the lower area causing ashes and sparks to jump into the air. In a short period of time, there was nothing left of the prison but a pile of hot iron bars and smoldering wood.

As one, the rag-tag army turned and headed for Nogales. They'd done what they came to do and now it was time to return to their normal lives. Three of their men had been wounded but no one had died, at least on their side. Some of the prisoners rode along with them, while others headed south to places unknown.

This time it was Justin who brought up the rear. He wanted some time to think. Ever since he'd boarded that stage back in Lordsburg, things had been moving way too fast. That whole thing with Snake-eye, then his pa trying to shoot him, and his time in prison with that insane warden who inadvertently ordered the death of his mother and Julie.

There was also something else he needed to think about. He had a son now. How was he going to raise a son without Julie there to guide him along? He didn't know anything about being a father or raising a child. And how was he going to tell his father about his wife being dead? He felt sure his pa would blame him for that too, and might even draw his gun and shoot him. He didn't want to die, but he knew he couldn't draw against his pa.

They hadn't gone far before Elijah dropped back and pulled along side Justin, interrupting his thoughts.

Elijah noticed that Justin seemed to bristle up a little when he rode up beside him but understood the boy's apprehension. After all, he had sworn to shoot him. They rode in silence for while, which allowed Elijah to build up the courage to speak. Finally, he took a deep breath of air and let it out slowly before he said, "Son, I ah, I reckon we need ta talk."

Justin kept his eyes straight ahead, dreading what he had to say. Finally, he decided there was no other way but to come out and say it and take his chances. "Ma and Julie are dead."

Elijah reached over and grabbed the reins on Justin's horse and brought both mounts to a stop. "What'er ya talkin' about, boy? Elizabeth cain't be dead. She's the one thet sent Ephram and me down here after you boys, which didn't turn out exactly like we planned, but thet's another story. So you gotta be wrong, son. "

Justin turned his head and looked his father in the eyes. "The warden sent some of his guards after me, Jeremiah and Ben. Guess he told'em ta kill us, cause we was standin' out in the front yard when they attacked without any warnin'. Ma had just come out onto the front porch with some of her Irish coffee and one of the bullets caught her in the chest. In case you're ah wonderin', she didn't suffer none. The doctor said she died instantly. I'm real sorry, pa."

Elijah let go of the horse's reins and sat looking into nothing for a long moment, tears running down his face. He was choking back a sob as stepped down from his horse and walked away a short distance and bent over. In between the sobs, Justin could hear his father throwing up. Not knowing what to do, Justin just sat there, and waited.

After a while, Elijah stood up, wiped his mouth on his shirt sleeve, then walked back to his horse, mounted, and rode away at a hard gallop.

Justin watched his father ride away, wondering what to do next. He lit a cigarette and took a couple of puffs before making his decision. He touched the side of his boots to his horse and galloped off in pursuit of his father. When he saw the silhouette of Elijah in the far distance, he urged his horse into a hard run that would catch up to him before he reached the rest of the group. He had something more to tell him and he wanted to do it in private.

They were still a short distance behind the others when Justin caught up to his father. Elijah slowed his horse to a walk as Justin reined in alongside of him.

Elijah said nothing and kept looking straight ahead. He was very confused. He'd planned on trying to mend things with his oldest son, but this news had shaken him to the very core of his being.

Was it Justin's fault Elizabeth was dead? And what did Julie have to do with all of this? Maybe he should do like Ephram had said, talk things out with Justin, clear the air and start over. But how could he? He felt lost and bewildered, even betrayed somehow. How could he go on with Elizabeth gone? And after the way he'd treated folks, why had the whole town turned out to rescue him and Ephram? That was for sure something he hadn't considered. It was all so confusing and too much coming at him all at once. Best he ride off by his self for a while, get things straightened out in his mind. He was about to ride off into the desert when Justin said the words that brought him to an abrupt halt.

"Your grandson sure did love his grandma. And now he's gonna need you more'n ever."

Elijah pulled back on the reins, "What grandson?" he said as he turned in his saddle.

The moon shone brightly in the heavens, and the night sky was covered with stars as Justin told his father the entire story of what had happened since he'd gotten back. He even told his father about how he felt somehow responsible for their deaths.

Elijah sat there listening to Justin's story, really listening, and was beginning to understand a lot of things he'd pushed to the back of his mind. What a fool he'd been. Very slowly, Elijah reached out and put a hand on his son's shoulder and said, "I reckon they both know it weren't yer fault, son, jest like I do. I reckon it might sound a mite strange, but when Ephram and me was in thet prison, he said some things thet set me ta thinkin'. I begun ta understand ah lot about myself thet makes me feel ashamed. I could'a been ah better husband to yer ma, and I didn't treat you none too good, either." Ephram swallowed back a catch in his throat before he said, "Do ya think you can ever forgive me for the fool I've been?"

Justin leaned over and put his arms around his father, and after a moment, Elijah hugged his son back.

Ephram, Ben, the sheriff, and the doctor stopped following the others with the excuse of having a smoke, but the truth was, they wanted to see what was going on between Elijah and Justin, and what they saw made each man smile. The sheriff blew a puff of smoke that resembled a circle and said, "Let's go home, boys, things are gonna be alright."

CHAPTER THIRTY-FOUR

The funeral was held the day after they got back. The whole town turned out. Both Elizabeth and Julie were well liked by everyone. Even the saloon closed down for the occasion. There was just enough cloud cover to make things tolerable and just enough light breeze to make the day comfortable for the unpleasant deed that had to be done. They all figured the good Lord had made it so, on account of them both being such good people.

Over to one side, a group of Mexicans stood silently. The men all held their sombreros reverently against their chests, while the women crossed themselves and said silent prayers for the two white women they had come to love and respect. Not far away, one of the Mexican guards who had come to Nogales to see about work, stood alone with his head bowed. He was there out of respect for what the Hackers had done, plus, he wanted to pay his respects for this bad thing his comrades had done.

Father Sandy had said most of what he wanted to say at the church service held earlier that day. As he stood in front of the two gravesites, he simply said, "Dear Father in heaven, we don't understand why you have chosen to take these two wonderful women away from us at this time, but we know you must have your reason. So, in the name of the Father, the Son, and the Holy Ghost, we now commit their bodies to the ground because we know their souls are with you in heaven. Amen."

At this point, Father Sandy walked over and gave his condolences to Elijah, Justin Jeremiah and Patrick. Patrick stood next to Justin, holding tightly to his father's hand, his young jaws clenched tight. He was trying hard to be a man and not cry.

When Father Sandy finished, he walked down to the entry of the graveyard and waited to greet the people as they left. At that point, the rest took their turns, each expressing how sorry they were. Justin, Jeremiah and Elijah nodded and mumbled their thanks.

Then finally, it was over. The townspeople could be seen walking back toward town, accompanied by Father Sandy. Elijah, Justin, Jeremiah, Patrick and the four Mexican men who would fill in the graves were the only ones left.

The four Mexican men stood to one side, holding their shovels, waiting patiently for these last three men and the boy to say their goodbyes.

"Even with all the dumb things I did and the way I treated folks," Elijah said, as tears ran down his weather-beaten face, "you always stood by me. There'll never be another woman like ya and I'm gonna miss ya somethin' awful," he said as he scooped up a handful of dirt and dropped it into the hole. "I always loved you, Elizabeth Hacker, even if I didn't tell ya like I shoulda'."

Justin laid his hand on his father's shoulder as he stared into the other hole where Julie's casket rested. "I'd like ta think I found one jest like her," he said as he reached down and scooped up a handful of dirt and gently let it fall into the grave. "I'll never let a day go by without thinkin' of you, and I want you ta know that I'm gonna do all I can ta see that Patrick gets raised right and knows what ah wonderful mother he had."

Elijah reached down and lifted Patrick into his arms and started off down the hill, in the direction of town.

Jeremiah followed his father and Patrick, leaving Justin, alone.

After a moment, Justin gave a sigh and said, "There ain't much else I can say, cept, I'm sorry. I hope you and ma don't hold it agin me. I didn't know they'd come in ah shootin' like that."

Justin looked up toward the heavens and said, "God, I ain't much of a church goin' person and we ain't done much talkin', but if you can hear me, I sure would appreciate it ah bunch if you'd look out fer ma and Julie. They were two of the finest people you ever put on this earth. That's about it. Thank ya, kindly."

After wiping the tears from his eyes, Justin turned and hurried to catch up with the others.

They walked along in silence for a bit, then Elijah stopped and set Patrick on the ground and took his hand and began walking again.

"You gonna be okay, pa?" Jeremiah asked.

Elijah took a plug of tobacco from his coat pocket, bit off a piece and put the rest back. After a moment of chewing, he spit a stream of tobacco juice into the dry desert sand that covered that part of Arizona, and said, "Ya know, I been ah thinkin'. Maybe I ortta sell the blacksmith shop. I'm getin' too old ta be ah doin' thet kind'a work and I don't reckon you boys would want ta take it over, so maybe I'll get rid of it and move out ta Californie and buy me ah store of some kind. You know, somethin' easy ta run."

As Elijah walked on down the hill, he sneaked a couple of peeks at his two sons, who had flabbergasted looks on their faces.

"Course, even that'd be ah lot of work fer ah man of my years," he finally said. "But on the other hand, "if'en I had me ah couple of sons and maybe ah grandson thet wanted ta come along ta help out some, well, thet might make ah man think real hard about given'er ah try."

The boys slapped Elijah on the back and told him they thought that was about the best idea he'd ever had.

When they got back to the house, the first thing Elijah did, with the help of his brother Ephram, was to put a For Sale sign in the front yard.

And, as they were walking toward the front porch, a youngish man in a wagon stopped and called out, "Does the blacksmith shop and livery stable come with the house?"

THE END

ALSO BY JARED McVAY

Other works by Jared McVay

Jared McVay is an award-winning author who writes, Westerns: A western series: Historical Fiction: Action/Adventure: YA: Children's books: screenplays: teleplays: Short stories, does storytelling.

NOVELS:

Clay Brentwood western series:

Book 1 – Stranger On A Black Stallion

Book 2 – Unjust Punishment

Book 3 – Hammershield

Book 4 – Cinch Mountain

Book 5 – The Storm

Book 6 – The Chameleon

Book 7 – Ol' Son

Book 8 – Loralie

Historical Fiction: The Legend Of Joe, Willy & Red – award winner

Western: Hacker's Raid – award winner

Action/Contemporary - Not On My Mountain – double award winner

CHILDREN'S BOOKS

Bears, Bicycles & Broomsticks – 11 short stories

Randal Gets A Hit

SCREENPLAYS

The Hobos

Jared & the Warden

Talltree

Santa's Magic Ring

TELEVISION PILOT SCRIPTS

McClusky [6 episodes] - Drama/Comedy

ACT Acute Care Transport - Drama/Comedy

Melinda: Award winning short story

FROM THE AUTHOR

Thank you to all my readers. Your reviews and requests for more Clay Brentwood books is an inspiration to me. I'll keep writing them as long as you keep requesting them...

Jared McVay

MEET THE AUTHOR

JARED McVAY is a four-time award-winning author. He writes several genres, including - westerns, fantasy, action/adventure, and children's books. Before becoming an author, he was a professional actor on stage, in movies and on television. As a young man he was a cowboy, a rodeo clown, a lumberjack, a power lineman, a world-class sailor and spent his military time with the Navy Sea Bees where he learned his electrical trade. When not writing you can find him fishing somewhere or traveling around and just enjoying life with his girlfriend, Jerri.

THANK YOU FOR READING!

If you enjoyed this book, we would appreciate your customer review on your book seller's website or on Goodreads.

Also, we would like for you to know that you can find more great books like this one at

www.SixGunBooks.com

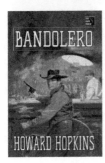

Stories so real you can smell the gunsmoke.™

CPSIA information can be obtained
at www.ICGtesting.com
Printed in the USA
LVHW091522210719
624773LV00004B/466/P